SUNSTONE
PRESS

BROKEN HEARTS

A NOVEL OF SUSPENSE

BROKEN HEARTS

BOB LEVY

SUNSTONE
PRESS

This book is a work of fiction.
Names, characters, places, and incidents are either the product
of the author's imagination or are used fictitiously.

Printed and bound in the United States of America. No part of this book may be reproduced in
any form or by any electronic or mechanical means including information storage and
retrieval systems without permission in writing from the publisher, except by a reviewer who
may quote brief passages in a review.

Sunstone books may be purchased for educational, business, or sales promotional use.
For information please write: Special Markets Department, Sunstone Press, P.O. Box
2321, Santa Fe, New Mexico 87504-2321.

FIRST EDITION

10 9 8 7 6 5 4 3 2 1

Library of Congress Cataloging-in-Publication Data:
Levy, Bob, 1953–
    Broken hearts: a novel / by Bob Levy.—1st ed.
        p. cm.
    ISBN: 0-86534-312-8
        I. Title.
PS3562.E9249 B7 2000
813'.54—dc21   00-029727

Published by SUNSTONE PRESS
            Post Office Box 2321
            Santa Fe, NM 87504-2321 / USA
            (505) 988-4418 / *orders only* (800) 243-5644
            FAX (505) 988-1025
            www.sunstonepress.com

For Debbie and Hampton Pitts,
whose courage, strength, and faith
in the face of overwhelming odds
will always be an inspiration

Acknowledgment

As with any writing endeavor, there are a number of people without whose help this book would not have been written. They took time from their busy, everyday lives to share the expertise that is woven into the following pages. To those listed I will be forever indebted; not only for their guidance, but for their friendship as well.

To Dr. O.C. Smith, Shelby County Chief Medical Examiner, and Dr. Steven A. Symes, forensic anthropologist at the University of Tennessee Medical School, who not only are integral cogs at the Regional Forensic Center but are also masters at bringing the subject of death to life. Also to Dr. William Bass, the Director of the Forensic Anthropology Department at the University of Tennessee, Knoxville, who will always be remembered for his creation, the Anthropological Research Facility.

To former Memphis Police Director Melvin Burgess Sr., who has been with me on this from the beginning. To Memphis Police Lieutenant Paul Sheffield and Captain Aurie Schwarting of the Charlottesville, Virginia Police Department, for sharing their wealth of knowledge in police and criminal procedures. To Gil Monroe, warden of Brushy Mountain State Penitentiary in East Tennessee, for his allowing me total access to a place most people would never hope or want to see.

To Dr. Bill West for his cancer expertise; Dr. Ben Beatus for his knowledge of the twisted human psyche, and Dr. David Lightman for his ocular insight.

To Gloria Belz, make-up artist extraordinaire, and to Mark Vorder Bruegge Jr., one of the finest legal minds ever produced by the Algonquin

9

J. Calhoun School of Law, who is and will always be one of my closest personal friends.

To Bunny Cohn, Tom Donahue, Ken Brown, Nick Nixon, Bill Cooper, Tom Bugg, Bonnie and Wayne Richey, Bill Thompson, and Susan Malone for their particular contributions.

To my "typing hands," Stanley Thompson, who so ably transferred my handwritten words into their present format—I can never thank you enough for being on call at all hours of the day and night, rewrite after rewrite after rewrite.

To my publisher, James Clois Smith Jr., who took a chance on me when others would not. I will not let you down.

To anyone whom I have omitted, please accept my humblest apologies and know that I will always be appreciative of your contribution. And to those of you offering encouragement over the years, and you know who you are, please realize you had a hand in this end result.

Lastly, let it be known that my family has had a profound influence on my life, as is the case with almost every writer. I thank my mother, Evy Halle Levy, and my late father, J. Lawrence "Dooley" Levy, for their love and the belief that, if you reach high enough, you just might grasp that star in the sky. To my brother, Bill, and my sister, Sue, I give thanks for their understanding and encouragement given in chasing a dream.

Most importantly, thanks and love are due my wife, Jane, and my two sons, Jim and Chris, who gave me the ultimate gift a writer can hope for—time. I had the ideas; they supplied the opportunity to transform them into the pages that follow.

. . . when you look into an abyss, the
abyss also looks into you.
—Friedrich Nietzsche
Thus Spake Zarathustra

1

April 8, 1943

"See how easy it is to change the way you look, Jimmy?" the young woman said with a smile. "A little touch here, a wave of a brush there. What do you think?"

"You don't look like you," the awe-struck youngster replied as he sat by her side. "Who are you going to be tonight, Mother?"

"You'll have to wait and see," she said, playfully poking at his ribs with long manicured nails.

She gently patted her newly bleached-blond hair, styled in finger waves. With the aid of a lipstick tube, her mouth took on a deep red hue as the metamorphosis continued. She carefully accentuated the bows above her lips.

After meticulously plucking her eyebrows, all that remained were slender, arcing half-moons above startling blue eyes. She dipped a tiny brush into a tin of make-up cake and slowly drew pencil-thin eyebrows, adding character and definition.

Next she picked up an eyelash strip, expertly applied a slight amount of adhesive and positioned it on her upper lid. After sweeping an eyeliner brush across the lash line, she fluttered huge round eyes at her son.

He stared, mesmerized, soaking up her every move.

Lipstick dabbed on each cheek and gently patted around her cheekbones produced a hint of color, while powder brought on a velvety soft complexion.

"Hey, big boy," she drawled in a voice dripping with sensuality, "like what you see?"

"I've known ever since you put on the lipstick," the boy admitted.

"Who then?"

"Godfrey Daniel!" slurred the youngster as he jerked his shoulders back in mock surprise, trying his hand at a high-pitched imitation of W.C. Fields. "You're Mae West from *My Little Chickadee*."

"You're getting good. Your imitation's not too bad either."

"I've seen that movie with you *nine* times. He's my favorite."

"She's mine," his mother replied. "How about we work on you now?"

"How about *I* work on me now?" the ten-year-old responded.

The mother sat back as her young make-up prodigy leaned toward the mirror. Strategically placing small dots of brown cream eyeshadow along the bridge and sides of his nose, he carefully tapped and stippled, dabbing lightly to create freckles. Reaching for a jar of Petrolatum, he combed a glob of it through the mop on his head, slicking back curly brown hair.

"Who am I?" he asked.

"Mickey Rooney!"

"Right," he squealed, flashing a snaggle-toothed grin.

They sat transfixed, studying their images in the mirror, as Mae West and young Mickey Rooney stared back at them.

"I don't remember seeing the two of them in a movie together," Jimmy said.

"Me neither," his mother replied, slowly shaking her blond hair sadly.

"We'll just have to make our *own* movie!"

Audrey Seabold beamed. "I am *so* proud of you, Jimmy. You'll always be my little man. Will you take care of me when I'm old? When even the make-up can't keep me young?"

"I'll take care of you *always*, Mother. Nothing will ever happen to you. Not as long as I'm around."

2

September 24, 1957

He sat motionless in the nearly deserted Jefferson theater in downtown Charlottesville, Virginia, as the figures on the screen flickered before him. His eyes were fixed on the young woman two rows in front of him. Tonight was the night.

Marilyn Larsen stared straight ahead, a smile etched on her face, captivated by the images of Frank Sinatra, Rita Hayworth, and Kim Novak in *Pal Joey*. She popped her last malted milk ball into her mouth and took a sip of Coke, then, in the darkness, set the almost-empty cup on the sticky floor under her seat.

Tuesday nights the striking twenty-two-year-old indulged her passion. Every week she sat in the same chair, in the same row, and lost herself in the make-believe world of the movies.

He focused on her petite frame, noticing every move like a wild animal stalking its prey. Each smile, each laugh, the way she ran a hand through her long blond hair, twirling it into a curl near her chest.

He appeared harmless. And quite ordinary. With his square jaw, thick neck, and stocky body, he could have passed for a wrestler at the nearby University of Virginia had he been a bit younger than his twenty-four years. Wrestle, however, he once did with the dark thoughts that had taken control of him.

As the final frames of the movie flashed on the screen, she stood up, not waiting for the credits or the house lights. The brown vinyl seat bottom, cracked and faded from decades of use in the old movie house, creaked gently.

15

Passing quickly through the ornate lobby, she pushed open the oak-framed theater door with ease. The salty aroma of popcorn, which had been so tantalizing moments before, was replaced by a rush of chilly September night air. She paused for a moment and inhaled deeply, then exhaled, amused as the vapor of her breath rose upward, vanishing in the glow of the flashing white lights on the theater marquee.

She clutched her camel hair coat tightly and turned the corner into the dark shadows.

Within minutes her light blue Chevrolet Impala sedan passed the train station on West Main Street. She glided along, lost in a fantasy with Frank Sinatra. Would she ever find the man of her dreams?

A red light at Fourteenth Street and University Avenue brought her back to reality. Her car vibrated as a passing freight train rumbled across the bridge above, almost drowning out Elvis Presley blaring on the radio. Soon the Chevy's tires came to a noisy halt on the short gravel driveway of her house at 222 Fourteenth Street.

The headlights blinked off. The engine fell silent. Lifting up on the handle, she gave the heavy metal door a shove with her left shoulder, slipped out, and forcefully slammed the door shut, all in one fluid motion.

A moment later, on the porch of her three-story, tan stucco house, she closed her eyes and again breathed deeply. Once. Twice. Then a third time, reveling in the first cold burst of autumn.

Out of the night, he moved effortlessly into position through the shadows, avoiding detection in the bright moonlight. He locked on to her, observing her, never letting her escape his sight, as if she were caught, helpless, in a bell jar. His heart pounded. Adrenaline surged through him at the sight of her silky hair shimmering under the solitary porch light. He wiped beads of cold sweat from his forehead.

She inserted the key into the dead bolt and pushed open the beveled glass front door. The inside latch locked behind her with a loud click. Walking into the narrow foyer, she flicked on a light and dropped her keys and purse next to a telephone perched on the marble-topped entry hall table.

Just as she hung her coat on an antique hat rack, a noise from behind startled her. A frenzied, metallic-toned rattling at the front door. Whirling around, her breath left her.

A wild-eyed young man clutched the doorknob, twisting it furiously. He mouthed out a silent command. "Open the door, bitch!" Fury flared across his face.

Her heart skipped a beat. Panic seized her. Shaking, she grabbed the black rotary-dial telephone. It crashed onto the hardwood floor with a hollow ring.

"Go away!" she screamed, fumbling for the phone. "Go away!" Cowering in the farthest corner of the entry hall, she pressed the receiver to her ear and dialed.

The beady eyes of the assailant narrowed. The stainless steel blade of his small axe gleamed under the bright porch light. Gripping the handle tightly with both hands, he reared his arms back like a batter at the plate.

"Operator," finally answered a placid female voice.

"Help me! A man is breaking into my house! He has an axe! I'm on Fourteenth—"

The front door exploded. Hundreds of sharp shards of glass zinged inward, pinging off the walls and floor. He flew across the room. In an instant he was on top of her. The receiver banged to the floor.

The thick fingers of his left hand closed around her neck. Frozen, she could only stare at his crazed face. One eye was pale blue, the other green. The right eye, the green one, began to twitch.

"Say goodnight!" he snarled through clenched teeth. He tightened his grip.

She tried to scream. Nothing. Only the muffled sounds of her straining to breathe. She tried to poke at his eyes, to grab his curly brown hair.

Just as she sank into unconsciousness, he eased his grip.

She wheezed, gasping under his weight. The last thing she saw was the upraised blunt end of the axe in his right hand, swinging down toward the side of her head.

The sound of the blow resounded through the open telephone line. "Hello? Hello?" pleaded the operator.

He picked up the receiver and gently placed it in its cradle. Then he ripped open the woman's tan blouse. As white pearl buttons bounced play-fully across the floor, he began to work. With short, knowing strokes he hacked, in search of his treasure.

3

"Haven't had one of these in a long time," the graying Charlottesville police chief remarked as he ambled up the porch steps at Marilyn Larsen's house, reflecting on life in the quiet college town. "Especially one that got me up in the middle of the night."

"Especially one like this," added a tall, red-haired detective, standing in the glass-shattered front doorway. His warm breath turned to vapor as he spoke, quickly vanishing into the dark of the cold night.

They walked across the threshold. Glass fragments cracked and popped under their feet. The chief's eyes darted about. Another detective, short and stocky, stood before them, feverishly taking shot after shot of the blood-drenched corpse with his Crown Graphic camera. Behind them the flashing red lights from police sedans reflected off the surrounding houses, illuminating the faces of the concerned neighbors peering from their porches.

"Whatcha got?" the chief asked. He looked away from the woman's body in a futile attempt to shield his eyes from the incessant blinding flashes of the camera bulbs.

The detective glanced at his notepad. "An operator got a distress call from the victim at about 10:30. Said a man was breaking into her house. The operator heard glass breaking. Then nothing for a little while—"

"What's a little while?" the chief asked.

"About a minute. Next she hears sounds like somebody's choking. After that a thud. Then she got disconnected."

"What next?" The chief motioned with his hand to hurry up.

"She called the station. The desk sergeant dispatched the radio car from Charlie's restaurant."

"Guess they just *had* to have some coffee."

"It *is* pretty nippy out tonight," the detective replied, rubbing his thumbs along the lapels of his navy topcoat. "Anyway, when the radio car got here, the patrolman on the walking beat had just made the scene." He nodded toward a young skinny rookie standing in the driveway.

"Anybody see anything?"

"Not a *damn* thing," the detective answered, shaking his red head. "Some neighbors heard glass break and dogs barking. Didn't see anybody suspicious. By the time the beat officer and the radio car got here, whoever did it was long gone."

The chief licked his chapped lower lip. "And that was?"

"10:40."

The stocky detective with the camera glanced over at the two men. "All yours, Chief," he said, stifling a yawn as he dropped the bulky black camera to his rotund side and walked out the front door.

"We got a big problem I haven't told you about," the detective warily added.

The chief looked curiously at him, glancing down at the murdered woman.

The detective kneeled down and pulled open the victim's blood-soaked blouse.

The chief winced.

"It's her heart." He frowned, pausing to look directly into the chief's eyes. "It's missing."

4

Warden Winston Carpenter shuffled the paperwork on his desk, picking up a fat folder marked *James Cagney Seabold*. A thunderstorm raged outside, as it had all day, caught in the mountains surrounding Brushy Mountain State Penitentiary in East Tennessee.

A booming clap of thunder rocked his office. He glanced out the window. All he could see in the darkness were raindrops streaking across the panes of wire-imbedded safety glass, backlit by the bright lights of the prison. A perfect night for an execution. Just like in the movies. Only this James Cagney was for real. With over thirty years of service as assistant warden and then head warden, he would preside. His first. And the first to ever take place at the prison since its construction in 1896.

Carpenter opened the folder and skimmed over the psychiatrist's notes on the condemned inmate's life history:

Born in 1933 in Charlotte, North Carolina. Moved to Richmond and raised by his mother, a door-to-door Avon saleslady, after his father's abandonment in 1935. Devoted to his mother who loved movies and was an expert make-up artist. Her hobby consisted of spending hours in front of a mirror in an effort to transform herself into movie stars of the era. When a boy of twelve, Jimmy, as he is known, witnessed his mother's death at the hands of a woman, the result of an argument involving a mutual love interest. In a fit of rage, young Jimmy knocked the woman out as she knelt in shock over his dead mother's body and stabbed her to death. Charged with manslaughter but, being a juvenile, he was sent to reform school. Initially thought to have a danger-

21

ous propensity for violence against females, he was success-
fully treated with therapy and released at the age of eighteen.

The warden looked up from his desk and out the window again at the heightened electrical storm. Jagged bolts of lightning flashed time and again, as if on cue, dancing with the towering trees on the surrounding mountains, followed by rumbling thunder. He slowly shut the folder and, closing his eyes, massaged his temples. Silently he recounted the rest of Jimmy Seabold's story, well-documented by the media, which had dubbed him the Hollywood Killer.

Ten murders occurred from the end of September to November, 1957, and seemed completely random. None of the victims knew one another or were related. Not a prostitute or criminal record among them. All led quiet, middle-class lives. Some worked, others were housewives, a couple were college students. All were considered attractive and well-liked. Their ages ranged from late teens to mid-thirties.

However, two glaring similarities were common to all; one public knowledge from the beginning, the other revealed only after the criminal's capture. The murders were all committed at movie theaters, except the first victim, who had been to a theater within twenty minutes of her death. The other similarity, revealed by the police after Seabold's apprehension, was that after striking a victim unconscious, the killer quickly eviscerated her heart. None of the hearts were ever found.

The state of Virginia pushed its case for prosecution there, since the first two murders took place in Charlottesville and then Roanoke. Tennessee would have none of that, with one victim each in Knoxville and Nashville, then six in Memphis, a city for which Seabold developed a particular fondness.

He had been captured by Sergeant Joe O'Riley, a Homicide Squad detective for the Memphis Police Department. O'Riley's wife, Evelyn, was Seabold's tenth and last victim. The sergeant, along with two other undercover detectives, subdued Seabold as he attacked his intended eleventh victim, an eighteen-year-old who suffered a blow to her head but survived.

The trial in Memphis lasted only three days. The jury found Seabold guilty of six counts of first-degree murder in that city and sentenced him to death in the state electric chair at Nashville on August 20, 1959. Governor Buford Ellington ordered a stay of execution only hours before the sentence was to be carried out. The date of execution was reset to November 12, 1959.

"Tonight's the night," the warden mumbled as he slowly opened his eyes, unaware his intercom button was on.

"Did you say something, sir?" buzzed back the perky voice of his secretary.

"Uh . . . yes," replied the warden, his stomach churning, startled but quick-thinking so as not to belie his mounting nervousness at the approaching execution. "I'm expecting that visitor at any time, Maggie."

"Sergeant O'Riley from the Memphis Police?"

"That's right," the warden answered. A slight smile cracked his somber expression. "What *would* I do without you?"

"Fix your own coffee, for one thing," came the giggling response.

"When Sergeant O'Riley gets here, send him right in, if you will please." He glanced at his watch. 6:15 P.M. "And," he quickly added, "be on the look-out for that media bus. It should get here by eight o'clock."

"Anything else?"

"No, that about covers it."

"Pepto-Bismol?"

A momentary silence was followed by a laughing reply. "Yes, a large order of Pepto-Bismol. But you better hold the fries."

The rain kept falling hard. Joe O'Riley clicked on the defroster fan of his unmarked Ford Fairlane detective cruiser in an effort to clear the vapor from the windshield. He strained to see the winding road as the wipers beat to and fro in front of him in a constant rhythm, barely able to do their job. His right hand waved across the fogged-up glass, quickly wiping away the slowly evaporating film.

Ten minutes later, the glow from Brushy Mountain State Penitentiary cut through the darkness and rain. The black sedan slowed to a crawl, coming to a halt at the entrance gate check point. An older guard, about sixty, stepped out, barely shielded from the rain by an overhang.

"Nice night for an execution," O'Riley remarked with a smirk, cranking his car window down only as much as necessary to keep out the rain.

"Wouldn't have it any other way," the guard responded, scratching a gray sideburn. "Your name please?"

"O'Riley. Sergeant Joe O'Riley. Memphis Police Department."

The guard scrolled down his clipboard. He finally stopped, checked something off, and handed O'Riley a clearance pass. "Just stick it in your pocket," he said. Raindrops splattered down on the black brim of his guard hat, trickling down the door's tan vinyl interior.

"Got a full house tonight?" O'Riley asked.

"You betcha," the oldtimer replied with a grin. "I could *really* make some money scalping for this one. Hotter than a ticket to the 'Bama-Vols football game. Guess you got a fifty-yard-line seat?"

O'Riley nodded. "If you're a betting man, I'll give you a tip. Give all takers the visitor and as many points as they want. Stick with the home team. You can't go wrong. The boy ain't gonna cover the spread tonight." He winked.

The guard smiled and faintly waved as O'Riley rolled up the window and headed down the narrow access road. Chain-link fences topped with barbed wire zig-zagged across the grounds. Within minutes he parked near the front of the gloomy, foreboding four-story prison and sloshed through the puddles toward the building entrance. His every move was watched closely by guards nestled in their cozy gun towers thirty feet up on the perimeter wall.

In the warden's office a few minutes later, the secretary announced over the intercom, "Sergeant Joe O'Riley to see you."

"Send him in."

"Yes, sir."

The heavy wooden door swung open. O'Riley walked in, holding a soaked navy fedora that had been only partially effective in keeping his rusty-brown hair dry. Water dripped from the black rubber raincoat covering his nearly six-foot frame, forming tiny puddles on the faded green carpet as he approached the warden's desk.

"Sergeant O'Riley," greeted the warden, extending his beefy hand, "Winston Carpenter." He had expected an older man, in his fifties like himself, not someone in his twenties. "Nice coat," he said, nodding at O'Riley's drenched slicker. "I've got one just like it."

O'Riley gripped the warden's hand firmly. "Police issue. Gets the job done. By the way, Warden, Joe will do."

"And Winston for me," Carpenter replied. He motioned for O'Riley to sit down. "I hope the weather didn't slow you down too much."

O'Riley peeled off his raincoat. "I tell you, that road up from Knox-ville is a killer." He paused. "No pun intended."

The warden forced a polite smile. "Let me officially welcome you to The End of the Line."

"That what you call this place?" O'Riley asked, sitting down in a dark-brown leather wing-backed chair facing the warden's massive cherrywood desk. The coat of his navy blue suit flapped open as he sat, exposing his once-heavily-starched white shirt, now creased and wrinkled, turned limp by the humidity.

"That's what everybody in Corrections calls it. The state pen in Nash-ville is The Wall. We're The End of the Line. They send the *real* sweethearts up here. The ones they can't handle. The incorrigibles. Plus the run-of-the-mill criminals from here in East Tennessee."

"Ever had any escapes?"

"An escape from here would be *very* ill-advised," answered Carpenter. He walked to the window and pointed into the darkness. "The people over in Petros don't take too kindly to escapees. If anybody busts out of here, they better pray our guards find them before the townspeople do. Last one was in 1939. Twenty years ago. A nineteen-year-old kid named Henry Hunter, in for a rape in Knox County. By the time we found him six hours after the escape, they had him hanging from a tree, using him for target practice. Looked like a piece of Swiss cheese." His blue eyes beamed with pride like a proud father. "There isn't a house within three miles of here that doesn't have a loaded shotgun handy. I swear I think every boy in these parts can shoot before he can ride a bike!"

O'Riley arched his eyebrows.

"I compare living around here to an old football saying," the warden continued. "The best offense is a good defense. Know what I mean?" He sat back down.

O'Riley nodded and tried to clear his parched throat.

"Can I get you a drink?" Carpenter asked.

"Sure," O'Riley replied, still trying to dry out. "I could use some water in me instead of on me." He reached up to loosen the knot of a navy tie squeezing his neck. "Never have liked these things," he muttered.

"If you had waited a bit longer, you could have come in the media caravan from Knoxville. They're due in about eight. It's gonna be quite a show. Most media credentials we've ever had for an execution in Tennessee." The warden poured a glass of ice water from a silver pitcher kept behind his desk. "Of course, this is the first one we've ever had here at Brushy Mountain."

O'Riley reached for the glass, gulping the water down as if it were his nightly ration of Bushmills Irish whiskey. "How'd you pull that off, Winston? Need to see your name in lights?" he joked.

"Not my doing. Governor Ellington's. Too much media attention in Nashville on this one. Move Old Smoky to the mountains in East Tennessee

26

and he figures fewer people will notice when it lights somebody up. Can't have too much liberal backlash, ya know? Not with another campaign on the horizon."

O'Riley nodded again, then suddenly sneezed.

"Bless you," Carpenter said.

"Must be the weather." O'Riley pulled a monogrammed white handkerchief from his back pocket and wiped his nose.

Carpenter ran a hand across the top of his balding head, brushing back some errant strands of gray. "I understand you're on a first-name basis with the Governor, Joe. Any chance for a last-minute stay? Like last time?"

"No way," O'Riley snapped. "*That* was a one-shot deal. Hopefully I can make the delay pay off tonight."

"You *better* make it pay off. You won't be getting a second chance. We tested the chair out last night while Seabold was sleeping in his holding cell over in solitary. Once the juice flows, he's bacon. You ready to go see him?"

"That's why I'm here."

The two men stood up. The warden adjusted his navy suit coat and motioned politely toward the door. "After you."

5

The hasty walk across the prison yard to the solitary-confinement cells, known as The Hole, was not a pleasant one. Winds swirled about, blowing raindrops that stung like grains of sand against O'Riley's face. The three guards who accompanied O'Riley and Carpenter wore bright yellow rubber prison raincoats with hoods pulled tightly over their heads. The full-length coats kept them dry, except for their faces and feet. Upon reaching the outside of a squat building, constructed of tan stone hand-cut by inmates, the five men quickly descended a flight of stairs and passed through a metal entry door, their water-logged shoes squishing with each step.

O'Riley stopped abruptly, jolted by the sight. At long last, revenge would be his. In the spacious, well-lit, thirty-foot-square area loomed the electric chair, neatly centered facing a massive floor-to-ceiling glass partition. The warm hues of the chair's dark brown oak clashed with the bright, antiseptic appearance of the makeshift death chamber. The dull brass buckles attached to the snake-like maze of leather straps hanging from the chair gleamed under the overhead fluorescent tubes. An ominous black power-control panel stood partially hidden in the far corner. Neat rows of brown metal folding chairs for the media and witnesses faced the glass, the same kind of chair common to funeral parlors.

"What do you think?" Carpenter asked, his ruddy face beaming at the efficiency of his work crew.

"Looks like you did a damn good job," O'Riley replied. "Especially on such short notice." The Governor's decision to carry out the execution at Brushy Mountain had been finalized just ten days prior. "He in there?"

The warden looked at the bars in front of the steel doorway to his left and the burly guard standing watch. "Yeah," he answered, "in The Hole."

nodded quickly and the guard unlocked the gate. It screeched on its hinges, slowly swinging open.

O'Riley's stomach growled as the peppery aroma of a grilled steak tickled his nose. Then he frowned.

"He's eating his last meal. I don't think he planned on you for dessert," the warden deadpanned.

"Seabold! You got a visitor!" bellowed the guard.

O'Riley slowly walked alone down the short, narrow hall that led to the three cells. The brown paint on the cold concrete floor was chipped and faded. But the smooth walls shone a lustrous white, freshly painted in a vain effort to mask the odors attendant to solitary confinement. He passed by the first two of the three cells, both empty, as the stuffy, stale air became more pungent, laced with the smell of sweat and an undefinable scent of fear.

The conditions were spartan, fitting for the last hours of any man who had shown no remorse in taking the lives of ten women. The four by eight-foot cell contained a thin metal bed bolted to the wall. There was no mattress or pillow. Near the top of the twelve-foot ceiling hung a single forty-watt light bulb. Two metal pails stood side-by-side against the wall, one for drinking water, the other for human waste. Bars covered the narrow cell door.

O'Riley's solitary footsteps echoed in the enclosed space, becoming silent as he reached the third cell. Before him sat Jimmy Seabold on the metal bed, dressed in a gray and white wide-striped prison uniform. He held a massive, thirty-two-ounce sirloin strip steak in his hands, pulling at it with his teeth.

"Good to see you again," Seabold said. "Didn't happen to bring any cutting tools for me, did you? This steak's a little tough. Maybe I shoulda ordered a filet."

The police sergeant shook his head, looking blankly at him. "Always leave 'em laughing, huh, Jimmy?" He paused for a moment. "Somehow I don't think they wanted you to have a knife."

"Aw, I wouldn't hurt myself with it."

"I don't think it's *you* they were worried about," O'Riley said, his mouth slicing into a thin smile that didn't reach his eyes. "I got a favor to ask."

"You want *me* to do a favor for *you*? I thought it's the dying man who gets a last request." He smacked as he spoke, chewing on the rare sirloin strip.

"My favor is this. I got a few questions I was hoping you'd answer. You have a problem with that?"

"I ain't got a problem with it."

"First question. It's an easy one. Why'd you *really* do it?"

Seabold squinted at O'Riley and shrugged. "I had to."

O'Riley frowned. "Don't feed me that *had to* bullshit. Nobody *has* to."

"You walk in my shoes and you'd understand. I couldn't help it." A faint grin crossed his thin lips. "Then I started to enjoy it. Next question."

"Why Memphis? Why'd you stick around there?"

"I got to like the place real quick. Took a trip there once when I was a kid. Had a great time. You know, home is where the heart is." Red juice ran down the corner of his mouth to the cleft in his chin. He dabbed it quickly with his sleeve. "Or hearts, I should say. And your last question?"

His voice soft, his tone sympathetic, O'Riley said, "In the name of God, Jimmy, tell me. Where *are* the hearts of your victims? Have mercy on the poor families of those you've wronged."

Seabold stopped eating and leered. "Why the hell should I? You think the man pulling the switch is going to have mercy on me? You think the Governor is going to have mercy on me?"

"You've inflicted a lot of pain on *so many* families. You haven't just taken away a young woman from each. You took somebody's wife, somebody's daughter, somebody's sister, somebody's mother."

Seabold's voice grew harsh. "I know *all* about that last one. You don't think *I* ever felt pain? But not anymore. I found a way to put an end to it."

"Please," O'Riley pleaded, "let my wife rest in *peace*!" He met

30

Seabold's gaze and held it, locking onto his strange dual-colored eyes.

The prisoner returned the glaring stare. He said nothing for a split-second. Then, a smirk spread across his face. "I'd rather she rest in *pieces*!"

The policeman's anger swelled up, nearly engulfing him. Face flushed red, he began to sweat. The veins poked out in his neck. In a commanding voice he said, "You know what's gonna happen when they pull that switch? Let me fill you in. Your body's gonna jerk as the voltage rips through you. If you didn't have a mouthpiece in, you'd probably break your teeth off from the force of the electricity. Your eyeballs will bulge out of their sockets as blood oozes from your eyes down your cheeks. And the smell. Oh, yeah. You'll start looking like that steak on your plate, your skin singed and the smoke from your burning flesh filling the room. Don't worry about it, though. They'll make sure you're plenty done before they unstrap you and throw you in a hole for the worms to feed on."

Seabold jumped to his feet and hurled his food tray, splattering a cherry pie against the wall. The tray clattered on the floor as the pie slowly slid downward, leaving a sticky red stain in its wake. "You . . . you had it all figured out," he stammered. "Coming in here with your sob story. Thought I'd go soft and pour my guts out. Like you tried to make me do in Memphis. Well, you know what, asshole? I don't give a damn about the victims or *anybody* who cares about them. As far as I'm concerned, you and the whole goddam Memphis Police force can go *straight* to Hell!"

"*You're* the one going straight to Hell! And damn soon!" O'Riley yelled.

Seabold balled his hands into fists, his chest rising and falling. "Don't bet on it. I got a stay before."

"Here's a dime, go call the Governor," O'Riley sneered, flipping the shiny silver coin at Seabold, who caught it in mid-air. "*I'm* the reason you got it in the first place. *I* went to the Governor to request it. Thought maybe with a little more time you'd show a little compassion."

Seabold laughed. "Guess you thought wrong."

"But I got one thing right." O'Riley's sneer softened, turning into a slight grin. "I picked the day you were gonna die. November twelfth. The same day you murdered my wife two years ago."

"I remember it well." Seabold smiled. "She didn't know what hit her. Since you bring her up, the red juice from this steak reminds me of her after I hacked her open."

"I'll kill you myself, you son of a bitch!" O'Riley screamed, grabbing wildly through the bars.

Two guards rushed in and, with one holding each of his arms, they half-dragged, half-escorted the sergeant out of the small area into the main room. His shouting reverberated throughout the prisoner's cell as the bars to solitary clanged shut.

"They're gonna fry you, Seabold, you hear me! And I'll be on the front row when they light your ass up like a Christmas tree, you filthy—"

The slamming metal entry door to solitary turned O'Riley's outcry into unintelligible muffled sounds.

6

Seabold took a deep breath. He kicked the food tray and the remnants of his steak into a corner. His eyes darted around the walls of the tiny, dimly-lit cell, finally fixing on one particularly smooth area across from his bed. With the silver dime in his right hand, he began to write.

An hour passed. Then another. And another. With each tick of the large, round, black and white clock mounted on the wall in the death chamber, the amount of time left for Jimmy Seabold grew shorter.

Rain continued to drum on the roof, sounding like surf crashing upon a shore. As the fog-shrouded first hours of Thursday morning approached, the wind whistled and howled relentlessly.

Seabold scraped the silver dime back and forth with blinding speed, his hand a blur, frantically trying to finish scratching the final letters on the wall. His forefinger and thumb bled but he felt no pain. His time was almost up. He would not be denied.

At precisely 11:10 P.M., the bolt on the massive steel entry door to the solitary-confinement cells loudly clicked and the door swung open. Next the Folger Adams lock on the gate released with its characteristic clang. The bars creaked inward, banging to a stop against the wall. With it came the bustling noise of voices and footsteps of four men. The death squad had arrived to prepare the prisoner.

Seabold dropped the worn dime to the shadowy floor. It pinged as it hit, coming to rest in the corner. He wiped his bloody hand on the leg of his prison pants and then smiled at his creation.

The voices fell silent as the cell key unlocked the latch to his tiny, private domain. The bars opened and before him stood four brawny men, all wearing the Brushy Mountain guard uniform of dark green pants, tan shirts, and matching green jackets. They stared grimly at him. He had never seen any of them before.

A guard with piercing dark eyes and slick black hair to match carried a lone, small wooden chair. He placed it in the center of the cramped cell and ordered Seabold to sit down. His voice showed no emotion. Another guard placed a white apron around the prisoner's neck. The monotonous hum of electric clippers drowned out all other noises, even the rain. Seabold's curly brown hair fell in clumps onto the floor.

Next, two of the guards gripped him tightly, one holding each arm. The third belted his legs together so he couldn't move. The lead guard lathered up the remaining stubble on his scalp with a shaving brush. A straight razor then glided across his head, leaving not a trace of hair in its wake.

Unexpectedly the two guards by his sides gripped his head tightly, tilting it back at a slight angle. Lather was quickly applied to his lower forehead and, with two deft strokes, his eyebrows were gone. They shook off the apron, wiped his face with it, and then unbelted his legs.

"Now," barked the guard who had wielded the razor, "take off those prison stripes and put these on." He tossed a rolled-up bundle onto the metal bed.

Seabold stood and unraveled the bundle. He stripped in the dim light of the cramped quarters, feeling humiliated for the first time since his childhood. Slowly he slipped on the garments he would die in.

First the white boxer shorts. The tight elastic waist uncomfortably gripped his stomach. Then the white cotton socks and black wool-blend slacks. He next slid his feet into black leather house slippers and began to button up the front of the white dress shirt.

"I think you guys forgot the undershirt," he joked.

"You won't be needing it," the lead guard replied. "Sit back down in the chair."

The other guards resumed their positions, two by his side, the other holding his legs. The guard then pulled out a pair of scissors and cut open the inside seams of Seabold's pant legs all the way up to his knees. Trading the scissors for a straight razor, he dry-shaved the prisoner's legs from his knees to his ankles.

"You boys look like you're having so much fun, maybe you'd like to do the rest of me too, while you're at it. Or," he grinned, "you could watch me do it. I'm pretty good with a blade."

Without cracking a smile the guards stepped outside the cell, flanking the open door two on each side, awaiting the arrival of the prison chaplain.

"Have any of you seen *Some Like It Hot* with Marilyn Monroe?" Seabold asked. "That's the one thing I miss most about being in here. No movies. What I wouldn't give to see Marilyn in that one. Just *one time*."

The guards stared at him flatly.

Shuffling footsteps soon echoed in the hallway. A moment later, a balding man of slight build dressed in a black cassock and slacks stood in the cell's doorway. His wire-rimmed spectacles accentuated gentle, aged eyes filled with tenderness and hope. A sympathetic smile graced his lips.

"Don't bother wasting no prayers on me, Father," Seabold offered. "It won't do any good."

"My son, accepting the Lord into your heart will give you eternal peace."

"Eternal peace ain't what I want. What I want is revenge on the guy who put me here."

"Your own actions are what put you into this situation, not those of any man. Feelings of unrepentance and a lust for revenge without accepting the Lord will only serve to damn you eternally in the hereafter."

"Those are the cards I've been dealt, Father. Win or lose, I ain't folding my hand now."

"The Lord doesn't bluff, my son. May He have mercy on your soul."

The chaplain closed his eyes and silently mouthed a prayer before he turned and walked away.

At 11:40 P.M., Seabold glanced up to see the face of Warden Carpenter staring at him from the shadows.

"It's almost time, Jimmy. Are you prepared?"

"It don't really make a shit if I am or not, does it, Warden?" he replied from his perch on the metal bed. "They got me looking like a cross between Mr. Clean and a goddam Thanksgiving turkey about to be popped in the oven." He rubbed his left hand across his pale scalp, which tingled to his touch. "At this point there ain't a whole lot you can do for me."

"No, but I can explain what the procedure will be so you won't get too alarmed as things go on."

Carpenter then spelled out the final steps. The inmate showed no emotion, nodding like a wide receiver acknowledging a pass route from the quarterback as he nervously gnawed his thumbnail. The warden then left the cell, motioning to the lead guard.

For the first time the guard spoke to the prisoner in a more civil tone. "If you would, on your feet please."

The guards wrapped heavy chains around his waist, clamped on the handcuff restraints, and locked the manacles to his ankles. When finished, they stood back for the warden to inspect their work.

He nodded. "Jimmy, I'm afraid it's time," he said softly. "Do you want me to call the chaplain back in?"

Seabold sucked in a deep breath and exhaled loudly. "Nope. He's said his piece. Let's get on with it," he declared, masking his fear in a shell of defiant courage.

Stepping out of the holding cell for the first time in four days, he turned to his left and, after eight short steps he was through the solitary-confinement entryway. Turning again to his left, he stopped cold in his tracks. Before him, just twenty paces away, loomed the newly built death chamber with the state's electric chair, imported from Nashville, placed precisely in its center.

A guard stood on either side and, grasping an arm, began to usher him forward. Warden Carpenter led the way with the remaining two guards trailing behind.

The witnesses, mainly law-enforcement officers, prison officials, and newspaper reporters, sat silently with their necks crooked, observing the last few strides the condemned man would ever take. The cadence of the entourage's shuffling footsteps mixed with the harsh jingling of chains scraping along the cold concrete floor. In no time they had all stepped into the chamber.

It was nothing like Seabold had imagined. For four days he had heard the hammering and the sawing and had been forced to inhale the sawdust that permeated the air and left an ever-thickening tan coating on every surface in his cell. He thought when they finished, it would be dark and gloomy with a lone light bulb dangling high over an ominous, leather-strapped wooden chair, like in *Frankenstein*. Instead, the chamber was bright, lit like a hospital operating room. Fresh. New. Seemingly sterile. Except for the old chair. His heart began to pound as the death squad led him to the seat that had been the feared last stop for those on death row. Tonight it was reserved for him.

This legendary Old Smoky was the official vehicle for Tennessee executions for decades. The dark oak finish shined glossy as a mirror and smelled of lemon furniture polish. Once in the grips of its leather-strapped and metal-buckled tentacles, there would be no escape. This time a call from the Governor with a last-second reprieve was not a possibility. Jimmy Seabold knew it. So did the witnesses.

The death squad sat the condemned prisoner down. A broad leather strap was placed around his chest and tightened, pulling him firmly against the back-slats. More straps were then wrapped around his forearms and wrists, binding them in place to the armrests. A strap around his waist was next, followed by another over his thighs. The ankle straps were last and, only when he and the chair had become one, were his handcuffs, chains, and manacles removed.

For the first time Seabold looked up, fixing his gaze on the glass partition that separated him from the witnesses. The glaring light in the chamber contrasted with the darkness on the other side, rendering the two dozen faces unrecognizable. He could make out the men in the predominantly male assemblage from the outline of their hats. He figured out the number of reporters by counting the white pads glowing softly in the darkness. Their hands seemed to move in unison, taking notes so people could read every disgusting detail.

An electrician knelt at his feet and, after parting his pant legs, strapped a leather anklet lined with copper to each of his calves. The copper felt cold against his shaved skin in the warmth of the increasingly stuffy chamber. The electrician then connected shiny electrodes to the anklets and rose to his feet, never once glancing at the prisoner as he left the small enclosure.

Warden Carpenter stepped into the chamber, his eyes unflinching. "James Cagney Seabold, do you have any last words before the sentence of the people and the state of Tennessee is carried out?"

Seabold squinted into the darkness of the witness room, scanning right down the front row, then left across the back. There, in the last chair on the row, he thought he saw Joe O'Riley. His right eye, the green one, began to twitch. Just as it had whenever he butchered one of his victims. He scowled at this faint visage of his nemesis.

"I left my last words in my cell."

The warden pursed his lips and walked from the chamber. He took his place behind the witnesses, standing next to a black telephone mounted on the building's white-painted stone wall, a direct line to the Governor in Nashville. A phone that would never ring.

O'Riley sat quietly in his chair at the end of the back row, hands clasped in his lap. His view of the methodical proceedings suddenly faded to black. Behind his closed eyes, in the deep recesses of his mind, he could see his wife, Evelyn, smiling at him with twinkling eyes. He wanted to reach out and touch her. Caress her. Feel the love that he knew would never come his

38

way again, no matter how long he lived. A pall of loneliness enveloped him like the low-level clouds hovering above the prison. The soothing image quickly disappeared, replaced by the image of Evelyn's savaged body lying on a table in the morgue.

The policeman's eyelids slowly opened and he began drumming the fingertips of his right hand on his thigh, alertly watching the proceedings once again. His impassive face hid his thoughts. "Let's get this show on the road," he mumbled, glancing at his watch. If they'd let him, he'd throw the switch himself.

It was five minutes until midnight. Five minutes until November twelfth.

7

The guards placed a thick, white mouthpiece between Seabold's teeth and ordered him to bite down while they fastened a leather chin strap tightly around his jaw, locking his head firmly into the chair's headrest. They pulled a black silk mask over his face, leaving only the top of his newly-white scalp exposed.

The lead guard grasped the steel cap from the back of the chair and bent it over, checking to make sure the sponge sewn into the headset was sufficiently soaked with the salty water that would conduct the voltage. He then lowered the death cap until it rested firmly on Seabold's head. Tiny trails of briny liquid trickled down his slick scalp, tickling his cheeks and nose. It felt as if a swarm of gnats had landed on his face.

The electrician returned. This time he plugged a thick, black, power line into the electrode jutting from the top of the steel cap. He then exited, followed closely by the guards.

Seabold tugged at his right hand, subconsciously trying to pull it up to his mouth to gnaw his thumbnail. The cold metal held his wrist firmly in place. He drew in a breath, outlined by the black silk's impression of his mouth, and quickly puffed out in an effort to alleviate his itching cheeks. He repeated this over and over, almost twenty times, until he neared a hyperventilated state.

The witnesses, many visibly shaken by this bizarre sight, fidgeted uncomfortably in their seats. The second hand on the large wall clock above the electric chair continued its relentless assault on the witching hour.

An intense wave of sadness engulfed Seabold, alone in the darkness behind closed eyes and the black death mask. Not a sadness in dying but a sadness that he would never again be able to revel in the euphoria that killing bestowed upon him. Never be able to bask in the sunlight of control over women. Never enjoy the thrill of the hunt in stalking his victims in the soothing, dark confines of movie theaters, where the stars on the screen so reminded him of his mother.

He fought the melancholy by thinking of his victims. Each face, each name, each murder scene flashed through his mind. But his sadness was replaced by an inner calm as he rejoiced in the memories of dominance and death. Anger then gripped him as he flashed to an image of his capture by Joe O'Riley. He seethed at the memory of the man who had robbed him of his only true enjoyment in life.

At the stroke of midnight, Carpenter nodded toward a partition in the chamber that concealed the two anonymous executioners. Neither would ever know which one controlled the actual live switch on the control panel. In unison they gripped the red handles in front of them and forcefully jerked downward.

The noise was not as loud as O'Riley had expected. A dull clunk was followed by a droning hum, accompanied by a slight dimming of the lights as the antiquated building's power surged to the chair.

The charge of electricity shot instantly into Seabold's brain, bolting him upright, his hands spasmed into fists. His chest heaved. The two thousand volts shook him violently from side to side. His body snapped quickly forward and fell back five times, his arms and legs straining against the leather straps that held him in place.

He emitted a faint gurgling whimpering cry as wisps of steam drifted up from the death cap. Purplish saliva drooled down from under the black silk mask, wicking into an ever-widening stain down the front of his white shirt. The incessant humming of electricity filled the air.

A sickening odor of roasting body hair, burning flesh, and singed sponge wafted from the chamber, smelling like meat left too long on a grill. Most of the witnesses looked on in horror, their faces pale with hands cupped over their eyes, their bodies shuddering.

Seabold slumped in the chair, his body twitching not from life but from the current still running through his corpse.

When two minutes had passed, Carpenter slashed a finger across his neck. The monotonous hum stopped.

"Contrary to what you think you may have seen," announced the warden, "let me assure you, James Seabold did not suffer. Electrocution instantly ends the body's ability to feel pain."

Not sure he believed it, O'Riley didn't care.

Carpenter nodded to an elderly man standing near the chamber door who held an old black leather satchel in his left hand. The prison doctor, seventy-eight-year-old Doc Sherman, ambled into the chamber, placed his bag on the concrete floor beside the chair, fished out his stethoscope, and gently set the earpieces in his ears. He stood still for over three minutes, waiting for the body to cool down. His rumpled, worn, brown suit coat hung loosely from sloping shoulders revealing that age had robbed him of a once-robust physique.

The doctor popped off what was left of a melted plastic button on Seabold's shirt and placed the disc of his stethoscope on the dead man's chest. He turned toward the warden.

"He's gone," announced the doctor, pulling the earpieces from his head and stuffing the stethoscope back in his satchel. "If you need me, I'll be at home."

"Thanks, Doc," replied Carpenter as the old man shuffled from the chamber. "Sorry to have you out so late on such a nasty night." He motioned to the death squad to get the gurney. "Unbuckle him and get him out of here. Show's over."

The guards carried the corpse from the building and placed it into a black Cadillac hearse waiting in the prison yard. The rain had stopped, veiling the prison grounds in a cool, thick blanket of fog. As the hearse drove off, a din of clanging tin cups against metal window bars erupted, breaking the silence of the night as hundreds of Brushy Mountain inmates tolled a final good-bye.

Thirty minutes later, Joe O'Riley remained as did four newspapermen, one each from the *Knoxville News-Sentinel*, the *Nashville Banner*, the *Memphis Press-Scimitar* and *The Commercial Appeal*, also from Memphis.

"What were his last words? What'd he leave in his cell?" the Knoxville reporter asked.

"It's not newsworthy," replied Carpenter.

"You fry a guy who killed ten women, a maniac who cut out their hearts and his last words aren't newsworthy?" questioned the exasperated *Commercial Appeal* reporter, his mouth wide open. He dropped his pad and pencil to his side. "I'd sure as hell hate to meet the S.O.B. *you* think would have newsworthy last words!"

"Let me rephrase myself," the warden answered. "His last words were not meant for the general public."

"Who to?" asked the Nashville newspaperman. "A relative? A girlfriend? Another prisoner?"

"He had no relatives, women didn't much care for him, and the other prisoners weren't allowed to mix with him in the short time he was here."

"Who then," repeated the *Banner* reporter. "A guard?"

"Gentlemen, please. Don't make this any harder than it is. Suffice it to say that it's a personal message to someone and we can't divulge it. I just won't invade that person's privacy. Now, if you don't mind," he said, lifting a muscular arm toward the exit door to the prison yard, "you had all best take advantage of my guard here to escort you back to the main building. You never can tell what might be wandering around this time of night." He turned to O'Riley, barely able to hide a growing smile. "Sergeant O'Riley, I need a word with you."

The newspapermen filed out begrudgingly, one of them vowing under his breath to find out Seabold's last words if it killed him. The warden dismissed the other two guards, leaving O'Riley and himself alone.

"You know me well enough by now," O'Riley said. "Curiosity killed the cat. What *did* he leave? A note? A letter?" He jingled the keychain in his front pants pocket.

"Just some graffiti." Carpenter pursed his thick lips.

"Graffiti?" repeated O'Riley, rubbing his nose in confusion. "Why the hell would he do that?"

"My guess is, he wanted to make a lasting impression on the person he intended it for."

"And that person is?"

"You."

O'Riley jerked slightly, his eyes widening.

"Come on," motioned Carpenter. "Take a look."

The two men walked the few steps down the solitary confinement hallway to the last cell. Stepping inside, the warden aimed the beam of his flashlight at the message crudely scratched into the wall:

> *With eyes of red*
> *My actions are blue,*
> *When your time comes, O'Riley,*
> *I'll be waiting for you.*

O'Riley slid his hands into his pockets and yanked upward, pulling his slipping pants back up on his waist. "He sure as hell wasn't a poet. What do you make of it, Winston?"

"Got rage in his eyes and cold-blooded feelings for you, I'd say. When your check-out time from this world arrives somewhere down the line, he's planning on meeting you there, I guess."

"That ain't the first time I've heard that from somebody I put away." A forced smile spread across O'Riley's face. "If that's the way the bastard wants it, he better take a number and get in line."

8

The Present

David Lancaster glanced at the other students scattered in groups near the front, filling fifty seats in the auditorium-type lecture hall at the University of Virginia School of Law in Charlottesville. Friday afternoon's Securities Regulation class, the last before the weekend, was about to begin. It was two o'clock. An air of uneasiness filled the room.

By the third year of law school, the scare tactics embraced by many professors in the weeding-out process of first-year students had been abandoned. Such was not the case in the classroom of Professor Albert Hightower.

A fourth-generation lawyer and grandson of a former Supreme Court justice, Hightower's résumé was impressive in its own right. After graduation from Yale Law School, he served two years as Law Clerk to Supreme Court Justice Lewis F. Powell before working first as an associate, then making partner in the Washington, D.C. office of the prestigious Jones, Day, Reavis, and Pogue law firm.

Several UVA Law faculty friends had convinced him to take up teaching. He embraced the challenge of a twice-weekly commute while still billing over three thousand hours per year on corporate mergers, acquisitions, financing, and other complex business transactions for his firm.

But, he had an ulterior motive.

The best student in class would be assured a spot with his firm. It was no secret. That was all the justification he needed to warrant his particular brand of classroom terrorism.

Lancaster knew if he answered the professor's questions correctly, his chances of receiving a good recommendation in pursuit of a corporate practice with a large law firm in a major money-center city such as New York, Atlanta, or San Francisco would dramatically increase. An incorrect answer would doom him, placing him in an unfavorable light from which there existed only a slight chance of redemption.

The entrance door at the rear of the auditorium slowly creaked open. All eyes turned, focusing on Professor Hightower at the top of the steps. He stood for a moment and surveyed the class, looking down on the students like a monarch over his subjects. His style of dress was impeccable and expensive and, with a glossy black leather briefcase by his side, he looked as if he had just stepped off a plane, fresh from a high-powered merger deal on Wall Street.

True to form, he began the class as soon as he started down.

"Mr. Algonquin," Hightower bellowed, spotting a lanky target on the front row near the podium. "A hypothetical. Three young entrepreneurs—Bill Gates types—have started and operated a small business for about a year. The business is doing well but cannot grow fast enough to meet demand due to lack of capital. They decide to give up some of their ownership in the business and obtain additional capital by selling stock representing a forty-percent interest to investors. They run advertisements for several weeks in a local business newspaper and in the *Wall Street Journal* soliciting investors. They also mail letters to approximately one hundred of their business acquaintances, suppliers, and customers to solicit interest."

The professor stopped halfway down the steep steps and pivoted in a half circle on the heels of shiny black wing-tip shoes, observing the relieved expressions on the faces of those not called upon. He resumed his descent after a momentary pause.

"The solicitation is successful. Three investors emerge who, together, purchase the forty-percent interest in exchange for one million dollars in badly needed cash. Unfortunately, the company is not successful. For the next three fiscal quarters, the company operates at a substantial loss. After a year, it is so strapped for cash that it must file Chapter Seven bankruptcy in order to stave off supplier lawsuits and pay off debt in an orderly fashion. Its bank seizes most of its inventory, plant, and equipment. Its unsecured creditors receive fifty cents on the dollar. The stockholders receive nothing."

Hightower reached the podium and whirled around to face Algonquin, startled by the professor's stare. "The stockholders are furious and feel betrayed," he said, his tone sharp. "They hire you as their lawyer and ask you to recover whatever part of their investment you can, from whomever you can. Although the company is bankrupt, you decide to sue the three entrepreneurs who originally solicited the investments. What is your plan?"

The student let out a deep sigh. "Since the company is in bankruptcy, and it issued the stock, I don't see how the investors have any remedy."

"Mr. Algonquin," Hightower replied, "I would suggest you consider an alternative means of employment if you should be *so* fortunate as to pass my class and graduate from law school. The law doesn't seem to be your forte."

A palpable wave of dread swept over the students as the professor's eyes scanned left, then right, across the auditorium in search of his next victim. Coming full circle, his gaze settled on a red-haired woman with dark-framed glasses sitting one seat over from Algonquin.

"Ms. Alexander?"

"Can we prove that the entrepreneurs lied about the financial condition or prospects of the company?" she responded hopefully. "If so, we could sue for fraud."

"*I* ask the questions here, Ms. Alexander," Hightower replied. "And no, I didn't assume any fraud in the hypothetical. May I encourage you to entertain thoughts of forming a partnership with Mr. Algonquin in whatever your life's work turns out to be after law school? You seem to be perfectly suited for each other." He was silent for a split-second, then added with a smile, "Intellectually speaking, that is."

Nervous laughter spread across the room, quickly subsiding as the professor eyed his next candidate.

"How about you, Mr. Lancaster? Would you like to try your hand at the question, or will you be joining your two *esteemed* colleagues?"

Lancaster took a deep breath, heart pounding. "We can recover the one million dollar investment from the three entrepreneurs—and we don't have to prove anything except the purchase of stock itself as described in your hypothetical," he said confidently.

"Excellent! Mr. Lancaster has *obviously* done his homework." Hightower glared at the duo he had berated before turning back to Lancaster. "Your proof?"

"Under the Securities Act of 1933, the shares of stock offered to the investors had to be registered with the Securities and Exchange Commission. This offering of shares could not be treated as an exempt private transaction because it was advertised to the general public. Because the shares were not registered," he went on, "the buyers of the shares have an absolute right to rescind their purchase and recover their money. The entrepreneurs are liable for the money because they participated in selling the stock."

"Absolutely correct," remarked the professor, nodding as he had throughout Lancaster's explanation. "Keep up the good work and you *just might* find yourself working in Washington when you graduate."

Hightower then brought up the subject of bank mergers and posed a question to another member of the class. For David Lancaster, the question went unheard. He was lost in his own thoughts. Lost in his own little world.

"*Finally,*" he mouthed in a barely audible whisper as he eased back in his chair. "It's about time something went my way."

9

Four days later Lancaster strolled along University Avenue in Charlottesville with a plastic grocery sack dangling from his right hand. The warmth of the Indian summer day had given way to a late September cold front, dropping the evening temperatures into the low sixties. A cool breeze skirted the clean-shaven face of the twenty-four-year-old, invigorating him as it tousled his sandy-blond hair.

A red-plaid *Polo* shirt covered his athletic barrel chest and long, muscular arms. Khaki pants graced a lean waist. His appearance, invariably, was meticulous. Shirt tail always neatly tucked in. Trousers the perfect length, never too short or too long, always with a cuff. Whatever he wore, his clothes were seldom, if ever, rumpled or wrinkled. If a garment became stained, frayed, or faded in the least, it was immediately discarded.

As with his appearance, so he was with his possessions. Everything in its proper place. He had to have order in his life. A life that had been turned upside down at the age of twelve.

Swollen lymph nodes in his chest as he approached his thirteenth birthday had been diagnosed as Hodgkin's disease. Successfully treated at St. Jude Children's Hospital in Memphis, he returned to his home in Richmond. The only side effect was a hypothyroid condition resulting from the massive doses of radiation. And the realization for a young boy that life could end at any time. Dreams must be pursued. His was of becoming a lawyer.

Valedictorian of his high school class in Richmond, he was accepted at the University of Virginia and received his undergraduate degree in political science four years later. He decided to stay in Charlottesville when he was admitted to the University of Virginia School of Law. His romance with his college sweetheart played a major role in that decision and they were married during the summer after his first year. Jean became a secretary to one of the senior partners in a prestigious local law firm in order to support the couple while her husband pursued his degree.

Then toward the end of his second year, he began experiencing severe headaches and instances of memory loss. Medical tests showed the presence of a malignant tumor in his brain. St. Jude agreed to treat him, as they would all former patients, and included him in a study on secondary malignancies. An operation performed in late May removed the tumor and follow-up treatment soon began.

Heavy doses of radiation were administered for six weeks beginning in June. Dementia, mainly in the form of forgetfulness, accompanied the radiation, leaving him frustrated and his wife particularly distraught when, in one instance, he couldn't even remember her.

During the month of July the couple agreed to his taking part in an experimental memory drug therapy program at St. Jude that overlapped the final four weeks of radiation treatments in hopes the drug would help combat the dementia. The results bordered on miraculous. Not only did his memory return, he even began recalling early childhood memories long-since forgotten. The couple returned to Charlottesville in late August for the third year of law school.

The wind kicked up. Lancaster leaned his five-ten frame into the gusts as he turned from University Avenue onto Fourteenth Street, under the shadow of the hulking, gray-steel, Fourteenth Street railroad trestle. His bulging quadriceps tightened as he trekked up the steep hill.

The small grocery sack swinging by his side, held tightly in his right hand, contained an expensive steak—a reward for studying hard all week-end, even avoiding the telecast of the Washington Redskins game. The brisk walk to the grocery seemed as much a reward as the steak itself. Anything to get away from the books, even for an hour.

In the top ten percent of his class, his grades were not coming as easily as they had before the operation. His mind didn't seem quite as sharp. He knew it and, deep down, it gnawed at him. But he prided himself in being not only a survivor but a fighter as well. Confident. Strong-willed. Deter-mined. He had to be to emotionally withstand the rigors of his illness, his final year of law school, and his slowly deteriorating marriage.

Studies took most of his waking hours. He couldn't spend much time with Jean. His schoolwork wouldn't allow it. They had argued about it al-most every night since the beginning of the semester.

His promises of a blissful future together hadn't helped. His illness had worn her down. She fretted about the cancer coming back. At any time. And the voice he had recently told her about. He said only he could hear it. She feared he was having mental problems. Maybe another tumor. It was more than she could bear. It had driven her into the arms of another man—her boss at the law firm.

Lancaster had sensed his wife was having an affair. At least, that's what the voice had been telling him. The first time he heard it was only three days after finishing his experimental memory drug treatments in Memphis. At first he had ignored it. Just his imagination. Then he fought it, sparring verbally with it. It was so unlike him. Crude. Angry. Uneducated. But, in the last few weeks, the voice began to make sense. He talked with it, as if a part of him. As if they were becoming one.

Nearing the bottom of the large hill on Fourteenth Street, Lancaster's eyes caught a glimpse of a three-story, tan stucco house on the right, its rear converted into an apartment building for student housing. He paused. He had seen it many times before but this time it seemed different.

The sack swaying from his hand hung limp. He stared at the porch and its overhang held up by four white columns. The black metal numerals above the front steps read 222.

Suddenly the scene before him vanished in a flash of light. In an instant he was inside the house, kneeling over a woman lying on her back in the entrance hall. A black telephone lay on the floor near a marble-topped table. Pieces of shattered glass littered the floor. The woman wore a blood-soaked tan blouse. In his right hand he held a heart, still twitching and vibrating. He closed his grip around the quivering organ, feeling a feeble beat. Then it was still.

Clutching it he ran to the back of the house and into the dark night as the screen door slammed behind him. After climbing a wooden fence, he slid down a steep hill. Pausing for breath, chest pounding, he heard the distant wail of a police siren.

Lancaster's head jerked and his eyes opened wide, startled, like a student dozing off in class, called upon by the professor to answer a question. It was still light outside, not yet night. Before him stood his apartment building, the College Court apartments on Thirteenth Street, not the house at 222 Fourteenth Street. The wrought-iron railings and black shutters of all twenty-eight units took on a pale orange cast in the fading beams of the setting sun.

Panting and out of breath, he glanced down at his right hand. It clutched something soft and wet. He slowly brought his hand up. His fingers gripped a bloody piece of meat. Appalled, he let the steak drop to the ground.

10

"What happened to the steak?" Jean Lancaster inquired, forcing a smile as her husband walked in the front door empty-handed.

"I changed my mind," he snapped. "Is that a problem?"

"Hey, don't get so testy," she shot back, glaring at him. "I'm just asking. I've already eaten."

"Sorry," he replied in a softer tone. "I'm just a little tired. That walk really did me in. I think I need a nap."

"You might want to check this out first." She tossed him a small white, purple and orange Federal Express box. "It came while you were out. From some company in Arkansas."

Lancaster wrestled with the box for a moment, then unwrapped a bone-handled, folding hunter knife and a pocket camp axe. His heart skipped a beat. He smiled at the two objects as if at old friends he hadn't seen in years.

Gripping the four and a half-inch knife handle, he extended the shiny, three-inch-long, razor-sharp blade. "This'll cut through just about anything. And this," he continued, picking up the short axe by its smooth, light-brown handle, "is small enough to fit in your pocket but sharp enough to quarter large game animals." He wrapped his fist around the blunt end of the axe and then rubbed his left forefinger along the two-inch cutting edge.

His wife frowned. "What's with this sudden interest in the outdoors? I don't get it."

"That little voice inside of me has been telling me I ought to try a little camping. Maybe some hunting."

She grimaced. "Ugh. Why is it men think it's so macho to go out and kill animals and birds for fun? It makes me sick. When did you ever kill anything?"

"Never have. That's what makes it so exciting," he replied, eyes shining.

"You have time for hunting? You don't have time for *anything* but studying. Certainly not for me."

"Jean, I—"

"How about a movie? Please?" she implored, toying with her neatly curled, shoulder-length brunette hair.

"I can't," he replied. "I've got a lot of work to do."

She forced her ruby red lips into a pout. "Well, do you think you and your little voice would mind if I went to the movies with Amanda?"

"No, go ahead. Which theater?"

"I'm not sure yet. Does it matter?"

"Whatever," he answered, concealing his swelling anger in a veil of indifference. She was going to meet another man. The voice had told him so.

"I've got to leave in a few minutes. I'll just walk over to her place. You sure it's all right?"

"Yeah, no problem." He placed the knife and axe on the coffee table in the den. "I'm gonna take a cat nap and then hit the books. I'll see you when you get home."

"Sweet dreams," she smiled, pecking him on the cheek.

He walked down the stark, pictureless hallway to their bedroom. A creeping trepidation clouded his thoughts. Scarcely two minutes after his head touched the pillow, he drifted into a deep sleep.

Opening his eyes, Lancaster was startled by a huge pane of glass, as big as a room, only five feet from his face. The bright overhead fluorescents made it difficult to see through to the other side but what appeared to be people, most wearing hats, sat in two rows of chairs. They gawked at him as if he were a piece of sculpture in a museum.

He tried to stand, to move, but couldn't. Paralyzed. Massive leather straps and shiny buckles firmly bound his arms and legs to a chair. His heart began to pound.

A burly man with piercing dark eyes and slick black hair, dressed in dark green pants, a tan shirt, and matching green jacket stared at him while another man placed a thick, white mouthpiece between his teeth. "Bite down on this," he ordered, his breath stale and sour.

A leather strap then gripped his chin, locking his head tightly against the chair's headrest. Next a black fabric mask dropped down over his face, leaving him in darkness.

The chill of a cold sponge pressed down on the top of his head. Salty water trickled across his forehead into his eyes, burning them, running down his cheeks. He wanted to beg them, anyone, to scratch his itching face but no words would come. Trying to inhale and exhale in short bursts barely helped. He felt claustrophobic, pressed on all sides, gasping for air.

Suddenly a dull clunk and then a humming noise. Hot knife points jabbed into him all at once, piercing every surface of his body, inside and out, burning him alive. His saliva began to boil and his head seemed ready to explode. He tried to let out a frantic cry for help. His jaw frozen shut, only a whimpering moan escaped his throat. With all his might he tried to scream—

"Stop! Please!" yelled Lancaster, bolting up in bed. Disoriented for a moment, he didn't know where he was. Cold perspiration dripped from his forehead, stinging his eyes and running down his cheeks.

The light blue stripes of the wallpaper in his bedroom brought relief. He was safe. At home. He took a deep breath. Never had he experienced such a realistic dream.

Unexpectedly the voice said, "What are you, blind? You *know* she's seeing another guy. Probably been biffing him during the day while you're in class. You'll see. You'll start listening to me soon."

"I guess I'll have to," Lancaster replied out loud, shaking his head.

"Find her," the voice urged. "Find her and you'll see. I *told you* what she's up to."

Lancaster rubbed his eyes. "I . . . I just can't believe she'd see another guy."

The voice mimicked his words in a squeaky, child-like tone. "I . . . I just *can't believe* she'd see another guy!" It quickly changed, becoming deep, forceful and taunting. "Bullshit! Sometimes you make me *sick*, sounding like a *goddam patsy*. You *better* start believing me. Just find her. Show her who's boss. Make her pay. Do what you have to do. Do what I'd do!"

Lancaster jumped up from the unmade bed and, grabbing his car keys from the walnut night stand, hurried out the sliding glass door in the den to his green Toyota Camry.

Ten minutes later he had parked in downtown Charlottesville and was walking past the Omni Hotel on the Main Street open-air mall.

He knew Jean would go downtown. Crowds on Tuesday nights at the mall restaurants and movie theaters would be sparse.

The modern, three-screen Regal showed only new releases. Close by, the historic Jefferson theater beckoned customers to its bargain admissions for second-run films. Built in 1912, the Jefferson had once been home to vaudeville, plays, and then movies. In a constant state of disrepair and renovation, the original auditorium had been subdivided into triple screens, one downstairs and two upstairs in the former balcony. It seemed to have a charm about it. Cozy. Comfortable. Most of all, secluded. Especially in the small balcony theaters.

If Jean were having an affair, *that's* where she would go. He knew his wife well.

Pulling open the tarnished, brass-handled entry door, the smell of fresh popcorn hit him in the face. The aroma turned his stomach, already on edge at the prospect of what he might find.

He bought a ticket to a romantic comedy starring Julia Roberts, passing on the main floor Bruce Willis action movie and the full-length Disney cartoon in the other balcony theater.

His heart pounded with each step up the dimly lit, narrow, curving stairway. The black metal handrail was scarred and in need of paint, as were the once-white walls, tanned with age. Bits of flaking paint dotted the maroon carpet, its surface stained almost black.

Only five other people sat in the nearly deserted auditorium. He squinted at first, eyes adjusting to the darkness. In the back row, he sat in the last seat next to the emergency exit door.

As the movie flickered, he could make out three people sitting alone, two men and a woman. Five rows in front and to his right sat a couple. The man was tall and wore glasses. His arm draped the woman's shoulder.

The silhouette in the darkness appeared to be that of Jean. Curled, shoulder-length hair. The shape of her slightly upturned nose. He stared intently for five minutes, never once looking at the screen. His right foot fidgeted constantly, tapping silently on the scuffed, sticky, hardwood floor.

All of a sudden, everyone in the theater laughed. Lancaster felt as if someone had driven a stake through his heart. The woman's high-pitched giggle was unmistakable. It was Jean's.

Dazed, he leaned his head back, eyes fixed on the ceiling turned red from the glow of the exit sign behind him. His marriage was crumbling, just like the aged theater's plaster above his head. He had seen enough.

He drove home, in shock, his mind a blur. He sat in the car with his head bowed as the engine grew cold.

"It ain't that bad. C'mon, cheer up. You still got me," the voice said. "I'm with you *all the way*. Let's take a walk. It'll do you some good."

"Maybe it will," Lancaster replied, slamming the car door and proceeding up Thirteenth Street to John Avenue in the cool night air. The sidewalk shimmered in the glow of street lights. He turned south down Fourteenth Street and sprinted down the steep hill.

"Take a load off," suggested the voice. "Over there, in the shadows.

We'll watch the traffic go by. Might even catch your bitch on the way home." The house at 222 Fourteenth Street loomed ominously across the street.

Two hours passed like only minutes. Maybe it hadn't been Jean. Maybe he hadn't heard her laugh. Maybe it was just someone who *sounded* like her.

A car door slammed gently at the top of the hill on John Avenue. Lancaster looked up to see a woman wave at a black Lexus sedan as it drove off. She quickly walked out of sight, toward Thirteenth Street. Jean.

He clenched his fists, rage boiling inside him.

"I told you that she's playin' around," chided the voice. "That movie was over *long* ago. What do you think she's been doing the last hour? Studying male anatomy in some motel, I'd say. There's only one thing to do." The voice paused and then yelled, "Kill the bitch! Make her pay for cheating on you! That'll show the whore who's boss!"

"You're right," Lancaster replied, a strange, rigid expression etched on his face. "It's up to us to show her the error of her ways."

He took off, running full-tilt up the street. In three minutes he stood at his front door. Ramming the brass dead-bolt key into its slot, he turned the latch, flung open the door, then slammed it shut.

"David!" called out his wife from the den. "What is it? You'll wake the neighbors!"

He walked wild-eyed into the den, his chest heaving.

"Where have *you* been?" she asked, bewildered and frightened at his disheveled appearance.

"Where have I been? Where have *you* been is the question? And who with?"

"At the movie, with Amanda. I told you before, we—"

"Bullshit!" he shouted, hands quivering, his face dark with rage. "Don't lie to me, you bitch!"

"David, you're scaring me," she cried, blue eyes darting between her husband and an escape route to the front door.

"I saw you at the movie. With a guy. Explain, dammit!"

58

"I didn't want it to come to this. We've been needing to talk. . . ." She buried her face in her hands.

"How long have you been seeing him?" he demanded.

"About three weeks. Since just after Labor Day. David, it just happened. . . ."

"Have you. . . ?" He couldn't bring himself to say it. He knew the answer.

His wife nodded, staring down at the gold carpet.

Lancaster's right eye began to twitch.

"Do it!" the voice urged. "Do it *now!*"

He lunged at her, throwing her to the floor. With his left hand gripping her neck, he held her rigidly. His body burned with anger, hate, and a compulsion to hurt, to kill.

Stunned, she lay on her back, struggling to breathe under the weight of his body and the strength of his powerful hand. Trying to plead, only guttural sounds came out. Her blue eyes widened in panic.

His left hand tightened savagely. "Say goodnight!" he snarled coldly at the helpless woman.

Her eyes rolled and she lost consciousness, just as he loosened his grip, reaching over for the pocket axe still on the coffee table.

The steel blade gleamed in the lamplight. Twirling the wooden handle, he held the axe high over his head and swung the blunt end downward. The sound resounded throughout the room, as if a ripe watermelon had been dropped from high above onto a concrete floor.

After ripping open her bright, French blue blouse and snapping off her bra, he again raised the axe. He looked down at her one last time before he struck, admiring her chest with eyes that had never before seen this woman's nude breasts.

The next morning a well-rested, clean-shaven David Lancaster walked down the hallway, a Hartmann suitcase in hand, and stepped over the blood-soaked body in the den, feeling no guilt. It was just the body of another woman.

He flicked off a lamp and with a casual step turned toward the sliding-glass door to leave. As he did, he caught sight of the darkened reflection of himself in the gilded mirror above the brown leather couch.

For the briefest of instants, an image formed in his mind. Before him was the concrete wall of a dim, shadowy prison cell. Scratched into the white paint, he could make out a message.

With eyes of red
My actions are blue,
When your time comes, O'Riley,
I'll be waiting for you.

His right eye began to twitch. Setting his tweed suitcase down, he walked into the kitchen and retrieved a can of yellow spray paint from his tool drawer. Then he headed down the hallway to the dressing table in the bedroom.

Shuffling through an unkempt array of compacts, brushes, sponges, curlers, and combs, he zeroed in on an eye-liner pencil and tube of red lip-stick and, after placing them in his pocket, returned to the den.

He picked up a small pad, printed a single word with a black Sharpie marker and tore the sheet off, placing it alongside the corpse. After shaking the can of paint, he sprayed the dead woman's brown hair, turning it a bright yellow, and fluffed it with the expert touch of a hairdresser at a beauty salon. He deftly used the make-up and, in a matter of only a few minutes, his creation was complete.

His eyes narrowed. The murder and the seething inner-hatred rejuvenated him, bathing him in a euphoric high. He knew what he must do. No one would prevent him from attaining his goal. Not this time.

Again he glimpsed at the darkened visage of himself in the mirror above the couch. The image of David Lancaster stared back at him. The corners of his mouth arched up in a smirking grin. A vow rolled from his lips.

"Your time, O'Riley, is now."

With that, he was gone, vanishing into the warm, bright sunlight.

11

The red and blue flashing lights could be seen from two blocks in all directions. The driveway and street in front of the College Court apartments were ringed with yellow police crime-scene tape and gave off a glow like the grand prize winner in a Christmas decorative lights contest. Three unmarked Buick Centurys, one black and two gray, with grille and dashboard beams blazing, stood parked under pine trees in the drive along with two gold and blue-striped Charlottesville patrol cars, their lights revolving nonstop. A Ford Aerostar van, containing evidence-gathering and forensic equipment, was nearby. The bright white glare from a television news crew filming a report added to the eerie sight of midnight's darkness turned light.

Porch bulbs burned at nearly every house down the street. Pajama and robe-clad neighbors warily peered out at the commotion, many gathering to catch a closer look. Voices crackled over the police radios as an ambulance, its idling engine rumbling noisily, awaited its passenger destined not for a warm hospital bed but the cold, stainless steel examining table of an autopsy room.

Two uniformed patrolmen on the ground level of the three-story brick building flanked the open front door of apartment twenty-seven, which was criss-crossed by additional yellow police tape that warned CRIME SCENE— DO NOT CROSS. Inside, the apartment was alive with activity.

An evidence technician, clad in navy coveralls, was carefully incising a piece of dry-wall bearing bloody fingerprints from a corner of the den adjacent to the back hallway. A forensic technician busily snapped 35mm photographs from every angle, illuminating the grisly corpse with each flash of the camera. The forensic technician supervisor gathered hair, skin, and fiber evidence while two detectives, both sporting navy blazers, nosed around the other rooms. Once the photos were completed, the medical examiner, covered from head to toe in lightweight pale-green protective gear, crouched over the body, slipped on a pair of gloves, and began his preliminary investigation.

Lieutenant Arliss Schwerting, in charge of the scene, looked on as his men performed their duties with the flawless precision that had earned them the reputation as one of the best forensic units in the state. Always dapper in his dress and appearance, the striking thirty-eight-year-old could have passed for a model with his broad shoulders, six-foot three height, and easy smile. He hoped to work his way to the top and succeed the incumbent chief, Bill Parker, upon Parker's retirement, supposedly just a few years away. Getting this murder solved quickly and efficiently would put a feather in his cap. As long as the chief's interfering nature didn't get in the way.

Thirty minutes later, Chief Parker arrived. Casually dressed in a yellow crewneck sweater to ward off the early morning chill, he rubbed the dark circles under his eyes. After elbowing through reporters' microphones and beaming video camera lights with a polite smile but no comment, the chief, in his late-forties, with a full head of black hair graying at the temples, quickly located Schwerting standing just outside the apartment door.

"Helluva way to start October," Parker said. "Damn month isn't even an hour old. What do you have, Arliss?"

Schwerting shook his head. "It's a horror show in there, Chief. If you've been snacking, think twice before going in. If the sight doesn't knock you for a loop, the smell will. Female. Twenty-three. Name's Jean Lancaster. Married to David Lancaster, third-year UVA Law School." He paused for a moment, squinting as the blue and red lights flashed in his face. "She's been dead about two days. The next door neighbor tried to call. Didn't get an answer. Hadn't seen either of them since Tuesday. Their car was here yesterday morning. It left about eleven. A green Toyota Camry. The neighbor didn't see who drove off in it. Just noticed it was gone. Got worried. We found the body when the apartment manager let us in. The husband's missing."

"Any chance he was abducted?"

"Very slim," Schwerting replied, shifting his weight to his left leg. "Almost nil. We ran a quick check on the car. It's *already* been impounded. Got towed in yesterday just after noon. Illegally parked on University near the Bank of America branch at The Corner."

"Is he our man?"

"Looks like. Good possibility he cleaned out their bank accounts. We can check it out when the bank opens. After getting his cash, I'm guessing he hit the road."

"This town's getting to be like the big city. Richmond. Hampton. Even D.C. Guess we're losing a bit of that old, small-town charm. That's the way of the world," the chief said, stroking his salt and pepper mustache. "You said he hit the road. In what?"

"I'd say a *brand new* used car. I'll bet he took his wad of cash and headed straight up to Pantops Mountain. Tell some of those jokers your name's John Doe and, if you got the cash, it's take your pick. No questions asked."

"Sounds like you got it all figured out," said Parker.

"Not really." Schwerting clenched his teeth for a second, flexing his jaw muscles. His brow wrinkled. "The crime scene's got me stumped. This ain't your normal domestic quarrel. It's ritualistic. *Really* bizarre. Like Charlie Manson or something. Hacked open her chest. Lots of blood."

The chief grimaced, his long face engraved with ever-deepening lines.

"That's not the bizarre part. There's a three-by-five slip of paper near the body with Marilyn written on it in black Sharpie. Her hair is spray-painted yellow, she has bright red lipstick on, and a little black beauty mark penciled near her mouth." His eyes widened. "Just like Marilyn Monroe."

"Was she molested?" Parker asked.

"Nope. Doesn't look like it. Her blouse was ripped open and her bra snapped off. The rest of her clothes were intact. Looks like he washed up afterwards and went to sleep in their bedroom. Got up the next morning, shaved, ate a bowl of Cheerios with skim milk, and went to the bank. Easy as one, two, three."

The chief shook his head. "A bonafide psychopath."

A short, stocky man with close-cropped brown hair emerged from the crowded apartment, ducked under the yellow police tape, and approached the pair. "I'll see your bonafide psychopath and raise you one demented nutzoid with a proclivity for sharp instruments." He grinned, pulling off bloody gloves.

Schwerting headed back into the apartment, smiling for the first time all night as the medical examiner, Vince Bishop, began briefing the chief. "You want to take a look?"

"No thanks, Vince. I'll look at the pictures later. I'm not up for any more of the scene than I can already smell." He paused. "Especially at this time of night. I've been here maybe five minutes and seen two officers puke their guts out over there in the bushes." He nodded at the low-level shrubbery just up from the breezeway where they stood. "I don't plan on being number three."

The medical examiner offered the chief a small blue jar of Vicks VapoRub. "You should try this. People not used to the odor swear by it. I don't need it, but a little dab under your nose'll block out the smell every time. Most of it, anyway."

"No thanks," Parker replied, "never liked the stuff. What's the story on her?"

"Been dead a little over two days. She was starting to bloat up pretty good. The thermostat was set on seventy-eight so she ripened up fast. There are ruptures of small blood vessels in her neck, face, and eyes resulting from occlusion of the jugular by, most likely, a hand."

"So strangulation was the cause of death?"

"I wouldn't bet on it." He scratched his bristly head. "She's got a fractured skull. Left temple. Most likely caused by a blunt object with squared edges. That's the imprint I found. She *really* got popped."

65

"So that did it?"

"There's more. Fragmentation of the sternum. Caused by some type of chopping tool. Probably a small axe. I'd say the blunt end of it left that impression on her head. Blood spatter patterns on the ceiling indicate a minimum of four blows to the chest. The sternum's cracked wide open."

The police chief winced. "So *that* did it?"

"To be honest, I don't think she died until her heart was cut out."

Parker stared in stunned silence at the doorway.

Bishop continued, "Appears a sharp knife was used. Maybe a scalpel. It was very neat. Precise. Like the guy knew exactly what he was doing. If the husband did it, he'd probably make better grades in med school than law school!"

The chief grunted.

"What I think happened, and I can't really verify this until I get the body to the lab for the autopsy, is she got strangled but not to death. Either she blacked out or got knocked out by the blow to the head. Her chest gets whacked open and the killer cuts out her heart. *That* killed her. The murderer then sits down on the couch with heart in hand. Left a big blood stain about five feet from the rest of the body."

"Did he leave it? The heart?" Parker asked tentatively.

"Sorry," Bishop said, raising his open palms and shrugging. "Haven't seen it. I guess your guys can look for it in the morning out back in the undergrowth. If they find it, I wouldn't expect there'd be much left. You know, between the bugs and other critters."

The drifting stench began to turn the chief's stomach. His face turned pale.

"You all right?" Bishop asked.

"I'll be fine. Just a little queasy."

"Did Schwerting tell you about the Marilyn thing?"

"Yeah." The color began to return to his cheeks. "What do you make of it?"

"Don't know. Maybe he's a fan. He sure could have made it easier on me."

"How's that?" queried Parker.

"By using a load of barbiturates like the real Marilyn." The medical examiner grinned. "Wouldn't have been *nearly* as messy."

12

Brilliant, hazy sunlight smacked Joe O'Riley squarely in the face. The brisk chill in the early Saturday morning air invigorated him. Squinting, he walked past a vacant shoeshine stand on the nearly deserted sidewalk and then bounded up the front steps of the landmark Memphis Police Department headquarters building on Adams at Second Street with the zeal and swagger of a man who walked as young as he felt. He firmly held a brown grocery sack under his left arm as a slight breeze ruffled his mop of brown hair handsomely laced with gray. Pulling open the weathered bronze door, he entered the building that held a lifetime of memories for the retired former Memphis Chief of Police.

Like most policemen, O'Riley had taken his career one day at a time, from his start as a rookie until his retirement. Generally in a law-enforcement officer's line of thinking, if one made it through the years on the force without getting killed, one took his pension with a smile and welcomed the chance to stay as far away from the police station as possible. That was where O'Riley soon differed from the others.

Retirement was at first effective. He became a creature of habit, his days varying little from one to another. Mondays, Thursdays, Sundays—it didn't matter. He woke up when he wanted, took it easy around the house, watched some television, then went to bed whenever he damn well pleased. He took comfort in his routine. But after a while, his restless nature took hold.

Sporadic visits to the Homicide Squad to check on his boys, as he affectionately termed the detectives, became more frequent, then a regular weekly event, then two to three times a week, often under the guise of bring-

68

ing doughnuts or some other treat to his beleaguered colleagues in downtown Memphis who were fighting the purveyors of death on the city's streets. As the former chief, he knew and respected the importance of the other departments. Vice, Robbery, all of them. But he had grown up living, eating, and breathing Homicide. It had infected his blood and there was no cure.

O'Riley was one of those policemen who might hang on to be one hundred, outliving everybody while making sure that the younger cops knew about their heritage. A Monday-morning quarterback, back-seat driver, and someone with twenty/twenty hindsight all rolled into one, he was there to comment on cases—what was done right and how it *should* have been done. Often his advice was sought out; other times avoided. Only in the rarest of cases would he actually become involved.

He could grumble and bitch with the best of them, often hiding behind the guise of retirement, but he couldn't hide his genuine interest in law enforcement and a heart of gold. Just ask him for help and he'd give you his full attention and anything else he could think of.

He ambled through the ornate gray marble entryway of the headquarters building and up the marble stairway to Homicide on the second floor. Clad in khaki pants, a navy blazer, and green plaid button-down sport shirt, he looked more like a senior member of a law firm dressing down on Friday than a retired policeman dressing up. The front buttons of his shirt pulled slightly in their holes in a vain attempt to conceal the added pounds he constantly fought to keep in check.

Today was special. Not like the other days he wandered down to the station to mix with the boys. He wanted to look good, to look sharp. He had an announcement to make. An announcement to share with the world. But his world as a retiree was limited to his friends at the police department. More specifically, in Homicide. And the present chief who had succeeded him, Charlie Perry.

O'Riley had fallen in love. He never thought it would happen again. After Evelyn's death, he had thrown himself into police work, making that the love of his life.

But his affections had been rekindled in the past two months in the form of Nancy Summerfield, a petite, attractive widow almost ten years his junior. She lived just four houses down the street from him on North Avalon in midtown Memphis. He was smitten by the tenth-grade English teacher at the affluent Memphis University School the first time he saw her working in her yard. He was in love. No one knew. Least of all Nancy Summerfield.

He stood outside the glass double-doors to Homicide, peering in. The detectives sat at their cluttered desks, stealing a few minutes before tackling the daily routine of tracking down clues and leads involving suspicious deaths and murders throughout the city. They sipped coffee and thumbed through the pages of the morning paper, its sections spread about the room like the remains of the homicide victim they had found in the posh Peabody Hotel the day before, a quickly solved casualty of a drug deal gone bad.

"Well, well, well," remarked Sergeant Jack Harris, O'Riley's closest friend on the force, as O'Riley's nearly six-foot frame slipped through the swinging doors, "look what the cat drug in. How come you ain't been coming down here to see us as much lately? I been losing weight on account of you slacking up on the doughnuts."

"If the truth be told, I've been spending a lot of time with a lady friend of mine," O'Riley announced loudly for all to hear. "She's not real fond of ill-mannered gorillas. Found that out on a trip to the zoo. I figured she wouldn't want to see the animals down here so I left her home. She wanted me to bring these to you guys, though. Made 'em herself."

He opened the brown paper grocery sack and pulled out a couple of white boxes. Gently lifting the lids, he exposed two dark-orange pumpkin pies ringed by a golden-brown flaky crust and covered with thick, billowy whipped cream.

"Those look better than *any* I've seen the Pie Lady make down in Orange Mound," called out another sergeant, Hap Crosby, patting his generous belly. "And, believe me, *I* should know. We need to meet this girlfriend of yours."

"In time," O'Riley replied, sitting down at the gray metal desk next to Harris, who had poured a mug of coffee for his former boss. The older man fingered the rim of the mug as it cooled. The room resounded with a steady clicking as detectives punched up information on their computer terminals. Never one to embrace new technology, he shook his head at how things had changed over the years since he had retired. Picking up his cooling coffee, he drank it down in three massive gulps.

Just then the head of Homicide, Captain Walter McAlister, walked through the swinging glass doors and nodded. "How's it going, O'Riley?"

"It's all jelly but the jar, Walt."

"That's what I like to hear," the diminutive McAlister said, running his hands along his trademark suspenders.

"What's with Billy Crystal over in the corner?" O'Riley asked of no one in particular, referring to Sergeant Ken Driscoll, at twenty-eight, the youngest detective in Homicide, whose balding pate with its sparse, curly brown hair bore a striking resemblance to the famous comedian. "He don't look too happy."

"He *never* looks happy," said detective Mark Harvey, two desks away from Driscoll.

Driscoll looked up from his cluttered desk and glared at O'Riley, raising the middle finger on his right hand.

O'Riley laughed. "He don't talk much either but he sure as hell knows sign language."

Ken Driscoll's haughty, arrogant nature and his disdain for old-style police investigating and anyone associated with it, such as O'Riley, won him few friends in the department. However, his brilliant knowledge of computers to assist in solving homicides entrenched him firmly as the first in what would become the new breed of the future. Even so, his abrasive personality made him the brunt of jokes. And O'Riley took advantage of the situation every chance he could get.

Driscoll scowled at the former chief, finally opening his mouth. "A

71

girlfriend? You? I guess sometimes even a blind dog finds water. What kind of wheelchair does she have—manual or electric? Oh, does she prefer Depends or plastic panties?" Laughing, he continued as O'Riley winked at Harris, waiting for just the right moment to strike back. "If she finds you attractive, she's probably so fat her calves have turned to cows. And wrinkles . . . I bet she's got enough to hold a four-day rain!"

"Unexplained mysteries," O'Riley finally said.

"Whatcha mean?" Harris asked, playing the foil.

"You know, unexplained mysteries. Like why kamikaze pilots wore helmets," the former chief said with a smile. "And why Driscoll's mother didn't put him up for adoption."

All the detectives, Driscoll excluded, laughed.

"You know, Harris, I swear he must have been dropped on his head when he was a baby." O'Riley paused thoughtfully for a split-second, placing a finger under his strong chin and cocking his neck to the side. "And, the more I'm around him, the more I think it was intentional!"

Driscoll swiveled back to face his computer and began typing.

O'Riley beamed like a medieval jester.

Twenty minutes later a telephone rang loudly at a desk on the far side of the department. Sergeant Trevor Mills placed the receiver to his ear, not missing a beat as he shuffled the folders on his desk.

"Homicide, Mills."

O'Riley looked up from the newspaper sports section, watching the thirty-five-year-old across the room. The detective, a cum laude graduate of the University of Texas at Austin, had been on the police force in Memphis for about a year after ten years in the homicide division of the Houston Police Department.

O'Riley had spoken to him on occasion during his forays down to the station. What little he knew about him educationally and personally was impressive. A double major in college in ancient history and psychology. Into new-age thinking and a proponent of daily meditation, the result of

72

alcoholism and a divorce six years prior from a wife who couldn't handle the stresses of being married to a cop. Memphis afforded him a new start. A real thinking-man's policeman, he hadn't had a drink in five years.

Exceedingly fit at 5'10" and 170 pounds, you couldn't find fat anywhere on his body. His thick blond hair, barely receding from a smooth, unlined forehead, was carefully cut, feathering over the tops of his ears. With startling deep Carolina blue eyes, he attracted more than his share of dreamy glances from women.

He was always meticulously dressed in a suit or sport coat, his tie pulled up to his neck at all times. O'Riley had once asked why he always looked as though he just stepped out of a fashion ad. "You never get a second chance to make a good first impression," he had answered. "Why loosen my tie and look like a slob? Somebody will think that's the way I am and I'm not."

O'Riley felt a bond with Mills, who seldom dated, seeing in him the same drive and tenacity toward his work that he himself had exhibited following his wife's death when he was young.

"Hey, Chief," Mills yelled across the room. "Phone. Line two."

O'Riley's lips parted. "Who the hell would try to find me down here?"

"Probably your proctologist," Driscoll yelled.

"Yeah, you're probably right," snapped O'Riley. "I'll tell him I don't need him anymore. I'll just bend over and let you do it. I know you're damn good at sitting down all day with your thumb up your ass!" He picked up the white plastic receiver. "Hello?"

"That you, Joe?"

"Yeah. Who's this?"

"Bill Parker. In Charlottesville."

O'Riley's eyes lit up. "I'll be a son of a bitch!"

"How's it going?"

"At my age, it's downhill all the way. How'd you track me down here at the station?"

"Got your answering machine at home. I asked myself, 'If I was a retired, bored police chief, where would I go?'"

"Pretty perceptive. I knew you'd make a good chief someday."

"I understand my old man helped your guys out on some ATF business a while back."

O'Riley smiled, his mind filling with memories. "Yeah, he did. It was just like in the old days, back when you were an annoying little kid running around shooting everything that moved. Not too long after that I set you up in your patrolman job with the Charlottesville police when you graduated from UVA. What was that, 1973?"

Parker laughed. "You got a good memory."

"Like a goddam elephant," O'Riley replied. He began tapping his pencil lead on the top of the desk. "Look at you now. Chief of Police. You've come a long way, Bill."

"Thanks to you," Parker said. Then his tone turned serious. "I need a favor, Joe. Think you can help me out?"

"You name it. I'll do what I can."

"There's a murder we're investigating. A woman. Twenty-three years old. Married. We found her night before last in her apartment. She'd been killed two days before that. The prime suspect is her husband, twenty-four. He's still at large."

"How'd he do it?"

"Blow to the head to knock her out. Then he cut out her heart. Wasn't a pretty sight."

O'Riley paused. "Did he leave it or take it with him?"

"Took it. We searched a quarter-mile radius yesterday and didn't find shit."

O'Riley's mind again flooded with memories, none of them good. "I've seen it before . . . a few times. I don't care to ever see it again. Your dad must have filled you in on that case."

"He did," Parker replied softly. "You still touchy about it?"

"I'm over it. There are a lot of sick sons of bitches out there." He paused momentarily. "It didn't happen in that same house on Fourteenth Street, I hope."

"No, but just around the block. Thirteenth Street. The husband's in his third year at UVA Law School."

O'Riley shook his head, propping the receiver to his ear with his left shoulder. "Was she seeing somebody else?"

"We're all over it from that angle. The autopsy showed traces of semen in her vaginal canal. Turns out she'd been practicing the horizontal mambo with her boss the night she was killed. He's a hot-shot criminal lawyer in town, our local gigolo. Once you cut through his bullshit, you find the bastard's covered with Teflon. Nothing ever sticks to him or his clients."

"You think he had something to do with it?" asked O'Riley.

"Nah, he's clean. Came forward with his story the minute he heard about it."

"Everything points to a whacked-out sicko committing a crime of passion, if you ask me. Anything else besides the mutilation that sticks out?"

Every keyboard in Homicide fell silent at the utterance of the words whacked-out sicko and mutilation. Six sets of eyes descended on O'Riley. All ears strained.

Parker replied, "There was a piece of paper inscribed with the name Marilyn on it."

"And?"

"Make-up had been applied to her face so she looked like Marilyn Monroe. Right out of the 1950s. Hair was even spray-painted yellow. Name's David Lancaster. We've talked to his parents in Richmond."

"How'd they react?" O'Riley asked, puffing out his chest at the gawking detectives, acting like an old pro showing a class of rookies how it's done.

"Just like Hinckley's after he shot Reagan. McVeigh's after the bombing of the Federal Building. Shock . . . disbelief. Then they offered to help.

Any way they could. Promised to contact us if they hear from him." Parker paused to catch his breath. "We've checked on hotels, hospitals, jails, and morgues. Also pulled all credit card receipts and run cellular phone checks for all other family members and friends of the couple. We're drawing a big blank. It appears he closed his bank accounts, abandoned his car, and evidently hit the road. I was hoping you could help shed some light on the situation."

"Anything, of course." O'Riley shrugged. "But I got *no idea* how I can help."

"There's a medical angle we need some help on. Lancaster was treated in Memphis at St. Jude Children's Hospital. Twice. First time when he was twelve. Then again this past summer for a brain tumor. The doctor's name is Peter Morgan. I figured you might check it out for me."

O'Riley's lips spread into a wide grin. "It'll give my ass something to do."

"I'll call you back tomorrow to see if you had any luck. I've got your number at home," Parker said.

"Let me call you," O'Riley said. "I'll be out and about. Can you give me till noon?"

"You got it. I'll expect your call right after church. Oh, one more thing," added Parker.

"Yeah?"

"Lancaster . . . he's heterochromia."

"Hetero-*what*?"

"Heterochromia."

"I figured he was *some sort* of sexual deviate," responded O'Riley. "What does that mean? He does it in old Buicks?"

"No, no," Parker replied, "it's got nothing to do with sex. It's his eyes. They aren't the same color. The left one is blue. The right one is green. That should make him relatively easy to track down."

A chill shot down O'Riley's spine. He held the receiver to his ear, saying nothing.

"Joe? You there?"

"I'm here," he finally answered. "That just took me by surprise. I've only known of two people like that."

"With different colored eyes?"

"Yeah. One is David Bowie, the rock singer."

"And the other?"

"The guy who got the chair for murdering my wife and nine other women." O'Riley drew in a deep breath and exhaled before unleashing a name from his lips he had hoped to keep trapped forever in the farthest corners of his mind. "Jimmy Seabold."

13

At 4:15 that afternoon, O'Riley sat in the small cluttered office of Dr. Peter Morgan on the fourth floor of St. Jude Children's Research Hospital. The doctor had readily agreed to forego his Saturday off to meet with the former chief when he learned it involved police business linked to one of his recent successful patients, David Lancaster. O'Riley leaned back in a brown-tweed swivel chair opposite Morgan's walnut desk, pressing his fingertips together as he awaited the doctor's arrival.

The quick shuffling of footsteps came from down the hall. A diminutive, frail man with thick, black-framed glasses and thinning light brown hair pulled back in a pony tail suddenly bolted through the doorway, his white lab coat flapping behind him like a kite tail whipping in the wind.

"Mr. O'Riley," he said apologetically, extending his hand, "sorry I'm late."

"No problem," replied O'Riley, standing and firmly gripping the eccentric-looking doctor's hand. "I kept myself amused reading your wall." He nodded at framed diplomas and awards as well as a small bulletin board covered with *Far Side* medical cartoons. "Thank you for seeing me on such short notice."

Morgan sat down, fumbling amid the piles of folders hiding the top of his desk. "Lancaster, Lancaster . . . let's see," he muttered, "I know she must have found it after I asked her to—ah! Here it is. Both of them actually."

"If you could just recap his medical history, I'll try to take a few notes." O'Riley pulled a black Bic pen from the inside breast pocket of his blazer and angled a yellow legal pad on his crossed leg for support.

The doctor flipped open the first of the two manila folders. "We first treated Lancaster here when he was twelve years old. His home was in Richmond. He exhibited symptoms of swollen lymph nodes, profuse sweating, and weight loss. We saw a shadow in his x-rays of a mediastinum mass in his chest." He paused, pushing his glasses up the bridge of his well-endowed nose, and looked directly into O'Riley's eyes. "Hodgkin's disease."

The former chief scribbled on his pad.

"He was treated with mantle radiation. That is, we radiated the bottom third of his head and also his upper abdomen. The young man came through with flying colors. We watched him closely for a year, then checked him twice a year until he was eighteen. A minor drawback arose when he turned nineteen. Nothing serious. He seemed depressed, lethargic. We found he had become hypothyroid. Happens sometimes as a result of radiation. We put him on a daily thyroid hormone replacement which did the trick. No more problems."

"Until?"

Morgan reached for the second folder and opened it. "Until this year. Late May. He was plagued by headaches and forgetfulness. Even though he's an adult, we wanted to bring him back here for diagnosis and treatment. Once a patient at St. Jude, always a patient, no matter what your age, we like to say." He smiled broadly.

"Did he experience any amnesia? Or just forgetfulness?"

"Only forgetfulness," responded the doctor. "Forgetfulness is a disturbance of retrieval in the brain whereas amnesia is a disturbance of learning. This pointed to a brain tumor. An MRI confirmed it. It was malignant."

"So he had a recurrence of cancer after all those years."

"Actually, no. We term Lancaster's problem a *secondary* malignancy."

"Caused by what?"

"Probably one of two things." The doctor again adjusted his glasses. "Either he had a genetic predisposition for it or it was a result of the radiation from the treatment of his Hodgkin's. Brain tumors, like most cancers, arise after mutation or altered expression of several growth-controlling tu-

79

mor suppressor genes and growth-promoting oncogenes."

O'Riley put down his pen and nodded. The doctor was speaking a foreign language.

"We found the tumor in the frontal lobe of his brain. A low-grade glioma. Technically, astrocytoma. On the up side, that particular type is slow-growth."

"How'd you treat it?"

"Through resection and high-level radiation. That is, we performed a craniotomy, cutting open his skull. After removing the tumor, we replaced the section of bone we took out with a small plate. Then we put him on a regimen of six weeks of daily radiation at one hundred fifty rads a day. We radiated a broad area of his head for four weeks and then cut the field size to the area of the tumor for the last two weeks."

O'Riley nervously tapped his left foot on the floor. "Any side effects from all that?"

"There usually are. Too much radiation causes some dementias. The symptoms are a lot like Alzheimer's. Forgetfulness. Wobbly on your feet. Since Lancaster had experienced forgetfulness even *before* the radiation, I decided to include him in one of my experimental groups."

O'Riley raised his eyebrows.

"We treated his memory loss with an experimental memory drug we developed and have been testing here at St. Jude for a couple of years. He received it in conjunction with his last four weeks of radiation."

"What exactly does it do?"

"I call the drug Alzheimerone. It's my baby. We developed it in hopes of curing the lost memory symptoms of not only early and late-onset Alzheimer's victims but also memory problems resulting from brain tumors and accidental brain injuries, like those associated with automobile accidents and falls. It stimulates the cells in the memory portion of the brain, much like steroids are used to stimulate muscle growth and development in weightlifters. Hopefully this stimulation of the memory cells will lead to the recovery of lost memory function."

O'Riley nodded, impressed. "What happened in Lancaster's case?"

"I was greatly encouraged by his progress. By summer's end he was good as new. Able to go back for his final year of law school." He leaned back in his chair and made a steeple with his fingers, beaming. But his mood quickly turned somber. "It's a shame if he's responsible for the murder of his wife. I hope it's not David. He was always such a nice, pleasant young man. I can't imagine what would make him snap like that. That is, if he is this killer."

14

"It's out of my hands now," O'Riley said after finishing his noontime telephone conversation with Bill Parker in Charlottesville. The chief had thanked O'Riley for his work in uncovering Lancaster's medical background so quickly, promising to return the favor someday. O'Riley had wished Parker luck on solving his case and had hung up, intent on enjoying a Sunday afternoon nap.

He leaned back in the dark green recliner nestled in the corner of his small, cozy den. His left hand gently stroked the thick black and tan coat of his German shepherd, Bullet. The aged dog's eyes were tightly closed, twitching slightly. He was oblivious to the affection being heaped upon him but secure in the mutual love shared with his master, evidenced by the well-worn spot in the beige carpet where he lay.

Just as he loved this old dog, O'Riley loved his old house. He had known no other, having lived there all his life. Built by his father in the early 1920s when North Avalon was a street on the fringes of the city, it was now firmly entrenched in midtown Memphis.

The English bungalow-style home had remained virtually unchanged by the passage of time. The same furniture. The same oriental rugs. The same unique smell each house takes on over time. The only changes had been the loved ones who had come and gone through its doors over the years.

He thought of his mother, Louise, who had passed away when he was but five years old from complications of appendicitis. And his father, Paddy, a lieutenant with the Memphis Police Department, shot and killed while trying to settle an altercation between two drunks when Joe, known then as

Joey, was only sixteen. Also his best childhood friends, Jenny Adair and Will Harrison, killed in an automobile accident when they were eighteen. And his wife, Evelyn, whom he had married in 1951.

His life had revolved around her. Her inability to have children was never a source of conflict between them. The gentle manner and sweet disposition she possessed had filled his world with happiness. They had each other, sharing a peaceful idyllic existence. Until tragedy struck, taking from O'Riley not only his beloved wife but also his desire to ever love again.

Time would never be able to give her back. But it had finally returned his will to love. It gave him Nancy Summerfield.

He sat up in his recliner, eyeing the half-filled bottle of Bushmills Irish whiskey perched on the small table next to him. Normally reserved for consumption during the nightly 10 P.M. newscast, O'Riley felt a twinge of temptation he couldn't resist.

He picked up the bottle, unscrewed the cap, and took a swig. He winced at the slight bitterness that gave way to a warm, soothing sensation that slowly spread down his throat. He took another sip.

Within minutes the contented former chief leaned back in his recliner, his eyelids slowly drooping. The hardwood floors in the old house creaked gently as O'Riley, comforted by the seeming presence and memories of almost everyone he had ever loved, quietly drifted off, joining his dog in sleep.

When he awoke in the early afternoon, his first thoughts were of Nancy. After swapping his worn white terrycloth robe and house slippers for a pair of olive pants and plaid flannel shirt, O'Riley soon found himself four houses down the block, standing at her front door. He rang the bell twice. No response. He had a sneaking suspicion where he'd find her.

He walked to the back yard. With one hand on the rose-painted wooden gate and the other shading his face against the daylight glare, his eyes fell on her. Black slacks and a white cotton sweater covered a petite, five-foot one frame. The soft rays of the sun beamed down on her through the trees as she knelt in a vegetable garden, illuminating her brunette hair and making her features appear delicate and fragile.

O'Riley was enthralled by everything about her, from her beautiful looks, poised manner, and sweet yet sometimes feisty demeanor down to her often-animated gesturing and a special gleam in her eyes. He hadn't felt that way about a woman in years. Since he was young. Since Evelyn.

"Whatcha doing? Picking dinner?" he asked as she gripped a tomato with white canvas gardening gloves and plucked it from its vine.

Nancy turned her head, her eyes finding O'Riley's. A sincere smile crept across her face. She was radiant even though she had been toiling in the garden for over an hour. Her dark-brown eyes sparkled, just as they had the first time she had met the former police chief. The date had been the fifth of August and, to her surprise, she had committed it to memory.

"Might be," she replied. "You had lunch yet?" Her hand made a pass against her hair, gently fluffing it with a few light pats.

"Nope," he replied as he walked through the gate to her side.

"How about a late lunch-early dinner?"

"Is that an invitation?"

"You're getting *pretty* sharp in your old age," she said, her voice thick with pretend sarcasm.

O'Riley smiled. "I'm also getting used to your cooking. Meatless spaghetti again?"

"No, I'll be a little bit fancier for you this time."

"How fancy?" he asked, preferring a meat-and-potatoes diet.

"I'll take some of my home-grown onion, squash, zucchini, and red bell pepper, then add some black olives, sauté it all in olive oil and garlic, throw in some chopped tomatoes, pour it all over some fettuccine pasta and top it off with a bit of grated Parmesan cheese."

O'Riley shook his head. "*That's* how you vegetarians stay so damn slim. I just couldn't do it all the time."

"It's done wonders for your weight."

"Yeah," he grinned. "I used to be an *overweight* tub of lard. Now I'm just a tub of lard." He stuck his hands into his pockets and gave a tug, pulling his loose pants up on his hips.

"Don't be silly," she chided. "How many pounds have you lost?"

"About ten."

"Then stop your bellyaching. You're looking real good. About fifteen years younger than you are."

"Hey, don't get me wrong," he blurted, holding up his palms, "you're one helluva cook. But every now and then I just *got* to have a big, thick, juicy, rare New York strip. I just start cutting and then listen to it." He bellowed out a loud mooing noise.

Nancy's smooth face wrinkled in disgust. "Ugh! I don't see how you do it. If it's got a face on it, *I* don't eat it!"

She continued picking vegetables, placing a few yellow squash in a brown wicker basket as O'Riley looked on. Clouds streamed across the face of the sun, bathing the yard in alternating intervals of shade and bright light in the cooling afternoon air. A light wind through the trees lifted her hair as she stood up.

"You ready to come inside and cook?" she asked.

"I'm ready to come inside and watch *you* cook. I could watch you do anything." He grinned, unable to take his eyes off her svelte figure.

She smiled.

"You know," O'Riley said, patting his mid-section, "the way to a man's heart really is through his stomach."

"I've known that about you for almost two months now!" She laughed as O'Riley picked up the basket of vegetables.

They walked to the back porch door and into the house, soon standing in the middle of her renovated kitchen with its new appliances, cabinets, and countertops shining a bright white. Two short-stemmed yellow roses in a crystal bud vase rested on the end of the breakfast bar near a wall phone.

85

"I bet this cost a pretty penny," O'Riley said, drying the vegetables after Nancy rinsed them in the sink.

"Considering how much time I spend in here, it was well worth it." She pulled a vegetable cleaver from a drawer and began to slice each one, carefully roll chopping them into julienne strips and then dropping them into a deep, stainless-steel mixing bowl as her favorite visitor looked on.

Suddenly she tilted her head. "How much do you drink, Joe?"

"Aw, not much. A couple of shots of Bushmills Irish whiskey every night before I go to bed."

"Only at bedtime?"

"Well, sometimes before a nap. Like today."

"Is two shots the most you ever have?" she asked with a knowing smile.

"Ummm . . . occasionally maybe three." He paused for a moment. "Or four."

"That can't be good for you, not at your age." She continued to cut, filling the kitchen with the constant tapping of metal on wood.

"Whattaya mean, at my age? How do you think I got *this* far?" He chuckled. "Besides, the doctors tell me I got the heart and reflexes younger guys would kill for."

"I know about the heart, but you'll have to demonstrate those reflexes sometime." She grinned. Then her smile faded. "Tell me, how long have you been doing it? The drinking routine."

"Since I lost Evelyn."

"So you retreated into a bottle, like so many others."

"Hell, no!" he replied defensively. "Now look, Doctor, I didn't retreat anywhere. I caught her killer, worked my butt off to get to be Chief of Police and didn't let up until I retired. Does *that* sound like I retreated into a bottle?"

She smiled at him again, instantly defusing the sudden burst of anger. "Then why do you do it?"

"I enjoy it. I like the way it tastes. Why do you plant all those different vegetables in your back yard almost year round?"

"It relaxes me," she responded.

"Why do you teach all those kids over at M.U.S?"

"It's my job," she answered quickly. "And, believe it or not, it relaxes me too!"

"Well, drinking relaxes me."

"I should hope so. Three or four shots straight up of *anything* would relax most people." She laughed. "But you didn't do it before your wife died?"

"No, not every night. Once or twice a week."

"As I said, retreated into a bottle."

O'Riley gripped the white countertop with both hands, gazed down at the smooth red brick floor, and let out a sigh of frustration. Then he stared into Nancy's brown eyes. "If I didn't know better, I might think you were trying to analyze me. Like a shrink."

"No," she assured him, "just trying to get to know you better."

Deep down she had struck a sore spot and he knew it. He became melancholy, and made no attempt to hide it. He had never spoken about the aftermath of his wife's death with anyone. "I did retreat into that bottle, in a way," O'Riley confessed. "It eased the loneliness, dulled the pain."

"What was the worst part for you?" Nancy asked.

"Her absence. It never faded. And the little things you take for granted. I missed that smile when I came home at night. That touch that told me I was loved." He stared out the window, eyes wistful, as memories flashed through his mind. "She loved being a wife, doing things for me like washing and ironing my uniform and fixing my meals. All of a sudden she was gone and I was helpless around the house." But in a split-second, he snapped back. "What about you? What did you miss most?"

That same faraway look stole into Nancy's eyes. She ignored the olive oil heating in the skillet on the stove. "I missed all the little things you men-tioned. But I missed the big things too. Like being invited out in groups with married people. You aren't included because people think you'll feel uncomfortable, like a fifth wheel. Couples can't relate. It's not intentional but you just feel isolated."

O'Riley nodded.

A slight sizzling noise filled the air as she dropped four pods of freshly-minced garlic into the skillet. Vapor laced with a heavy garlic fragrance rose upward, bringing tears to her already-glazed eyes.

"With Tom's cancer," she continued, "I had time to prepare. But when the time finally comes, you find you weren't really prepared. You can't be. They're gone and, suddenly, you have nobody to talk to. Nobody who *really* understands."

O'Riley smiled and slowly nodded, watching as Nancy cooked and bared her soul at the same time.

She eased the fettuccine into the boiling water in a ten-quart Dutch oven and poured the vegetables on top of the golden-browned garlic. An enticing aroma accompanied the loud sizzling and fizzing as she sautéed, stirring the vegetables in well-rehearsed, fluid strokes.

She said, "Going to bed was the worst part. Crying myself to sleep. You just feel cut in half when you lose your mate. You can't trust your innermost secrets to anyone."

"I know just how you feel. But you know something else? We've been through all that. It's in the past. Now we need to enjoy the present."

She began to smile, still stirring the vegetables. "How did we ever get on that subject?"

"I tell you one thing. Before I go to bed tonight, I'm having at least two shots of Bushmills!"

"Tonight, I may do the same!" Both laughed.

A few minutes later they stood before two heaping plates.

"You're a wizard in the kitchen," O'Riley said. "Got any plans for dessert?"

"Fresh pumpkin pie. I couldn't make a couple for your police buddies and none for you."

"Anything else?"

"Besides *real* whipped cream on top?"

"Yeah. I've been thinking lately about maybe, uh, a little something special for dessert sometime." The corners of his mouth arched up in a sly smile.

"Joseph O'Riley, are you making a pass at me?" she blurted, frowning.

"N . . . no," he stuttered, "I mean, y . . . yes. I think so."

Her mock anger melted. "Don't be so skittish. I'm not mad. I'm just teasing you."

O'Riley sighed, his broad shoulders relaxing.

"I thought we were just friends," she said. "Are we becoming something more?"

"It kinda scares me but I think we are."

Nancy took him gently by the hand. "It scares me, too," she replied as he pulled her toward him. "I like being scared," she whispered in his ear.

15

Tuesday night settled quietly over the mountains surrounding Roanoke, Virginia.

He was happy he had surrendered to the persistent urges. Trying to fight them had left him exhausted. With the battle over, exhilaration was his.

He sat at the make-up table in his room at the Roanoke Marriott. The bright bulbs surrounding the large, oval dressing mirror illuminated his face. He applied the make-up with the deft, professional skill of a mortician preparing a corpse for eternity rather than a killer retreating into the anonymity a disguise would afford him.

Each stroke had a purpose in the transformation. Sporting darkened hair and eyebrows, he looked totally different. Almost. Then with the insertion of a single blue contact lens in his right eye, the sham was complete. He admired himself in the mirror.

A burst of light suddenly flashed in the deep recesses of his mind, so brilliant he couldn't see. He kept staring into the mirror as his vision slowly cleared, startled at the two images he found there.

"I have to leave for my sales conference in a couple of weeks, Jimmy. Remember?"

"Aw, don't go, Mom. Please?" begged the young boy, his eyes full of distress.

"I have to. It's only once a year. If I don't show up, Avon will give my job to someone else. With no job, we'd have no money for rent or food. You like to eat, don't you?"

The youngster nodded as he stared down at the faded blue area rug on the living room floor. "No money for movies, either," he murmured.

Audrey Seabold lovingly cupped her son's chin in her soft hand and tilted his head slowly upward to meet her gaze. "But this time will be different. I'm taking you with me."

"A trip! Where to?"

"Memphis. They have *lots* of movie theaters there. Big ones. Little ones. All sizes. We'll take the train."

His eyes widened like a child seeing something wonderful for the first time. "The train!"

"But this won't be an ordinary trip. We'll make it a vacation and stop overnight to see movies in towns along the way."

"Can we play the make-up game?" he asked, chest heaving.

"As much as you want. We've got our own sleeper compartment. You'll have the time of your life," she replied, running her fingers through his curly brown hair. "You'll never forget *this* trip. I promise."

Lancaster picked up his axe and began sharpening the blade. The harsh, grating sound of metal against whetstone filled the room, fueling his compulsion.

He held the axe up to his face and closely examined the shiny edge. Running his forefinger down the blade, he drew blood. Quickly he stuck his finger in his mouth.

After packing his gear he grabbed the car keys and walked from his room on the sixth floor. The door shut softly behind him.

Three and a half miles and twenty minutes later, he was parked across the street from the Grandin Theater in the upper middle-class Raleigh Court/ Wasena section of Roanoke.

The warm lights of the theater marquee cut through the chilly darkness, somehow soothing him. He stood silently, gaze fixed on an upstairs window of the old, two-story red-brick building as the cozy, comfortable sensation intensified, engulfing him. It was as if he had been there years before. Yet he had never been to Roanoke in his life.

Suddenly his eyes squinted. There she was. Right on schedule. Like the night before. And the night before that. She took a deep drag on a cigarette before snuffing it out on the window sill. Then she ran her fingers through her light brown hair before closing her eyes and massaging her temples. She vanished as quickly as she had appeared, returning to the solitude of the projection booth.

His breathing quickened. She would be perfect. Not too big and not too small.

"Looks like you picked a winner," he said to himself.

"No," he replied with a shake of his head. "*You* picked the winner."

After crossing the street, he eased up to the brown-tiled ticket booth of the multi-screen theater.

"Must be a slow night," he remarked to the young high school girl behind the counter.

"School night," she replied. "It's always busy on Fridays and Saturdays. What movie you seeing?"

He shrugged. "Doesn't matter. I haven't seen any of them. You pick."

"Well, what kind of movie do you like most?" she asked. "Comedies? Action? Violence? Love stories? Human drama?"

His right eye began to twitch. "Violence," he replied. "I like violence a lot."

The young girl pushed a button. After a momentary whirring sound, a ticket popped out from under the shiny metal counter in front of her. She tore it in half, handing him a stub. "Six dollars," she said, taking a ten-dollar bill from his outstretched hand and returning his change. "If you don't like this movie, I'll tell them to give you a refund," she promised.

"No need to worry about that. I'm sure I'll get my money's worth."

He turned to his left, gripped the handle of the glass entry door, swung it open, and stepped inside the muted light of the narrow lobby.

✳

The next morning at ten-thirty, there was chaos on Grandin Street. Blue-uniformed policemen diverted traffic away from the crime scene, blocked off by four Roanoke city patrol cars, their blue lights flashing non-stop, and three unmarked detective cruisers. Yellow police tape ringed the sidewalk and entrance to the stately old theater.

Television crews in vans with mobile antennas stretching skyward taped segments for the noontime news shows and prepared for live, on-scene reports. Gawkers, thrill-seekers, and the simply curious jostled for position behind the tape, craning their necks for a better view.

A detective, well-dressed in a tweed sport coat and tie, stepped through the lobby door into the bright sunshine. Easing on his sunglasses, he spotted the homicide squad sergeant approaching.

"Is it as bad as they made it sound?" asked the sergeant, buttoning his blazer as newspaper cameras clicked monotonously.

"Worse," responded the detective. "Come see for yourself."

They quickly walked through the rose-painted stucco lobby with its marbleized green and black columns on the way to the second-floor auditoriums.

"The stiff's the theater projectionist," the detective said. "Female, white, twenty-one, five-foot three. About a hundred and fifteen pounds. Name's Margaret Tisdale. Single. Lives alone."

He gripped a black, wrought-iron handrail as did the sergeant. They quickly scaled the dark green and burgundy carpeted stairwell.

The detective continued, "The body was found by the manager when she opened up a little after nine this morning."

They paused for a moment on a landing. The glow from the light in the recessed oval ceiling fixture reflected off the sergeant's bald head.

"The front door was unlocked, the upstairs projector exhaust fans were on, even the rectifier was on."

"What the hell's a rectifier?" asked the sergeant.

"The power supply to the projector."

"How do you know all this shit?"

"I'm a detective, ain't I? Actually, the manager filled me in. Anyway, the house lights were on. So were the amps and the marquee lights. Almost *everything* was on."

"What wasn't?"

"The concession stand." They continued up the remaining steps to the upstairs lobby. "A couple of high school girls shut it down at 10:15 last night. Gave the money box to the projectionist at 10:30. That included the box office proceeds. They hit the road. The projectionist was the only one left. Along with about fifteen customers split between the five screens. The last shows started about 9:15. She's in the projection booth. Blunt trauma to the head. Chest hacked open. The medical examiner's doing his prelim right now."

"Have you ruled out an inside job?"

"Not a possibility. The high school kids look like candy-stripers. The money box was near the body. Looks intact. Whoever did it wasn't out for cash," the detective added, stroking his chin.

The two entered the upper south auditorium.

"This place is spooky," the sergeant said, eyeing the medieval-styled concrete block stone walls with wooded gargoyles jutting out near the ceiling. "How old is it?"

"Built in the early thirties. Divided into multi-screens in the mid-eighties. Come on," he urged, "the best is yet to come."

They walked three more paces forward to a wide-open green door on their left. Trudging up the worn concrete steps, they felt like they had traveled over sixty years back in time.

The work room, adjacent to the projector room, looked like a cluttered graveyard of antique cinema artifacts. Wooden shelves sagged, filled with old movie posters, platter holders for film reels, film cans, film clamps, and broken ash trays from an era when smoking was encouraged.

Venerable theater seats broken by the hand of time littered the room along with an old make-up table and various pieces of obsolete projection machinery making navigation across the floor difficult. Other detectives and forensic personnel were observing, photographing, and noting everything they saw, letting no obstacles stand in their way.

"What do we have here?" the sergeant asked, nodding at a white porcelain wash basin attached to the outside of an old-fashioned toilet closet.

A forensic technician hovered over the sink, discolored by decades-old lime stains and blood stains less than twelve hours old. He glanced up at the sergeant. "My steak to your hot dog this blood matches the lady's in the next room."

"You're on," the sergeant replied. "You want mustard, ketchup, or both?"

The technician grinned. "Just mustard. I've seen enough red today."

"Here's what you've been waiting for," said the detective as both men maneuvered into the projection room.

One wall was covered by a huge, black, outdated power-switch panel that had once controlled the house lights, curtains, and marquee lights. With its knobs, buttons, and switches, it resembled a control panel for an electric chair execution from an earlier era. At its base lay the body of Margaret Tisdale, her white sweater turned dark maroon by blood. The medical examiner knelt over the corpse.

"This is the work of a *major* head case," the sergeant said, shaking his head.

A three-by-five slip of paper with the name Elizabeth printed in black Sharpie lay close to the body. A black wig covered her brunette hair. Facial make-up brought to mind a young Elizabeth Taylor.

"It's the same guy as in Charlottesville last week," the detective claimed.

"You sure it's not a copycat?" countered the sergeant.

"No way. It's the same guy. No doubt. I saw it on NLETS last week," he said, referring to the National Law Enforcement Teletype System. "Same M.O. Left a note with a movie star's name on it. That detail wasn't released to the media. They got Marilyn Monroe. We get Liz Taylor. I already called up the Charlottesville P.D. A Lieutenant Schwerting and a detective should be here within an hour."

"Try to find any connections between the suspect and *anybody*, business or social, both in Charlottesville and here in Roanoke."

"Looks like the only one who saw it happen was Sgt. Pepper over there in the corner," the detective said, pointing to a beat-up mannequin propped behind the projection equipment. He wore a tattered navy bellman's jacket with gold trim and gold fringe hanging from his shoulders. "And he ain't talking."

"You got a pretty good idea of the time of death, Doc?" the sergeant asked the medical examiner.

"Indications point to sometime between eleven and one. I'd say closer to eleven," he replied, scratching his ear with the back of his gloved hand.

The sergeant turned back to the detective. "You said the house lights were on. That means the murder would have occurred sometime after the last show let out around midnight, right?"

"I thought the same thing but the manager told me there's something called sensing tape at the end of a movie reel. Automatically turns up the house lights. So it could have been either way."

The sergeant sighed.

"Don't feel so bad, guys. You're on the right track," the medical examiner said. "Looks like she's missing a very important piece of her anatomy."

The sergeant read the medical examiner's thoughts perfectly, hearing the words ring in his head before they were spoken.

"Her heart."

16

The shade furnished by the billowy, majestic oak trees that had towered over Court Square in downtown Memphis for well over a hundred years slowly gave way to the changing of the seasons. Some of the once-green leaves clung to the branches, transformed into hues of bright yellow and fiery red. Others slipped their tenuous grip, drifting gently to the ground below.

Court Square, built on a short city block near the downtown legal court system in the mid-1800s, offered a brief respite from the hustle of the workaday world surrounding it. The Hebe Fountain's cascading waterfalls invited visitors to sit on the worn, wooden park benches as mist sprayed into the shifting breezes.

The Porter Building, adjacent to the south side of the park, soared above the only patch of greenery and trees on Main Street. When built in 1895, the ten-story skyscraper was the tallest building between Chicago and New Orleans. Converted to condominiums in the 1980s, the red-brick and terra-cotta structure was now overshadowed by modern towers.

Affording magnificent views of the Mississippi River from its upper floors, residents on the lower floors were quick to purchase any units available in their quest to move up. A widow on the second floor was one exception. Annie Shepherd had purchased the very first condominium after the building's residential conversion. Moving to enhance her view would be pointless. She had been blind for over four decades.

A dinging chime signaled the arrival of the elevator. A moment later the blue door opened and a woman stepped out into the lobby. Her faded-brown hair, sparsely streaked with gray, was pulled back in a loose barrette. A mahogany cane tapped against the white marble floor and echoed off the walls.

The lobby was small but seemed large with a winding, spiral staircase rising on the right side. A wood-framed, forest-green love seat was pushed against the salmon-colored wall on the opposite side, all illuminated by a brass chandelier.

The woman walked slowly past the love seat, through the front door, and down the eight pink granite steps to the sidewalk. After a few short strides on Main Street, she turned into Court Square, her left arm tightly gripping an eighteen by twenty-four-inch French paintbox easel.

A slight wind kicked up sending her full-length cotton caftan whipping behind her. Pausing for a split-second, she clutched at her brown leather vest to keep it from flapping. At 5'9" and one hundred thirty-five pounds, her slender figure was concealed by her preferred style of dress.

Nearing sixty years old, her face possessed a natural beauty highlighted by a hint of softly iridescent lipstick. That beauty, however, was partially hidden by ever-present sunglasses.

Although she used her cane, she could have easily found her spot near the Hebe Fountain without it. She made the short trip every day of the year without fail. On days too cold she would stay just long enough to feed the park's pigeons and squirrels. They depended on her. No one else did. Without them, she too would be alone in the world.

By the time mist from the fountain had landed gently on her face, she was being followed by a swell of cooing pigeons and an army of squirrels, as if she were taking a group of students on a field trip.

Once seated, she opened the wooden paintbox and extended its three legs, quickly converting it into an easel, and arranged her paint, brushes, and a small palette. She then dipped her hand into a small bag, grabbing a fistful of bird seed and peanuts, and threw it to her right. In the darkness of her mind she reveled at the sound of scampering paws and hundreds of fluttering wings accompanied by coos of contentment. Her furry and feathery friends then dispersed, leaving her alone in the warm morning sunshine.

✳

Joe O'Riley left the police station and glanced at his watch. 11:30. His desire to aggravate Ken Driscoll had been sufficiently sated, capped by the sergeant's profanity-laced tirade aimed at the former chief as the detective stormed from Homicide.

At first O'Riley headed for his Lincoln but then decided to walk down the few short blocks to Court Square. Walk and think about this second murder in Virginia, noticed by the detectives on the police wire, which also involved a missing heart. Jimmy Seabold's 1957 rampage swirled in his mind. Perhaps a little time idly sitting under the trees near the fountain, observing others doing the same, would ease his apprehension.

The morning stroll was soothing. Exercise was one thing he knew he needed more of. The sun warmed his face, its rays flashing off the windshields of the traffic passing down Second Street. The sidewalk bustled with people wandering about on their lunch breaks.

He entered Court Square near the old pavilion and noticed four artists sketching portraits and caricatures of passersby. They all sat on one side of the Hebe Fountain, the north side. On the other side a woman with a small easel sat alone. Her outstretched right hand almost touched the concrete sidewalk. Squirrels cautiously approached her and then gently snatched peanuts in the shell from her grasp, scampering into the grass to devour them.

O'Riley walked over and asked why the other artists were busy and she was not.

"They charge twenty-five dollars," she replied, her voice barely audible over the rushing waters of the fountain. "My price is fifty."

He sat down on the brick wall near her easel, his lips forming a slight smile. "What makes you so special? You need to cover the cost of the peanuts or something?"

She cocked her head slightly. "They're all artists who sketch surface portraits. I sketch portraits from within one's soul."

99

He frowned. "How do you see things other artists don't?"

She tapped her dark sunglasses twice with her left forefinger, then the side of her head once.

He gulped, his face flushing red. "Sorry, I didn't realize—"

"No offense. Happens all the time."

"My name's O'Riley. Joe O'Riley." He hesitated, unsure whether or not to extend his hand.

"Annie Shepherd," she replied, holding out hers. Their hands had no trouble connecting.

"I don't get it. How can you be blind and paint portraits?"

"It's not unlike a high-speed typist. They don't have to look down at the keyboard to see what they're doing. They *know* where the keys are by feel."

"Yeah, but painting's different."

Annie shook her head. "Not really. What I do is an extension of an art school exercise where we all had to sketch contour drawings while not being allowed to look at the work in progress. That taught us how to feel our hands with our minds as a guide. Needless to say, mine were the best drawings anyone had *ever* done on that little exercise."

O'Riley laughed. "Hell, I guess so!"

"Of course, I had an unfair advantage. My vision."

"I don't follow you."

Annie's slender face became serene. "Sometimes I feel what someone sitting here feels. I see things that they see, sometimes in their present, sometimes in their past."

"All right," smiled O'Riley. "That's worth the price of admission right there. You're on! Gimme fifty bucks worth."

"Lean forward," she said. "I need to feel your face."

Skeptical, he did as she requested.

Her hands softly glided along the contours, paying close attention to his prominent jaw, high cheekbones, and straight nose as well as every wrinkle, every imperfection. A finger grazed a small scar on the left side of his forehead. She said nothing, then returned her hands to her lap.

"I hope your hands are clean," O'Riley joked.

"As clean as the squirrels," she replied.

His stomach flipped. "I think I better go get a rabies shot."

She snickered. "These squirrels are cleaner than a lot of the humans who come here," she said, nodding to an area where some of the homeless who frequented the park were sleeping on benches. "And don't smell nearly as bad."

"I apologize," replied O'Riley. "I didn't mean to disparage Rocky and all his little squirrel friends."

They laughed. Had he met her before? Where? When? Why was she so familiar?

"Normally I paint a present-day portrait in the middle of the canvas along with a smaller portrait in the upper left-hand corner of how I visualize my subject would have looked when they were younger. In this case, I want to paint two portraits for you. On two different canvases."

"Why two? You gonna charge me double?"

"No. On the contrary, I hadn't planned on charging you at all. I can sense you're a little wary of clairvoyants."

O'Riley puffed out his chest. "Hey, I ain't scared of nothing."

"I didn't say scared. I said wary. Like unsure of."

"All right," O'Riley challenged, "tell me—what am I thinking?"

"I haven't the slightest. That's not what I do. I'm not a mind reader. I'm clairvoyant. I sense things about people, sometimes situations. Most of the time from the past. There's something I sense about you from the past. That's why the two portraits."

"I'll believe it when I see it."

"That old scar I felt on your forehead. Your left side," she paused, her irridescent lips scarcely moving. "An old injury?"

"Yeah, a bullet grazed me a few years back."

"It never ceases to amaze me that a scar from the path of a bullet can so resemble a scar resulting from a fall off a bicycle in one's youthful years."

O'Riley ran his left thumb across the scar. "How'd you know that?" he sheepishly asked.

"I've been trying to explain it to you for the last ten minutes." She smiled. "Now, shall we begin?"

"You're *way* behind if you're waiting on me."

Annie began the first portrait, carefully turning the easel away from O'Riley's voice.

Approaching the canvas with a loaded flat bristle brush, she rendered the contour of O'Riley's round face with five or six quick strokes. She next blocked in the shadow areas utilizing the blue tones from her oval wooded palette rather than reds, visualizing her subject's personality as more passive and laid-back than hot-tempered. Her palette was arranged as on a color wheel from cool to warm hues. She knew exactly the placement of each color, her brush finding whichever shade needed after a quick turpentine dip. She worked wet onto wet paint, building up a thick impasto on the canvas, giving the painting a Van Gogh-like expressionist quality.

After forty-five minutes, she was finished with one canvas and about a third of the way through the second. O'Riley caught a fleeting glimpse of himself on the first before she concealed it from him.

"Incredible! It looked like me from over forty years ago."

"Now, now," Annie chided. "You're not supposed to peek."

"Couldn't help it. I won't do it again." Pausing for a moment, he finally had to ask. "How on earth could you paint what I looked like that long ago?"

"With most people it's not too hard. They don't change drastically. In the past, their faces were a little thinner or a bit fuller. They usually had more hair which had more color. With my special gift, it's pretty easy for me to visualize. You're different, though." She put down her brush and picked up some bottled water, taking two quick sips before resuming.

"How so?"

"Yours is one of the last faces I ever saw. At the Luciann. The night you caught Jimmy Seabold."

"Oh God!" O'Riley stared at her, his mouth open. "*You're* the girl. Ann Morrison."

Annie continued the fluid brush strokes, not missing a beat.

"I never knew what became of you. I mean, I realized you lost your sight from the blow to your head. I just lost track of you after you got out of the hospital."

She stopped painting for a moment, as if staring into the distance over waves in a dark sea. "I remember everything about that night. It's like it happened yesterday. You were standing near the concession stand eating popcorn out of a red and white box. You were trying to be nonchalant, eyeing everybody who came into the theater. I don't think other people noticed you. But I did."

O'Riley slowly shook his head. "If only I'd been a little quicker."

"If you hadn't reacted as fast as you did, we wouldn't be having this conversation at all," she replied, resuming her painting.

The wind rustled through the trees, sending a light blanket of colorful leaves drifting toward the ground.

"What happened to you in those years?" O'Riley asked softly.

"I started painting about a year after the attack at the Memphis College of Art. Got married to a wonderful man, Russell Shepherd, in 1960. He was the light of my life. We moved to Jackson, Mississippi." She let out a deep sigh. "He was killed in a car accident five years later. Drunk driver." Her pained expression suddenly blossomed into a bright smile. "No one can *ever* take away those wonderful memories."

"I know just how you feel."

"I know you do," she replied. "I remember your wife's picture in the paper. After Russell's death, I moved back to Memphis and became a Court Square artist. I kept up with you on the local news while you were chief. I knew our paths would cross again someday."

Twenty minutes later she put the final touches on the second portrait using quick strokes with a sable brush. Trading it for a smaller, number-two sable, she dipped it into the black paint and signed her name with a flourish at the bottom of the canvas. She then turned the first portrait around, the one he had briefly glimpsed.

"I'll be damned," he said, peering at the portrait of himself as a police sergeant years ago. A small rendering of Evelyn O'Riley graced the upper left corner. "That's a young me with my wife!"

"*That* was the easy one. This one was a little harder." She turned the second canvas around. The present-day O'Riley was neatly centered in the middle. In the upper left corner was a small portrait that resembled Nancy.

O'Riley's eyes widened in surprise. "I . . . I don't believe it," he stammered. "You couldn't have known. She's . . . she's someone I care about. Her name's Nancy Summerfield. How could you . . ."

Annie smiled. "I saw her. I saw her in your heart."

He continued to shake his head, amazed.

"I sense a link between the two—your wife and this woman. The emotions are very strong. You love her, don't you?"

"I never talked about it to anybody." He pondered the question for a few seconds. "Yeah, I guess I do," he finally admitted.

Annie motioned for him to take the canvases, refusing any payment.

He thanked her and promised he would keep in touch, now that he knew where to find her. He then headed back toward Second Street.

She called out, "Remember, Joe, just because you can't see something with your eyes doesn't mean it's not there. Three things never seen by anyone are a blade's edge, the wind, and love."

"*Where* did you come up with that?" O'Riley yelled back, again amazed. "My father used to quote me that old Irish proverb when I was a kid."

Annie beamed. "I felt it in the gaze of your eyes."

17

On October nineteenth, two weeks to the day after the murder in Roanoke, the authorities in Virginia had no real leads on the whereabouts of David Lancaster. Numerous reported sightings of him across the state were all unsubstantiated, most of them false, given out by people thirsty for media limelight.

He had found safety in Tennessee. With the ability to change his appearance, he roamed the streets of downtown Knoxville invisibly. Night had fallen. Cool, crisp, and deadly. It was time to move.

He stood on the sidewalk under the dazzling marquee of the elegant old Tennessee Theater, a relic from the era of vaudeville and the golden age of the Hollywood studios. The pulsating neon illuminating the theater's name flashed across his face, turning his features red, then green, over and over again.

The maroon letters attached to the white marquee beckoned him inside. *Marilyn Monroe in Some Like It Hot*. This classic film series promotion to raise funds for the aging theater's renovation had provided an irresistible stage for his own performance.

Then she walked up. He eyed her as she bought a ticket and sashayed through the entry doors. Blond. Sexy. Alone. Looked like an animal entering the slaughterhouse. She'd be easy to spot in the sparse crowd.

His pulse began to race. He felt lightheaded. He wet his lips.

"Do you think you're up to it?" he asked himself.

"I'm *always* up to it," he replied with a smirk.

He approached the black marble ticket booth and asked for a single seat. His windbreaker concealed an uncharacteristically hefty stomach.

"Five dollars," said a college-aged man dressed like a woman.

Lancaster handed him a five-dollar bill and said, "I don't suppose you wear clothes like that all the time?"

"It's for the movie. Next week won't be too bad. *Lawrence of Arabia*. I wear a turban and robe for that one." He grinned.

"Much of a crowd tonight?"

"Not too bad for a Tuesday. About fifty or so. We'll pack the place this weekend. Probably get about eight, nine hundred. It's just starting—if you hurry up you'll get to see the *Movietone* newsreel. It's a scream."

Lancaster nodded and walked toward one of the five sets of doors lining the front, all heavily covered with gold-leaf. He ran a thumb and forefinger across his black, lace-tied mustache, making sure it still stuck tightly above his lip, admiring the reflection of his jet-black hair in the entry-door glass.

He took in the elegance of the interior, feeling as if he had been transported back in time. He seemed to remember it. The Moroccan-style arches lining the lobby, flanked by ornamental pink marble columns. The walls, painted in colors of red and gray mixed with more gold-leaf, giving the illusion of tapestries. The six-foot-tall gold and crystal chandeliers looming high overhead, casting off just enough light to define the eerie shadows that lurked beneath them.

He quickly proceeded up one of the many winding stairways to the first of the two balconies in the cavernous auditorium and found a seat on the aisle in the second to last row.

Once the movie started, he sat spellbound, staring at the screen for over thirty minutes, unable to take his eyes off the images flashing before him. A warmth wrapped its arms around him. He felt secure. Like a child whose mother is close by, always there for him.

His eyelids slowly closed. Marilyn Monroe faded from view, replaced by two women embroiled in a heated argument.

"We used to be friends—not anymore!" screamed a woman made up to look like Rita Hayworth.

"*He* made the decision. He didn't want to hurt you," yelled Audrey Seabold. Her blond hair and make-up had transformed her into Betty Grable. She suddenly noticed her twelve-year-old son peeking around a corner into the kitchen. "Jimmy! Upstairs, young man. Now!"

The boy vanished.

"If you hadn't thrown yourself at him, he *never* would have left me, you two-bit whore! I always was better than you at everything. Loving. Putting on make-up. Everything."

Audrey's eyes narrowed. "If you hadn't put on that extra flab, he never would have looked anywhere else. Who are you trying to look like now? Sophie Tucker?"

The woman's hands quivered with rage. She grabbed a butcher knife off the kitchen counter. "Shut up!"

"Marie Dressler?" Audrey mocked.

"One more word and I'll kill you. I swear it!" she shrieked, holding the knife aloft. The eight-inch steel blade gleamed in the overhead light's glare.

"W.C. Fields?" taunted Audrey.

The woman lunged. The shiny weapon disappeared, buried deep in the young mother's chest.

Audrey gasped. Staggering back, wild-eyed and disbelieving, she was unable to cry out. As her son peeked around the corner in horror, she collapsed in a heap, blood rapidly flowing from her heart into an expanding pool on the floor.

The woman's rage instantly turned to shock, then terror. Kneeling, she pulled the knife from her victim's chest and laid it on the floor beside her. "What have I done?" she sobbed, burying her face in her hands. "What have I done? Audrey, I didn't mean to—"

A dull thud silenced the woman in mid-sentence, knocking her hard to the floor. She lay sprawled on her back, barely conscious, bleeding profusely from a crack in her skull.

Jimmy Seabold stood over her, face flushed, eyes bulging. He clutched a heavy, lead-crystal ashtray in his right hand.

All of a sudden the woman felt a sharp pain in her chest, then a flaming sensation. She tried to take a deep breath but could not. She desperately tried to defend herself, to ward off the attack, but was powerless. Once, twice, and again the paralyzing blows of the blade found their mark.

The room grew darker. She wondered what was going through the boy's mind as her eyes fixed open on his baleful expression. He seemed to be enjoying himself. It was the last thought she ever had.

Then, with tears suddenly streaming down his cheeks, he stood up, his blue pajamas soaked with blood. His right eye twitched uncontrollably.

Dropping the knife to the floor, he ran to his mother's side. He lay down, clutching her lifeless body in a tight embrace, afraid to ever let go.

Lancaster's eyes abruptly blinked open. Confused and unsure where he was, he rubbed his fingers together, expecting them to feel wet with blood. The flickering image of Marilyn Monroe on the screen brought reality back into focus.

His right eye began to twitch. The time was right.

18

Later that evening, a shrill ringing in the office of Brian Davenport, the Shelby County medical examiner, pierced the uncharacteristic midnight silence at the Regional Forensic Center in Memphis.

He slapped at the glass-topped coffee table next to the couch as if he were at home, attempting to turn off a bedside alarm clock. He opened his eyes, recognized his office, and lunged toward the desk to catch the phone on the fourth ring. His knee whacked the corner of the table with a loud thump. He winced, cursing.

"*What?*" he yelled into the receiver, blaming it for his agony.

"Brian? Is that you?" asked Casey Corliss, a former assistant medical examiner who had trained under him. Bright, energetic, attractive and, at twenty-eight, almost ten years his junior, she had not only learned forensics from her bachelor mentor but had taken a personal course in anatomy as well. She also was the new medical examiner for Knox County, just finishing up her first week on the job.

"Yeah, it's me. Sorry about the scream," he replied. "I just banged the ever-loving *hell* out of my friggin' knee trying to get the phone."

"Did I wake you?"

"Don't worry about it. Had a break in the action. Just taking a little snooze. It's been a busy night already. You'd think it was a Saturday instead of a Tuesday. One a gunshot victim. Another a stabbing. They ain't going anywhere." He paused a moment. "How's the new job going in Big Orange Country?"

"It *was* going just fine until tonight. My first homicide. It's a real doozy. I wanted to call to fill you in on it. See if I'm leaving anything out."

Davenport leaned back in his chair, crooked his neck from side to side, gently popping it, and rubbed sleep from his eyes. His pulse quickened in anticipation. Details of deaths fascinated him. Even outside his locale. No matter what time of night. Sleep always took a back seat to death. Especially violent death.

"Whatcha got?" he asked anxiously.

"You been staying abreast of those murders in Virginia the past few weeks?"

"The bank teller homicides in Richmond, Norfolk, and Virginia Beach?"

"No, the other ones. In Charlottesville and Roanoke. The missing heart murders."

"I've seen a little about it."

"Well, looks like he's hit Knoxville."

Davenport rubbed a hand along his close-cropped hair, scratching the top of his head. "I'm all ears," he said, reaching for a half-smoked cigar propped up in a colorful Hermés porcelain ashtray on his desk.

"Female. Twenty-three. Single. Found in a wash closet on the first balcony of the Tennessee Theater."

He relit his cigar. "A movie house?"

"Not originally. More of an old-time theater for plays and vaudeville. Built sometime in the 1920s. Real ornate and pretty. It's getting renovated. They were showing a movie tonight. Some revival series. A Marilyn Monroe picture."

"Blow to the head?"

"You got it. Sternum then hacked. Appears to be a meat cleaver or small axe. Medium velocity blood spatter on the walls. Castoff on the ceiling indicates four blows. No other souvenirs taken except the heart."

The Memphis medical examiner's eyes lit up. "A messy removal?"

"Cleanly excised, considering the circumstances. Looks like he used a knife or scalpel. Whatever it was, it was damn sharp. And he knew what he was doing. The detectives act like they're on to him. A guy named Lancaster.

They just can't find him." She paused a second, then continued. "There's one other thing and this is *really* weird."

Davenport laughed as a thick smoky haze blanketed his office. "Right up my alley."

"A piece of paper near the body had J-A-Y-N-E printed on it in black marking pen."

"What was the victim's name?"

"Melissa Murdoch. She also had a blond wig attached to her head, bright red lipstick on, and towels stuffed in a 38D bra on her chest. It's a Marilyn Monroe flick and he makes his victim up to look like Jayne Mansfield. What do you make of it?"

"Likes blonds, I guess. Maybe he's got his old movies confused, who knows?" He thought back to the blood spatter. "How big is that wash closet?"

"Not very. About six feet square. Pretty tight."

"Must've been real messy for him."

"He did a good job cleaning himself up, I'd say. Blood stains are all over the wash basin. Fingerprints, handprints, hair—I think the only thing he didn't leave was his driver's license. I'm betting he had a change of clothes with him. The north side of the theater near the wash closet has a side exit stairway that empties right out onto Clinch Street. He probably didn't get noticed by anyone."

"You sound like a detective and a medical examiner rolled into one."

"I had a good teacher," she replied.

"Looks like you're gonna have your hands full the rest of the night."

"Any pointers I need to be reminded of for the autopsy?"

"You were my best assistant ever, Casey. You tell me what you need to do," he prompted, like a professor giving an oral quiz.

"Forensics 101?" She laughed. "All right. First I save the bone that's been cut. Even the spine to match up puncture marks just in case we find the weapons. I'll also x-ray the body to see if any fragment of a blade or cutting edge was retained. How am I doing?"

"Cruising to the top of the class again. Don't stop now."

"I'll do an en bloc excision of the tissue damaged by the weapon so we'll have the cut margins." She paused. "Won't formaldehyde shrink it, though?"

"Yeah, but not that much. Smart question. And last but not least?"

"Get *good* shots with the Macro," she intoned.

Davenport remembered the words drummed into her head whenever he took close-up shots during autopsies with his Polaroid Macro 5 SLR camera. The corners of his mouth arched upward. "You get an A+."

"Thanks to your lenient curve."

His tone suddenly turned morose. "Damn."

"What's the matter?"

"I just wish something like this would happen here in Memphis."

"You better be careful," she warned.

"Why's that?" he asked playfully.

"Sometimes you just might get what you wish for."

19

The pulsing bulbs of the old Belle Meade Theater spire lit up the night in the Belle Meade section of Nashville, enticing patrons to come inside. Its curved white marble facade had remained unchanged for over sixty years. However, bright letters four feet tall now spelled out BOOK WORLD, cutting a red neon swath through the darkness. The illuminated marquee attached to the box-shaped art-deco-style building advertised upcoming author signings rather than newly released feature films.

In the restaurant next door, he sat at the same table he had for the three previous nights. By the windows. A table that overlooked the well-known landmark.

He picked at his steak, pretending to read the movie section of the *Nashville Banner*. Not once did he take his gaze off those who entered or left the bookstore.

Then he saw her. The young brunette who worked the night shift. A shivering thrill trembled through his body. He almost let out a laugh. Enough of the foreplay; it was time to finally meet her face to face.

"You're getting pretty good at this," he softly whispered to himself.

"Nice of you to notice," he replied.

"I got to hand it to you. You're on a roll now."

"Yeah, I sure am. And this one is *just* right."

He left a twenty on the table, more than enough to cover a large tip for the waitress, and walked from the restaurant toward the bookstore.

He stared curiously at the building from its parking lot for over five minutes. The vapor from his warm breath moved quickly upward into the cool air, distorting the beams of the blinking lights. Clutching the sides of his bulky, navy blue parka, he finally moved toward the looming, art-deco structure. Gripping the curved metal handle of the heavy, etched-glass entry doors, he entered the former lobby of the theater. The black and orange colors of Halloween, just five days away, were everywhere.

"Doesn't look like I remember it," he mumbled under his breath.

"Did you say something, sir?" asked the bright-eyed brunette behind the check-out counter.

A wall display of famous author hardcovers was in the exact location as the old concession stand. "It's changed a lot," he said, confused, scanning the converted theater. "I don't recall it looking like this."

"You got me," she said in a high-pitched voice and shrugged. "I've only been here three months." She studied his features, attracted to his milk chocolate-colored eyes. His scalp appeared freshly-shaved and reflected the bright fluorescent lights above. A diamond stud earring clung to his left ear lobe.

"Pictures," he replied, gazing around at the hundreds of framed pictures adorning the entry walls. Some were photographs of the Belle Meade and its employees during its heyday as Nashville's premier movie theater. Most were movie star photographs of actors and actresses who had visited the Belle Meade in person. "I've got pictures in my mind, just like on these walls. This part still looks familiar."

He seemed strange yet alluring to the young woman. She continued to eye him as he approached the photograph wall for a closer look.

Lancaster lifted his round, wire-rimmed glasses, as if near-sighted, to better read the autographs on the pictures. He moved his lips as he read them, enthralled by the faces he remembered from a past not his own. His eyes darted from name to name. Maureen O'Hara. Bob Hope. Doris Day. Donald O'Connor. Celeste Holm. Bert Lahr. Suddenly the photographs faded, replaced by a long, shiny, glass-topped concession stand.

"Do you want the same thing you got in Knoxville, Jimmy?"

"More," the young boy replied. "A *bucket* of popcorn this time. With *lots* of butter. And Jujys. And a Coke big enough for both of us. Plus a Hershey's bar."

Audrey Seabold frowned. "You'll get sick if you eat all that."

"No I won't. It's a double feature. C'mon, Mom."

She nodded to the man behind the counter.

"Look!" squealed the youngster as he ran toward a wall covered with autographed photos. "The Cowardly Lion from *The Wizard of Oz*."

His mother followed, leaving the treats on the counter for a moment and pointing to the picture of a dark-haired woman. "Can you guess who that is?"

The boy read the autograph out loud as he stared at the woman's face. "Margaret Hamilton. Hmmm. . ." Seconds later he answered, "The Wicked Witch?"

"You *are* good," Audrey said with a smile.

"She looks pretty, not like in the movie," Jimmy observed.

"She's just good with make-up."

"Like you."

"Yes," the proud mother replied, gently massaging the small of her son's neck, "just like me."

Lancaster stood motionless in front of the Margaret Hamilton photograph with eyes closed, basking in the warmth of a mother's love.

After a few minutes, the young woman called out, "Any particular type book you're looking for?"

The memory vanished in an instant, replaced by the burning compulsion. He whirled around without hesitation. "True crime. Serial killers."

"Third aisle straight ahead. Hang a right at the bestseller display." She smiled, seductively eyeing him. "You a student? Doing research?"

"Yes and no," he replied. "Fourth year at Vanderbilt. Not doing research though. I just like serial killers. I personally find them fascinating." He lightly touched the back of his neck, making sure his skullcap was still intact.

"I'm first year at Vandy," she said, her brown eyes shining. "Maybe I'll see you soon."

"You can count on it," he replied.

✳

The next day a light drizzle fell from the overcast morning skies above Memphis. Joe O'Riley raised his umbrella, trying to keep his freshly starched plaid shirt dry. Reaching the street, he picked up his newspaper, hurrying to keep from getting splashed by a red Corvette speeding by.

The rain began to fall more heavily, streaming down in torrents. Many of the leaves, now turned yellow and red, had dropped to the ground and street, making walking slippery.

Uncharacteristically dressed before breakfast, he had decided to go down to the police station, taking breakfast biscuits from a fast-food restaurant for everyone to enjoy. Glancing down at Nancy's house sent a warm feeling through him, even though he knew she had already left for school. He successfully managed his way up the sloping, slick driveway to his Continental without falling, just as he had done on countless occasions over the years.

Entering Homicide he nodded to Trevor Mills, who was shuffling papers on his desk in the corner, a phone receiver pressed hard against his ear. After glancing sidelong at Driscoll, he turned to detective Harris.

"Hey, Harris, whataya think of Driscoll here?" He paused momentarily, not giving the sergeant a chance to answer. "Only cop I know who can count to three and screw up two of the numbers!" He paused, then added, "Damn shame he works here, robbing a village somewhere of its idiot."

Harris leaned back in his chair and chuckled loudly. "What'd you bring us, Chief? I'm starving."

"Bacon, egg, and cheese biscuits." He dumped the brown sack on a spare desk.

The detectives all made a mad dash for the food. All but Mills and Driscoll.

Driscoll turned his flat, unfriendly stare toward O'Riley. "What are you trying to do? Kill us all with an overdose of cholesterol?"

"Not everybody. Just you."

Driscoll shook off the remark. "You still got that girlfriend?"

"You better believe it. Seeing her every chance I get. Mainly on weekends. Being a teacher, she ain't got a whole lot of time on weeknights."

"What do you do for sex at your age, O'Riley?" the young detective blurted. "Don't tell me she's satisfied if you just flop it out and lay it on the bed like a dead garden snake."

"Hey, now," he replied, "don't project your own problems on me. Have you tried one of those penile implants yet? The only drawback is you'd wear it out playing with it!"

The detectives continued to eat, all eyes and ears enjoying the verbal sparring match escalating between the two antagonists.

"You sure this girlfriend of yours isn't a nurse?" Driscoll asked. "Before you know it she'll be spoon-feeding you Gerber's baby food and bitching at ya 'cause you keep shitting in your drawers!"

"We are what we are cause we ain't what we used to be. You'll find that out as soon as you get older. I do the best I can. Ain't had any complaints so far. You married yet?"

"No, why?"

"Do yourself a favor. Take a couple of days off and do what you do best."

Driscoll's eyes narrowed into thin slits. "Yeah, what's that?"

"Go stump-break a cow. You could use the relaxation."

Driscoll bristled, his pale face turning red. "Why don't you take a hike? Vanish, vamoose. Get the hell out of here so I can think."

"From what I've heard, your thinking's impaired whether I'm here or not!" O'Riley whirled around, facing the other detectives. "Gentlemen, if I were you, I would not allow this man to breed."

A ripple of subdued laughter rolled across the room.

"But I tell you what," O'Riley continued, turning back to face Driscoll. "I'll do my Houdini stunt."

"Your *what?*" questioned Driscoll, cooling slightly.

"My Houdini stunt. You ever heard of Houdini?"

"Sure. One of those magic guys. Like David Copperfield."

O'Riley shook his head. "Not one of. Probably *the* most famous magician who ever lived. Other than Merlin. Copperfield's an illusionist. Houdini was world-renowned as an escape artist. Died in 1926. When I was a kid, about four or five, I wanted to be a magician because of him. I learned how to do his rope stunt."

All the detectives smiled. Most had heard of O'Riley's prowess but none had actually witnessed it. None except his longtime Driscoll collaborative foil, Harris.

"Here's what we'll do," O'Riley began. "Harris here will tie my hands behind my back with a piece of rope. If I can't free myself, I'll leave. *Then* you'll be able to think."

"And if you *do* get free?" inquired Driscoll.

The retired chief knocked on a gray metal desk with his knuckles. "I stand up here, drop my trousers, and you kiss my ass!"

"Sounds fair," the sergeant leered, "but there's one condition."

O'Riley raised his eyebrows.

"*I* get to tie up your hands."

"Knock yourself out," replied O'Riley, nodding at Harris.

Harris pulled open a drawer of his desk. Amid the clutter were two lengths of heavy rope, one treated with lanolin. He handed it to Driscoll.

The balding young detective began to tie O'Riley's hands together, knotting the coarse rope numerous times.

"You're pretty good," O'Riley said. "You must get a lot of practice doing this in your bedroom at home."

"Not really." Driscoll gritted his teeth as he forcefully tightened another knot. "I just have a thing for burned-out, overweight, retired policemen."

O'Riley laughed. "That leaves me out. Hey—easy on the rope. I'm not real fond of burns."

"You got a time limit?"

"Five minutes."

"I'll give you two."

"Two? Hell, I couldn't get out of this in two if I had a knife. Four."

"Three."

"Three it is," agreed O'Riley. "Starting now."

His face contorted as he worked his hands behind his back.

"I bet five bucks he gets out," Harris announced.

"Count me in. Ten on the chief," chimed in Hap Crosby.

"Five more," added another sergeant, Mark Harvey.

"You're all on," bellowed Driscoll. "Get out your money. Looks like I'll be eating lunch at the Peabody instead of McDonald's."

Sergeant Mills remained on the phone in the corner of the room, staring down at his desk as he spoke, grim-faced.

Two minutes and ten seconds later, Driscoll's confidence, along with his wallet, was suddenly torpedoed.

The strained expression on O'Riley's face eased. "Better have 'em hold your regular table at the golden arches," he said, holding up the rope in his right hand.

Driscoll clenched his teeth as he reached for his wallet, cursing unintelligibly under his breath. He flipped a twenty-dollar bill onto Harris' desk and headed toward the Homicide doors.

"What about me?" O'Riley called out, playfully unbuckling his worn, brown alligator belt.

"I wouldn't kiss your ass if you looked like Christie Brinkley!" Driscoll yelled, his stare so cold a popsicle stuck on top of his bald head wouldn't have melted. The glass doors swung shut behind him.

"If *I* looked like Christie Brinkley, I'd be finding a way to kiss my own ass all day long!"

Echoes of laughter again spread through the room.

Trevor Mills placed his telephone receiver back in its cradle. His smile, the one that sent women swooning, was missing. He motioned to O'Riley. Toying with the tight knot of his expensive Italian tie, he asked, "You been keeping up with these missing heart murders, haven't you?"

"As best I can," O'Riley replied. "Curious more than anything."

"A BOLO came across the wire this morning," the sergeant said, referring to a be on the lookout advisory. "The guy hit again. In Nashville yesterday."

"What time?"

"Last night. Tuesday night again. Both Virginia murders and now the two in Tennessee occurred on Tuesdays."

O'Riley's face tightened. "A movie theater?"

"A bookstore," Mills answered.

O'Riley breathed a sigh of relief.

"I just got off the phone with Nashville Metro. The victim was a female employee, white, eighteen or nineteen. College kid. First year at Vanderbilt. Name's Pam Miller. Found her in an old rest room used for storage. They said it looks like he washed himself off afterwards, slipped down a back stairway and out the back door without anybody noticing a damn thing." He leaned back in his chair and rubbed his blond eyebrows, pausing a moment to massage his temples before continuing. "Same M.O., no sexual assault. Blow to the head. Heart cut out and missing."

"Did he leave a note?"

120

"A name. Debbie. The girl had a wig and make-up on to look like Debbie Reynolds."

"Debbie from the late 1950s, not older like the Debbie of today, I suppose?"

"Bingo. The Nashville police weren't too receptive to me butting in. Kinda pissed me off."

"Don't get your panties in a wad over it. They want to handle it themselves. Nobody likes outsiders coming in and taking any credit. Just like when the FBI gets involved. They take all the local police info the detectives have scraped up on a case and won't give jackshit in return." He paused, glaring suspiciously at Mills. "You didn't try to piss them off first, did you? The guys in Nashville?"

"No, not really. I didn't try to, at least. Told them about my Tuesday findings. Suggested they check their hospitals for any runs on heart transplant operations." He grinned.

"Oh, I bet that went over *real* big."

"Not as big as when I told 'em we've been down that road before when you just strike out all day long and look for help anywhere you can get it. That's when they got pissed. I was a gentleman. Told 'em I wasn't trying to be intrusive but, if they didn't want to talk about details, we'd get details another way."

"A regular Mr. Congeniality."

"Damn straight." Mills laughed. "Back my ass in a corner and I'm damn congenial. Remember, I'm from Texas."

He began typing an E-mail to all the detectives in the department. His fingers flashed up and down in a blur on the computer keyboard.

"I'm telling everybody to be on the lookout next Tuesday. Just in case. Seems to be his designated night for some reason."

"Maybe Monday he's watching *Monday Night Football*," O'Riley joked.

"I'm hoping he's a country music fan," Mills said, still peeved at the

Nashville police, "and keeps his ass where it is. Those cops up there deserve him."

Before walking away, O'Riley looked down at the manila folders covering Mills' desk. His gaze blurred, his thoughts registering only what he was thinking, not what he was seeing. Something was about to happen. He knew it. He could feel it.

Something horrible.

20

Tuesday night, November second, passed quietly in Memphis, much to the relief of Trevor Mills.

But three nights later, a 911 call came in from the manager of the Orpheum Theater at South Main and Beale Street downtown. A husband had reported his wife missing as a Broadway touring group's performance of *The King and I* at the historic old theater was ending. She supposedly had gone to the rest room and to make a quick phone call home to check on the couple's two small children. She never returned.

A frantic search throughout the public areas after the show was over turned up nothing. But a probe into the cavernous storage areas below the building was another story. She had been brutally murdered in a maintenance room. Patrol officers and then the homicide detail arrived within minutes of the frenzied emergency call.

Mills had delighted in numerous events at the renovated Orpheum since his arrival in town. Plays, concerts, and classic films had all been enjoyed in the airy confines of the main floor or one of four spacious balconies. He often found himself distracted by the sheer beauty of its gilded moldings, enormous sparkling crystal chandeliers, and lavishly tasseled maroon velvet brocaded draperies.

Tonight he roamed through the backstage dressing rooms and deep into its bowels below, his footsteps echoing throughout a maze of engine rooms and storage areas filled with props and equipment. A single light shining at the end of the circuitous route marked the entrance to a theatrical nether world he would never forget.

The bulb dangled at the end of a fraying black electrical cord, providing the only light for a twenty-two by eighteen-foot maintenance room. On the dusty, stained, concrete floor directly under the light lay the body of a woman sprawled on her back surrounded by a halo of blood.

"Give me just a few minutes, guys," Mills told the two uniformed patrolmen hovering near the corpse. The other detectives at the scene, including Harris and Harvey, stood outside the weathered white door peering in, nervously anticipating the upcoming ritual.

Upon his arrival in Memphis, Mills' investigative technique had seemed strange. But with his success in the field, his intuition was not taken lightly by anyone in the department.

He slipped off his blazer and handed it to Harris. Stepping inside he closed the door, leaving only a sliver of light leaking in from the hallway. He looked down at the woman below him, just as he envisioned the killer had done.

He stood silently, drawing into play each of the five senses one at a time: smell, taste, hearing, touch, and sight. He wanted to feel and share this world that the murderer had experienced in hopes of prying into his mind.

First he closed his eyes and inhaled deeply, detecting a musty odor tinged with the scent of mildew and industrial cleaning supplies. He inhaled again, this time with his mouth open. Grinding his teeth, he felt and tasted tiny particles of grit that pulled him back to childhood days spent playing baseball on a dusty diamond, baking in the hot Texas sun. Next he listened, hearing murmuring conversations floating around him, hushed whispers speculating on details of the crime. He blocked those voices from his thoughts and imagined the muffled sounds of singing from the finale of the musical above creeping down into this subterranean killing chamber.

Rolling up his blue shirt sleeves, he dropped his arms to his side, eyes still shut. A dampness in the air chilled his skin, just like in the basement of his grandmother's house in Wisconsin that he visited as a boy.

His lids opened slowly and his blue eyes scanned the walls. Makeshift wooden shelves lined one wall, filled with jugs of cleansers and concession stand supplies. A floor buffer and three upright vacuum cleaners stood in one corner, their cords tangled and intertwined like a bed of snakes. Brooms and mops hung from nails on another wall with a jumbled assortment of dust pans and hand sweepers below them. In another corner, attached to the cinder-block walls covered with flaking white paint, was a porcelain sink, stained red with blood.

His gaze dropped to the floor. Purposely avoiding the body at first, he now began to take in the sight, the likes of which he had never seen.

On a three by five-inch slip of white paper, the name Sophia was printed in crude black letters. A playing card, the seven of hearts, lay face up nearby. An awkwardly attached brunette wig clung to the victim's head. Black eyebrow pencil, heavily applied across the murdered woman's brow, was accompanied by blue cake shadow across both eyelids. There was no mistaking the intent—she resembled a young Sophia Loren.

A cardigan sweater embroidered with a schoolhouse scene of young children had been ripped open, as had her now blood-soaked blouse. Buttons were strewn across the floor. Her grotesquely hacked chest was bare.

To the left of the body lay a bloodied pair of men's khaki pants. A similarly-stained blue pinpoint dress shirt and a pair of brown Rockport shoes rested next to the trousers.

Mills knew his intuition was correct. He had come up against the killer he had been dreading, the killer lurking in the back of his thoughts. He knew this one was special, in the most dangerous way. The orderliness of the murder scene and those that preceded it pointed to an obsessive-compulsive psychopath, not the least bit irrational, his thought processes cool and detached.

"C'mon in. Join the party," Mills said dryly as he pulled the creaking door open. He took his blazer from Harris and put it on. "No piece of evidence is too small for this one," he announced.

"Think we ought to vacuum it after we all get finished?" asked detective Harvey, stroking his pointed chin.

"What are you, nuts?" Harris answered, his jaw dropping. "We'd find shit that's been down here for fifty years!" He paused. "After the photographer gets his shots, we'll pick up anything that looks important. With gloved hands. I ain't playing housekeeper for nobody."

"First off we need some more light," Mills snapped. "Get a couple of halogen tripods in here for the photographer." He split the detectives into two teams of two each. "Crosby and Norton, work the witnesses. I want to know if *anybody* smoked a cigarette, threw down a piece of trash or so much as dropped a lint ball anywhere near the body before we got here. Harris and Harvey, you work the scene. And somebody get a call in to Davenport. Pick him up if it'll get him here quicker. He needs to get a good look at the body before it's disturbed." Smiling for the first time all night, he added, "I bet he'd jump on a bush hog to get to this one!"

Alerted by police radio that the medical examiner was on the way, Mills waited on the sidewalk under the flashing yellow lights of the Orpheum marquee. He glanced at his watch. 11:15. A phalanx of police squad cars and unmarked detectives' vehicles straddled the curb.

A white Ford Crown Victoria sedan suddenly maneuvered around the television news crews' cameras and past the yellow police tape, pulling up to the theater. The front door swung open and out stepped Davenport, already dressed in protective clothing.

"You look like a big blue baggie," Mills said, shaking the medical examiner's hand.

Davenport smiled. "Actually, it feels more like going to work in a garbage sack. You should try it sometime."

He was covered from shoulders to ankles in the standard disposable garments of his trade, coveralls and an apron made of plastic sheeting material bonded to tough paper cloth. His right hand clutched a head cover, shoe covers, and heavy gloves that would be slipped on at the start of his examination.

"So you think this is the same guy as the Knoxville and Nashville cases?" Davenport asked as the two men walked through the lobby.

"And two in Virginia," responded Mills. "No doubt in my mind."

They then took the stairway to the lower lounge area where Mills pointed out two enclosed telephone booths in an alcove near the women's rest room. A white door with a gray metal *Employees Only* plaque attached to it was opposite the phones.

"The victim's husband said she left her seat to go to the rest room and make a phone call when the show was about over. The concession booth down here was closed by that time. Hardly anybody'd be going to the can that late either—wouldn't want to miss the finale. Looks like she was abducted after her call. The baby-sitter said she talked to Mrs. Howard—that's the victim—at quarter till ten." Mills pointed at a red stain on the frame of the restricted entry door. "Based on what I know, I'd say that stain got there about quarter till ten."

"She suffer a blow to the head—like the others?"

"Right side. One blow."

The medical examiner's eyes narrowed as he pulled on his gloves. "With one blow there'd be no spatter. Without a drip it's hard to determine the position of the victim at the time of the strike but I'd guess he was behind her when she came out of the booth. He probably swung and she never saw a thing. A blood trail would begin when she starts to bleed in two, maybe three seconds."

Mills pointed to six dark spots in the carpet near the door. "Looks like blood to me."

"Can't be sure just looking. The damn carpet's red, too." Davenport glanced at an officer behind them. "Shine your flashlight on this, will ya?" He touched one of the spots with a gloved forefinger and nodded. "Blood."

Davenport then turned to the stain on the door frame. "That hair transfer pattern tells me he picked her up and, in a hurry to get out of sight, banged her head against this door as he rushed through it."

They passed through and within seconds were standing on a small steel platform attached to three steps leading down to the boiler room. Heavy machinery whirred and hummed.

"Spatter on the stairs," Mills noted.

"Technically," corrected Davenport, "blood drip pattern." He lowered his voice into a squeaky, guttural tone. "Follow the yellow brick road!" He sounded like a munchkin, but looked more like an overgrown smurff.

Mills, Davenport, and the officer quickly followed the trail through the engine room, past a service elevator, up a wooden ramp through a gray metal fire door, and down rows of wire-caged storage areas.

"He's a pretty strong guy," Davenport remarked as they stopped. "He's carrying her all this way by her torso, not over his shoulder."

A wrinkle creased Mills' forehead. "Enlighten me."

"Drag marks. The victim's shoes got dragged through drops of blood just after it dripped from her head. He carried her head first on his hip. His right hip."

"That checks. The suspect in the other murders is right-handed."

Resuming their quick pace in the dimly lit dungeon, they turned right at a large ventilation shaft. Thirty feet ahead was a melange of police personnel, each bustling about with their assigned tasks.

"This must be the place," Davenport said, noticing bloody fingerprints on the maintenance room door frame. He entered and stared down at the victim. "Ready for me to do my thing?"

Mills turned to the crime-scene photographer. "You got all your shots?" The man nodded. He turned back to the medical examiner. "It's your show."

Davenport knelt over the body.

"Well?" Mills asked, after five minutes had passed. "What can you tell so far?"

Davenport spoke in slow, measured words. "Her blouse spread laterally indicates the victim was at the mercy of the assailant as we've already surmised from the blood drip evidence. The lack of defensive wounds on her hands also indicate this, suggesting the head laceration came first, followed almost contemporaneously by the chest injury from a chopping instrument. The weapon would be moderately sharp like a machete but the abrasion is wider with skin scraped away indicating a more blunt instrument like an axe or thin shovel. It took multiple blows, I'd say a minimum of four from the cast-off on the ceiling and walls, to get through the breastbone. There's a wedge mark on the bone's left side and a crush mark on the right, like something was forced in there, holding the breastplate apart."

Suddenly a loud commotion erupted outside the doorway. Harris and Harvey were holding a man in his early thirties securely by his arms. The man was screaming hysterically, tears streaming down his face. The two detectives led him down the hallway, trying to console him.

"You might want to go talk to the husband," Davenport said to Mills. "He's freakin' out. Give him some assurance, will you?"

"Assurance of what? That we'll make sure as few people as possible gawk at her? I don't wanna lie to the guy."

Davenport glanced up, nodding.

"In life, people have privacy. In a violent death like this, privacy is history. First the killer sees her this way, then you got pictures of her pored over by detectives, experts in any given field, attorneys, jurors, judges. Am I leaving anybody out?"

"Sometimes tabloids," added Davenport.

"Tabloids," Mills repeated, shaking his head. "They flaunt anything they can get their hands on."

The medical examiner poked a gloved finger into the victim's open chest.

"If someone needs to assure the guy about his wife's privacy," the detective continued, "it better be somebody who's *damn* good at poker. It sure as hell ain't me."

Davenport's eyes abruptly widened. "We got a problem." His stare focused on the bloody torso. He pried the sternum apart just enough to peer into the chest cavity. "It's like the ones out of town. The heart's missing."

He continued his examination for a few minutes while Mills turned away from the grisly sight.

"The heart was sharply excised," said Davenport. "Poke marks in the pericardial sac indicate a sharp object like a knife. There are no tug marks or hack marks in the sac at all. It appears he cut through the sac longitudinally, picked up the heart and cut the aorta, the pulmonary artery, the superior and inferior vena cava, and the pulmonary veins. No pulling at all. Wasn't ripped or hacked out whatsoever. It was clean. Like a surgeon."

"Or somebody who's had a lot of practice," Mills added, nostrils flaring.

"He knows what he's doing."

"Was she dead when he did it?"

"Fifty-fifty," replied Davenport. "Knowing who we're dealing with and judging from the amount of drip marks between the body and the sink, I think her heart was still beating when he cut it out."

Mills winced.

"You know, normally I'm not this thorough at the scene. I just figured you'd want to find out some of these things as soon as you could, under the circumstances."

"A real prince of a guy," Mills said. "I think you've enjoyed finding some of this shit out yourself. Then what'd he do?"

"Probably took the heart over to the sink, rinsed it off, and bagged it." He nodded at the blood-stained clothing on the floor. "What's the story on that stuff?"

"Waist size 34 khakis. Dress shirt 16-34. Shoes a 9 1/2 medium width. About the same size worn by the suspect in the other murders."

"What's his name?"

"Lancaster. David Lancaster. Word is he goes for women first. Medical examiners are his second choice."

Davenport glanced at him deadpan. "I thought detectives were next."

"Nah. Couldn't happen. Everybody knows we're heartless to begin with."

Davenport grinned, turning back to the body. "Another thing about those clothes. It's very probable he was on both knees as he came down repeatedly with the blunt instrument. Look at the back legs of the pants. There's spatter on the calves but not the thighs. Also spatter on the shoulder of his shirt."

"And on the *back* of his shoes," observed Mills.

The medical examiner smiled again. "You're getting pretty scary with your accuracy. I think you've been hanging around me too much."

"Unfortunately."

"I'd say he washed himself up after he rinsed off the heart, changed into some other clothes and *very* carefully watched his step to avoid blood as he performed the movie-star make-up routine," continued Davenport.

"Then it was exit, stage right. Up the short back stairwell and he's out the side exit onto Beale Street unnoticed," added Mills.

"I'll know more after I get the autopsy done. One thing I can do is compare this one to the Knoxville murder. I'm tight with the medical examiner there. We worked together long enough to know each other's thinking. It'll be like having two homicides in one area. I'll let you know what I find out."

"You finished with the body?" Mills asked.

"For now," Davenport responded.

Mills bellowed, "Crew can move her."

Within minutes the Medic ambulance crew appeared with a stretcher, already double-covered with white sheets. After an identification tag had been banded around her ankle, Lisa Howard's body was lifted into a cheap white plastic body bag for the ride to the Regional Forensic Center.

"Hold up a second," Davenport said. "I got something else for you to drop off." He hung the killer's discarded clothes on wire hangers and covered them and the shoes with brown wrapping paper. Then he handed everything to the driver and winked. "For DNA analysis."

After Davenport pulled off his contaminated protective gear and placed it in a red biohazard garbage sack, he and Mills left the maintenance room and quickly headed up the stairwell they suspected the killer had taken and pushed through the secluded side exit onto Beale Street. A welcome blast of cold air filled their lungs, erasing the stench of death from their nostrils.

"Your suspect was either extremely lucky or he's been in town casing out the lay-out of the Orpheum in the ten days since that Nashville murder," Davenport observed.

"He's also been doing some shopping."

"How so?"

"There's an Oak Hall label in the pants," the detective said. "One in the shirt, too. He's no K-Mart shopper. He knows nice things. We're running a check to see if any clothes were left at other murder sites. If so, where they were from. Also checking out wig shops to see if some guy's buying 'em like futures in the stock market. Might give us a lead."

Davenport shrugged. "Worth a shot."

"We've got to figure out what's causing this guy to travel. We need to put some order to the disorder. If we can build up some kind of process, it'll get us inside his head. So far it's like we're putting together a picture puzzle, underwater, with gloves on, and the water's muddy. He's *got* to have a reason. We just don't understand it yet."

"He's intelligent, no doubt." Davenport nibbled his lower lip. "And devious. That's a very dangerous combination. He's looking for notoriety. Enjoying the attention. Thriving on it. Probably keeps the newspaper clippings."

"What's got me bumfuzzled is he's an anomaly. Most serial killers aren't transient. They usually stick to one area."

"What do you do next?" Davenport asked.

"Pray," replied Mills, looking up into the sky. The moon hovered between gently gliding clouds and then disappeared completely as the night became ink-black.

"Pray?"

"Yeah, pray. Pray the sick son of a bitch keeps moving down the highway."

He sat alone in a restaurant window overlooking Main Street near the Orpheum, balancing a cup of coffee on his knee. It was his fourth cup and he was excited, his heart still racing, not wanting to leave. When not watching the mayhem left in his wake, he was studying his reflection—deciding he looked good with medium-length black hair slicked back with styling gel and small wire-rimmed glasses resting on his nose. Dressed in a tweed sport coat and tie, he looked as if he'd taken lessons from the Duke of Windsor.

His return to Memphis had been flawless. The newspaper would call it a triumphant performance had he been an actor. After all, he did hear a thundering standing ovation from the crowd when his work was done. What more could he ask?

A heavy-set man in a wrinkled gray suit stumbled up to the window next to him. "Now that's a good-lookin' lady," the man slurred in a Southern drawl, swaying as he closed one eye to better focus on the leggy blond standing on the sidewalk. "I'd love to get my hands on her."

Lancaster warily observed the middle-aged man for a moment. Probably a traveling businessman so drunk he wouldn't remember a thing in the morning. Most likely wouldn't even remember being in a restaurant. "Have a seat," he offered. "I think you could use some of this." He pushed his cup to the other side of the table.

The man sat down. "Never touch the stuff. Wouldn't mind touching *that* stuff though." He pointed out the window at another woman, this time a flaming redhead.

"Sounds like you got one thing on your mind."

"Damn straight. All the time. Sometimes I think it's an addiction."
The man's wide forehead deepened into a frown.

"I know just how you feel," Lancaster said. His somber expression
relaxed, transformed into a grin. "Where do you like to do it most?"

"Just about anywhere. Whatever it takes to get rid of the urge."
Lancaster nodded.

The man continued, "Guess my favorite place is in the shower. How
about you?"

Lancaster picked up a fork and studied its prongs. One was bent slightly
forward. He flipped it over and pressed it against the side of the table once,
twice. He examined it again, then pointed it at the drunk. "Someplace public
but secluded. Like a rest room or maintenance room."

The drunk leaned forward and tapped the tip of the fork with his forefinger. "I did it in an airplane lavatory once. Hot little stewardess from Omaha
on a red-eye to the West Coast. But I've never done a woman in a maintenance room." He eased back in his chair.

"It's quiet. Out of the way. Usually has a sink to rinse off in. A rule of
thumb I always use is you gotta do it just right. You have to make it memo-
rable."

"I think I've met my match," the man conceded. "Name's Rick Magee.
I'm from God's country," he said with a wink as he extended his manicured
right hand. "Jackson, Mississippi."

Lancaster set down the fork. "James," he replied, firmly shaking the
man's hand. "James David. Sorry, but I've got to go. Busy morning ahead."

"Been nice meeting you, Jimmy."

"Likewise," he answered, standing up and walking away.

Within minutes Lancaster was behind the wheel of his car, pressing
hard on the accelerator as he barreled away from the downtown area on
Madison Avenue.

"What do you think we should do next?" he softly asked himself.

"The table's set, the bird's in the oven, and the guest of honor will be arriving soon," he firmly replied. "Time to turn the heat up."

21

O'Riley awakened, eased out of bed, and ambled over to the windows. He opened the curtains, flooding his bedroom with the bright light of a glorious November Saturday morning. He flinched at first but his eyes soon adjusted.

He thought of Nancy. He had found himself living for the weekend and, with it, the chance to spend as many hours as he could with his new love.

In no time he was heading down the steps to the street, one by one, as he had done day after day, year after year, decade after decade, since the death of his father. Brown leaves crunched under each step, ceasing only when he reached the sidewalk.

The belt of his fraying white robe hugged his waistline. He drew in a deep breath. The crisp air chilled his lungs, invigorating him with a stiff jolt, just like the morning mug of black coffee held tightly in his right hand.

Peering down, he paused. Attached to the orange plastic bag enclosing his newspaper was a note. He bent over, picking up the bag partially covered by a clump of dead leaves, and pulled off the message. His eyes widened.

With eyes of red
My actions are blue,
This one, O'Riley,
Was just for you.

"No," he mumbled, shaking his head. Seabold flashed into his thoughts. "No way."

Who could have done this? And what does it mean?

He gently pulled the newspaper from its wrapper. The bold front-page headline screamed: WOMAN MURDERED AT ORPHEUM THEATER.

His heart began to pound and his breathing became labored. The coffee mug slipped from his grip, shattering with a pop on the sidewalk. The houses and trees on the street began to spin. The brilliant sunlight dimmed to murky gray. He quickly sat down on the first step of his walk and closed his eyes to combat the dizziness.

In a few seconds he regained his balance and his composure. He slowly opened his eyes and read:

A Memphis woman was found brutally murdered in the basement of the Orpheum Theater at 10:30 last night, only fifteen minutes after the conclusion of the Broadway show, The King and I, attended by almost two thousand people.

The victim has been identified as twenty-seven-year-old Lisa Howard, the wife of Memphis insurance executive, David Howard, who had accompanied her to the Friday night performance at the downtown theater. Mrs. Howard left her seat at approximately 9:45 P.M. to make a phone call home to check on the couple's two small children. Her husband became concerned when she did not return. The theater manager, Eric Weaver, upon searching the basement of the vaudeville-era showplace, discovered the young mother's blood-soaked body.

Police declined to give details as to the weapon believed used or the exact type of injury sustained by the victim. However, several witnesses said the death appeared to be the result of stab wounds of some kind. Homicide detective Trevor Mills, in charge of the investigation, declined comment when asked if the murder could be related to a recently reported string of slayings stretching from Virginia across Tennessee. He stated there would be a press conference later today.

Two black and white pictures accompanied the text, one a photograph of police squad cars at the front entrance of the Orpheum and the other of detective Mills greeting Brian Davenport, the medical examiner. The former chief knew what was coming. Like it or not, he would soon be pushing open the doors to the Homicide Squad room.

This time he would be entering on business. Nancy would have to understand.

Less than an hour later, O'Riley leaned back in a brown leather swivel chair waiting for Chief Charlie Perry, the first African-American to head the Memphis Police Department, to return. Eyeing the dark walnut bookcase of his successor, filled with volumes of police manuals, true-crime novels, and personal mementos of a career on the force, he remembered that it appeared just that way when he was chief.

Perry entered his office in a hurry, looking dapper in a dark gray pin-striped suit. Almost six feet tall with close-cropped salt-and-pepper hair, he sported a narrow mustache the same color. Thin-rimmed tortoise-shell glasses framed round, smiling eyes.

"You look sharp, Chief," O'Riley said, rising slightly from his seat, offering a firm handshake.

"I feel sharp, Joe." Perry laughed, sitting down behind his neatly arranged desk. "Down to a trim one-eighty."

"Competing with Mills for best-dressed on the force?"

"I always did have a thing for nice clothes, you know that." The sixty-year-old chief rubbed his hand along his coat lapel. "Glad I ran into you downstairs. As I said, no need in you going over to Homicide when I got the guys due here any minute. That murder last night has us all hustling."

"You getting involved?" asked O'Riley, a hint of surprise in his voice.

"You can take the cop out of Homicide but you can't take Homicide out of the cop. You trained me—you know that as well as anybody. Stick around. You might be able to add to the discussion."

"Maybe so," he replied, clutching a rolled-up newspaper in his left hand.

A parade of detectives soon filed into the spacious office, exchanging pleasantries with both the chief and former chief.

"Have a seat," offered Perry, gesturing toward the blue-leather, high-backed chairs surrounding a large, dark walnut conference table.

O'Riley sat at one end, with detectives Mills, Harris, and Driscoll on one side and Norton, Harvey, and Crosby on the other. They spread out neatly tagged bags of evidence in the middle of the table as Perry took the chair opposite O'Riley at the other end.

"I ran a check of optometrists in Roanoke," Harvey began. "Found one, a Dr. Clayton Kingsley, who fitted a guy with an assortment of contacts. Six sets in three colors. Two brown, two blue, two green. He said the guy had heterochromia."

Puzzled expressions spread across the faces of the other men. Except for one.

O'Riley said, "That's when the color of somebody's eyes is different."

Everyone nodded, impressed.

Harvey continued, "His left eye is blue and his right one green. Just like our suspect, Lancaster. Kingsley said the guy seemed nervous. Noticed his eye twitching. Paid cash for the contacts on Monday, October fourth. The day before the second murder, the one in Roanoke."

"That helps explain why nobody's seen the bastard even with his picture all over the news," chimed in Harris. "The old disguise routine."

Mills cleared his throat. "I've checked with the police in Charlottesville, Roanoke, Knoxville, and Nashville. Every victim sustained a blow to the head, had their chest chopped open, their heart was missing, and they had make-up on to look like a 1950s Hollywood star. Plus a note telling who they were supposed to be in case nobody got it. Just like ours. Only we have something they don't." His gaze swept around the table, glancing at each man. "No clothes were left anywhere but here."

"Maybe he wanted us to find them," Driscoll remarked.

"*No doubt* he wanted us to find them. This guy's sharp. He hasn't made a mistake yet," maintained Mills. "And the playing card. The seven of hearts. The other cities didn't have any cards left at their scenes."

The hair on the back of O'Riley's neck stood up as a chill formed on his shoulders. He nervously jingled the keychain in his left pants pocket, staring at Mills as the sergeant kept talking.

"It doesn't add up. We got five dead bodies between here and Virginia. His count includes two we don't know about. I checked VICAP," he said, referring to the FBI's Violent Criminal Apprehension Program. "No other murders with missing hearts anywhere in the country."

"That they know of," O'Riley said quietly.

Mills turned his eyes to O'Riley and said, "That they know of."

"Why would he change his M.O. here?" Crosby asked. "Do you think we need to ask the FBI to get involved?"

"Hell no!" snapped Mills, his eyebrows almost meeting in a frown. "If they come in, they take control. They can't tell us anything we can't find out ourselves." He drew a deep breath and exhaled, tempering his sudden anger. "We *know* who the S.O.B. is. We just need to catch him."

"If he's still here," added Harris.

"I hope he's in Oklahoma by now," Mills replied. "The FBI definitely won't be getting involved. At least not here. They already offered. This morning."

"And?" the chief asked, dreading the wrong answer.

"I told them it's a jurisdiction problem. That we might get together with Nashville, Knoxville, and Virginia to develop a task force to study the situation."

Perry chuckled. "I bet they loved that."

"They said that would be premature. So I told them their getting involved would be premature and, if they wouldn't mind, they might want to pull their premature noses out of our assholes!"

Everyone laughed except O'Riley. He stared down at a yellow legal pad in front of him, doodling on it with a pencil, drawing small pyramids. "It's the same as before," he said softly.

Mills and Perry exchanged perplexed glances.

O'Riley looked up. "The movie theater killer I put away."

"I remember you telling me all about that when I was a rookie," Perry said. "The Hollywood Killer. The one who murdered your—"

A stunned silence fell over the room. Mills eased forward, resting his elbows on the table, hands clasped.

O'Riley exhaled. "That's the one."

"Can't be him, Joe," said Perry. "He got the chair. Besides, we already got a positive I.D. on our man. You've been keeping up with it. He's a hit-and-run serial killer. Strikes at an old movie house every time. Except the first one—the one they called you on."

O'Riley's brow wrinkled. "I thought in Nashville it was a bookstore?"

"It was," replied Mills. "Used to be a theater."

O'Riley muttered, almost to himself. "The Grandin in Roanoke. Tennessee Theater in Knoxville. The Belle Meade in Nashville."

"You been keeping up with these locations on the wire, right?" Mills asked.

He shook his head, staring into space. "It's just like before," he whispered.

"What are you talking about?" Mills asked.

"He's not going to move on," responded O'Riley, his soft tone becoming more assertive. "He's planning on hanging around here for a while. Just like before. Nobody here's old enough to remember." He glanced from Mills to Perry, then back to Mills. "Just like Jimmy Seabold. Years ago."

All eyes focused intently on the former chief as the neatly filed years in his memory opened wide.

"He started in Charlottesville. At a private residence. Then he struck at the three theaters I mentioned. He cut out the victims' hearts. All female. The hearts were never found. He didn't start leaving cards until he hit Memphis. Used the ace of hearts through the six of hearts. Six murders. The first one here was at the Malco Theater downtown."

"Holy shit!" Harris blurted. "That's the Orpheum now!"

"When we captured Seabold, he was going after Memphis victim number seven. He had the seven of hearts in his pocket. Looks like last night's killer is taking up where Seabold left off."

Mills twirled his gold Cross pen end over end in his right hand.

O'Riley picked up the bag containing the playing card from the center of the table. On the flip side of the seven of hearts were two mallards in flight. "W.C. Fields was on the other side of Seabold's cards." He grinned for the first time since they all sat down. "For you youngsters, he was a famous movie comedian in the 1930s and 40s."

Perry shook his head in amazement. "Any more ways you can enlighten us?" he asked half-jokingly.

O'Riley eased from his chair and walked to the other end of the conference table. Reaching into the pocket of his sport shirt, he pulled out the note that had been attached to his newspaper and handed it to Perry, who read it aloud.

"With eyes of red
My actions are blue,
This one, O'Riley,
Was just for you."

The chief frowned when he finished, looking curiously at his predecessor. "What's this supposed to mean?"

O'Riley then dropped the morning newspaper onto the table with a loud thump, its screaming headline facing up. "That note was attached to this."

"Why? A practical joke?"

"I don't know. The thing is, I got a message like this after Seabold was executed in 1959. It was in his cell. Scratched into the wall." He slowly repeated the rhyme, his eyes fixed straight ahead, as if he were reading the words off that cell wall all those years ago:

> *"With eyes of red*
> *My actions are blue,*
> *When your time comes, O'Riley,*
> *I'll be waiting for you."*

"You aren't thinking this guy's come back from the dead, are you, Joe?" questioned Perry, rubbing a hand over the top of his graying head.

"I ain't saying that," O'Riley responded.

"Sounds to me like someone's playing a little mind game. I doubt a dead man's leaving you any valentines. We'll have it fumed to see if we can get any prints. Anybody touched it besides you and me?"

"Nobody."

"Good. We might find something."

"It's definitely from our murderer," observed Mills, comparing the note to the slip of paper with SOPHIA written on it. "Same marker. Same three by five paper. Same royal blue sliver of gumming on the note's left side from a pad. What *really* has me worried is we might have a clever copycat on our hands."

"In case he is," said O'Riley, "I'd put men on a still-watch at every location that was a Seabold murder site."

"You know them off-hand?" queried Mills.

"Some things you never forget." O'Riley returned to his chair.

"Break out your pencils," Mills directed. "Let's all get this down."

"Like I said," O'Riley began, "the first murder was at the Malco, now the Orpheum. The second was at the Crosstown on North Cleveland. Today it's the Assembly Hall of Jehovah's Witnesses. Spot number three was the Bristol on Summer Avenue, about where the Junior League Thrift Shop is. Am I going too fast?"

The detectives shook their heads in unison, feverishly scribbling.

"The Loew's Palace on Union at South Main was number four. It's now a parking garage and a Russian restaurant, Cafe Samovar. The Memphian on Cooper was fifth and is a likely target, I would think, since it's still a theater even though it's used for live plays. Anybody know it's name?"

"The Circuit Playhouse?" answered Crosby.

"Wrong, but you still get some points," O'Riley replied. "Playhouse on the Square. Murder six was at The Guild on Poplar. *That's* now The Circuit Playhouse. Last but not least is the theater where we caught the killer. The Luciann on Summer near North Parkway. Let me see a show of hands if you know what that is now."

Every man's hand shot up, including Chief Perry.

"I shoulda known." O'Riley laughed, feigning disgust. "Norton?"

"The Versailles Adult!"

"Good man," said O'Riley. "You win a free sexual device to take home to your wife. Fix him up, will ya Driscoll?"

The men laughed loudly.

Mills abruptly turned serious, focusing their attention once again. "Everybody listen up. Keep in mind who we're dealing with. Our killer is fearless. He has to feed a need. If he gets frustrated, the urge is going to become stronger. Mark my words," he promised, "the intervals between murders are going to get shorter. The only thing that'll put an end to it is to catch him." He paused to look around the table, directly into the face of each detective. "We need a detail at every one of those old theater spots—twenty-four-hour surveillance. And I want four details at the Jehovah's Witnesses Hall. Everybody got it?"

The detectives nodded.

"Time's wasting. Let's get this show on the road, no pun intended," Mills exhorted. "Be *especially* wary come Tuesday night."

22

Nursing his third coffee, O'Riley weaved through the bustling aisles at Homicide, trying to stay out of the way. He then ambled over to Mills' desk in the corner, watching the detective give his computer a workout. A constant clicking of the keyboard filled the air. Then, silence, as Mills stared at the screen.

"Look here, O'Riley, one and the same," Mills said, gazing at the illuminated fingerprints before him.

"Yeah, yeah, I see it," he replied gruffly, his eyes fixed on the bright green images.

Mills looked up at the frowning former chief. "What's the problem?"

"I just can't get used to all these technologically advanced, high-speed systems you guys are using these days."

"Hey, cuts out a lot of legwork."

"I *like* legwork. In my day you did your legwork until you caught the suspect and had enough evidence to back up your charges. Then you grilled his ass until he cracked like Humpty Dumpty." He smiled. Eyeing the computer screen, he said, "But there's sure as hell one thing he's not doing."

"Wearing gloves," added Mills.

"Looks like he don't give a shit who sees his prints. Like he's advertising or something."

Mills shook his head. "I've never seen anything like it and I've been exposed to a lot of serial-killer cases over the years. Most of them around Houston and the Southwest."

"You an expert or something?" O'Riley asked.

"Nobody's an expert," he replied, "but I'm knowledgeable enough.

After what you just told us, this one has me worried."

O'Riley sat down. "You and me both. What are your reasons?"

"Almost all serial killers have this drive to kill. Many of them just *really* enjoy it," said Mills, his blue eyes locked on O'Riley. "Most stay on their own turf where they feel the most comfortable. But occasionally after they do the deed, a select few will leave town, not even waiting to read about their crimes. They wander down the highway, pegging victims from town to town. That's what I felt like this guy Lancaster was going to do. Charlottesville, Roanoke, Knoxville, Nashville, Memphis. Next maybe west to Little Rock, south to Jackson, or north to Saint Louis."

"And now?" asked O'Riley, taking a sip of coffee.

Mills thrust a fist in the air with thumb extended and jerked it back like a hitchhiker. "The son of a bitch has reversed his field. It's taking more to satisfy him. He's not content to hit and run. He's decided to become more daring. Taunting us by leaving clues. The card. His clothes. The note to you. He seems concerned with the account of his exploits in the paper, making sure *you* take note of it, probably getting off on the attention. Revenge seems to be in his equation but I'm not sure how it relates to you. What I am sure of is he's settling in here for a while. I hope to hell and back I'm wrong."

Just then Chief Perry walked up. Mills self-consciously fingered the knot in his red and black tie, making sure it was pulled tightly around his neck.

"I'm starting to feel underdressed around you two fashion plates," joked O'Riley, noticing Mills' reaction and hoping to put the chief at ease.

"You're retired. You're supposed to look like that," responded Perry, eyeing the former chief's usual khaki slacks and plaid shirt. "I wish I could dress like you do." He sat down in an old swivel rocker that creaked as he leaned back.

Turning serious, O'Riley looked over at Perry. "I got a favor to ask." He took a deep breath. "I want to come out of retirement."

"You want to *what?*" Perry asked, his eyes fixed on his friend.

"I want to come out of retirement," repeated O'Riley as Mills glanced over, grinning. "I want to work on this case."

"At your age?" His wrinkled brow smoothed. "You can watch from the sidelines. Like the coach."

"Screw the sidelines, Charlie. It's not that I want in the game," he said, his voice rising, "it looks like *I am* the game."

Perry studied him for a moment. "Look, you old buzzard, I know you've got a connection to this guy I don't understand. If it wasn't for that—"

The corners of O'Riley's mouth rose, forming a satisfied smile.

"I'm restoring your civil service rank. I'll handle the paperwork, Inspector O'Riley. And I want you to understand that this is just temporary duty. You need a gun?"

"Got it covered," replied O'Riley, patting the ever-present Walther .380-caliber pistol concealed in the right pocket of his pants. "That's one reason my britches won't stay up."

Perry waved an outstretched hand around the room. "Any preference on somebody to work with? Or, are you just going to solve this thing on your *own*?"

"I'll work on my own some. If I need help, I'll get with Mills. And maybe Harris."

"I'm here whenever you need me," Mills quickly volunteered.

O'Riley nodded. "Thanks. But, I'll start my investigation solo for now." He paused. "Beginning with finding out about that note I got this morning."

Perry shook his head. "I tell you, Joe, once you set your sights on something, you just don't let up until you get to the bottom of it. You're like a goddam pit bull."

"Let me know if something comes up," O'Riley said to Mills. He winked at both men and walked away, vanishing through the swinging glass doors.

The blue morning sky was now overcast, bright sunshine covered by dark clouds floating in from the west.

O'Riley hurried down Second Street toward his car. He wanted to discuss the case with someone. Not just anybody. Someone who would understand. Someone old enough to remember.

In a few moments the towering trees swaying in Court Square came into view on his right and, with them, a solitary female figure diligently painting near the Hebe Fountain, her ivory caftan gently billowing in the breeze.

He strolled up the curved walkway in the nearly deserted park, past benches occupied only by perching pigeons. Fifteen feet away, he stopped to watch, the sound of his footsteps masked by the waters of the thirty-foot fountain beside him.

She suddenly squeezed a generous mound of brown oil paint from a tube onto her palette and then resumed her strokes on the linen canvas. Using splashes of tans, grays and browns, her impressionist version of a Court Square scene was remarkably accurate. The fountain was framed by tall trees and walkways with wooden benches. Squirrels and pigeons, distinguished by tan or gray blotches, frolicked about under the shadow of the Porter Building, which loomed on the left side of the canvas.

O'Riley shook his head slowly. "I still can't figure you out."

Annie turned her head. Small smoky topaz drop earrings dangled from her ear lobes. "Hello, Joe," she said.

"That painting looks just like what I'm looking at right now, even the overcast sky. I'm . . . I'm just baffled how you do it."

She sighed. "Close your eyes," she commanded.

O'Riley's lids closed tightly.

"Pretend you're standing on the sidewalk in front of your house. What's the address?"

"249 North Avalon."

"What do you see?"

"A sloping yard filled with green ivy under two big oak trees. Steps in three tiers up to the front door. The house is a dirty white stucco. With an arch over the front porch."

"It's not so hard, is it?"

He opened his eyes. "That's different. I see my house every day."

"And I see mine every day, too. I sense it. I know what's around me." She paused a second, frowning, and placed her palette down on the taboret beside her. "Something is troubling you. What is it, Joe?"

"There was a murder last night. At the Orpheum."

"I know. I heard about it on the news. Like the ones from our past?"

"This is on the Q.T. Promise not to tell anyone?"

"I promise."

"The victim's heart was cut out." He hesitated for a moment. "And, the killer left a playing card. The seven of hearts." He didn't want to mention the personal note.

"Just like before."

"Yeah. Just like when you were attacked."

She winced. After a moment's pause, she inhaled deeply. "I don't think we have too much to worry about. Jimmy Seabold has paid the price. He's just a dark memory."

O'Riley shuddered, feeling strangely like the specter of death had stalked into his sheltered world.

She tilted her head and ran a hand through her hair. "So what's the matter now?" she asked.

"Are you ever afraid of dying?"

"What's there to be afraid of? People fear the darkness of death. I've been living it most of my life. I don't fear it at all. I take comfort in the darkness. It's there, in the constant grayness of my thoughts, that I experience and revel in every bit of happiness that comes my way." She buttoned up her leather vest to ward off an increasing chill. Then her fingers slipped through her hair, tucking a few loose strands behind her ear.

O'Riley let out a slight laugh. "You seem to have it all figured out. What advice can you give a tired old man looking for answers when he's not even sure what the questions are?"

"You already know the words you're about to hear. You never stopped being a detective when you became chief, nor did you stop being a detective when you quit the force. Your confusion is born of fear and self-doubt. The fear is well-founded. Your self-doubt is not."

He stared intently at her, scarcely breathing.

She continued, "When you search for answers, remember one thing. Everyone you come into contact with in this life knows a little something you don't know but need to know. Learn from them. It will serve you well. I don't mean to sound like a fortune cookie, Joe. But it's important for you now."

O'Riley thanked her and promised again to keep in better touch. After planting a good-bye kiss on her cheek, he headed back down Second Street to his black Lincoln.

Thoughts swirled in his head as the noisy rush of traffic sped by. Reasonable explanations had to exist for everything that was happening. He was certain he'd find out what was going on—who had written that note. He knew just the place to start.

Brushy Mountain State Penitentiary.

23

By mid-afternoon the next day, O'Riley's Continental was speeding along winding rural mountain roads, its six-hour journey across Tennessee nearly over.

He glanced at his passenger. How pretty she looked. Her brown hair had been lightly transformed, turning her into a captivating honey brunette. A wing-collared black and white polka dot blouse draped her narrow shoulders, coordinated with black worsted wool slacks and a matching black vest. With hair pulled back and up and clipped with a tortoise-shell barrette, a more attractive woman didn't exist in the world, O'Riley thought.

Nancy stared out the window at the bare trees flashing by and at the mountain tops, hidden in a veil of low-lying clouds.

As enchanting as the change in scenery was, his thoughts had shifted to his inner feelings. In the companionable silence he knew she belonged with him. Not just on this trip or back at home. She belonged with him for the rest of his life.

A few minutes later the car stopped at a traffic light. A white-brick general store stood to the left of the narrow two-lane highway.

"Are we in Petros yet?" Nancy asked as the automobile then turned right down an even narrower road.

"That *was* Petros," joked O'Riley.

They continued on, past scattered wood-frame houses that dotted the rustic landscape.

Nancy's fingers drummed restlessly on the white leather armrest at her side. In a deep tone to mimic O'Riley, she said, "Come with me to Knox-ville—we'll take a nice Sunday drive to East Tennessee. Take a personal day off from school. I'll have you back Monday afternoon. It'll be like a vacation."

"It will be. I promise," he countered, smiling. "We'll go to this special restaurant for dinner, then stay at the Hyatt tonight. Has a great view of the Tennessee River. Real romantic."

"As romantic as this?" she asked, nodding toward the entrance sign to Brushy Mountain State Penitentiary that resembled a cemetery headstone. "I'd hate to see your idea of a really *nice* vacation spot!"

The Lincoln slowed, then came to a stop at the entrance check-point. The prison loomed in the distance, a tan fortress nestled at the base of surrounding beige mountains laid barren of leaves and vegetation by winter's approach. Vapor belched skyward from the prison's steam generator, quickly joining the clouds that encircled the facility in a dense haze.

"Name, please?" inquired a middle-aged male guard dressed in a navy blue uniform.

"Joe O'Riley. And a guest. To see Warden Munroe."

The guard scanned his clipboard, quickly checking off the name, then peered in at the passenger. "Just a little information from you, ma'm." His gray eyes apologized. "Regulations. Name?"

"Nancy Summerfield."

"Age?"

She cringed. "Do I have to?"

"You have to. But," he paused, breaking into a slight smile, "you don't have to tell the truth."

"What the hell. Twenty-one. As you can see, I like older men." She laughed.

The guard broke into a full smile. "I should say so," he replied as he squinted at the driver.

"Be careful," O'Riley admonished, glancing at Nancy. "*You* just might get left here."

The guard handed them clip-on clearance badges and they were soon parked in front of the main entrance to the four-story prison. As they reached the front steps, a dark-haired man in his early forties came out to greet them. He wore a solid green v-neck sweater and tan khakis, just like O'Riley.

"We must have the same clothier," joked the man, extending his hand. "I'm Will Munroe."

"Joe O'Riley. And this is my friend, Nancy Summerfield."

"Pleased," said the warden, also shaking her hand. "Sorry about the weather. The place doesn't look quite so dreary when the sun's out. Sometimes clouds get trapped up here in the mountains and it rains for days."

"I know," replied O'Riley. "It seemed like it rained for days the last time I was here." He smiled at Nancy and then Munroe. "And I was only here for one night."

"When was that?" asked the warden. "We don't get many visitors here. At least, not ones who *want* to come."

"A long time ago. The Seabold execution."

Munroe's eyes lit up. "You were here for *that*? That's about the biggest thing that ever happened around these parts. That and the James Earl Ray escape in '77."

"I bet you were in junior high school when Seabold got the juice," O'Riley said with a sliver of a smile.

"Not even close," came the laughing reply. "I was in diapers."

They scaled the steps, passed through metal detectors after entering the building, and soon were seated in the warden's office.

The soft glow of the desk lamp illuminating the room and the light green striped wallpaper gave the office a homey feel. Nancy turned her head left, then right, popping her neck twice to ease her tension. O'Riley, in the meantime, yawned as he sunk down into a comfortable ottoman and propped his feet up. This police work was infringing on his afternoon nap.

"That old warden still kicking?" O'Riley asked. "What's his name? Parmenter?"

"Carpenter."

"Yeah, that's it. Carpenter. He still around?"

"You better believe it. Ninety-one years old and strong as an ox. Can't hear a damn thing, though. Lives down the road in Wartburg."

Unconsciously taking a deep breath, O'Riley said, "I got another question for you, Warden."

"I figured if you drove all the way up here, you probably had a few. Shoot."

"Would anybody know about a message that was left to my attention after Seabold's execution?"

Munroe's bushy eyebrows flew up over his green eyes. "You're *that* O'Riley! Hell, yes, everybody knows about that."

"You still got guys here who were around when it happened?"

"Sure. About eight of 'em."

"And they would remember him?"

"No doubt. Besides, everybody knows about Jimmy Seabold. We set up a prison museum for our hundred-year anniversary in 1996. Even have a goddam wooden chair with a dummy strapped in to honor him." His voice took on a mysterious air. "You know, the scuttlebutt I'm hearing in the yard is that some of the inmates think he's doing his thing again. Started up pretty good after that murder in Knoxville."

Nancy shifted uneasily in her chair, tapping her black pumps on the oriental rug at her feet.

"Just what we need," responded O'Riley, rolling his eyes back. "A celebrity murderer come back from the dead. It ain't gonna happen. I saw his ass get fried."

Nancy put a hand to her face.

"What's with the note you mentioned on the phone?" Munroe asked.

"Oh, I think somebody's playing a practical joke on me. Hell, after what you told me, it could be any one of about four hundred inmates."

"Got anybody in mind?"

"Yeah. He's over in the luxury condos you built."

"In minimum security? I guess you mean Terrence Baxter. The way the system works, when you get a former major corporate C.E.O. about to be freed after twenty years in with the general prison population, you have to make him comfortable. Nobody wanted him in the bright lights at River Bend over in Nashville. They decided to keep him tucked away out of the glare here at Brushy, just like they did Governor Blanton."

"I think I just might pay him a visit. If you don't mind, I imagine Nancy would rather stay in your office."

"With the door locked and bolted," she said, folding her hands.

"I'll be more than happy to stay here and keep you company," Munroe replied, smiling at her. He looked over at O'Riley. "But that visit is gonna cost you."

"How much?"

"A bottle of Bushmills. The entry gate guard radioed up that you had a few on your back floorboard. We don't get the good stuff in here very often. Thought you might be up for sharing a bottle."

O'Riley nodded, chuckling. "You know, you remind me of me. At home I even keep Bushmills by my bed at night." He paused momentarily. "Just in case I get bitten by a snake."

"Me, too," responded Munroe with a grin. "I keep the snake under my pillow."

✳

"Well I'll be. Joe O'Riley. It's been a long time, hasn't it?"

"Yeah, Baxter, a *real* long time," replied O'Riley, sitting across a heavy pine table from the tall, stocky, sixty-ish inmate. His short hair, about a half-inch all around, concealed a rapidly receding hairline. "How's the food?"

"You'd probably enjoy it."

"You look better in a suit," O'Riley said, nodding at the wrinkled chambray prison clothes.

"You never looked good in anything," snapped Baxter, his shiny dark eyes glaring. "If it weren't for you, my ass wouldn't be sitting here in this glorified shithole."

"You're the one who had your wife killed. If I hadn't caught you, somebody else would've."

"Bullshit. Everything you had was circumstantial. I could have made millions in the stock market by now if that jury had swung my way."

"Maybe you would and maybe you wouldn't. How do you know you wouldn't have blown it all on women and booze?"

"Not women. They're cheap," Baxter snarled, then his jowly face relaxed. "You might be right about the booze."

"I pissed you off big-time, landing your butt in here, didn't I?"

"You are very perceptive, old man."

"Did it piss you off enough to hire somebody to stalk me? Leave me notes about murders going down?"

Baxter smirked. "Murders? You know me. I wouldn't harm a fly."

"Well *somebody* had that in mind. My best guess was you."

"It's not a bad idea," mused Baxter. "I'm damn disappointed in myself for not thinking of it. The truth is, if I'd wanted you dead, you'd already be worm-meat."

"Tell you what," O'Riley said as he got up and walked to the door, "if I get any hot stock tips, I'll be sure to let you know."

With his suspicions still weighing heavily, he hurried back to the warden's office, where he asked if they could see the building where the Seabold execution had taken place.

Ten minutes later, O'Riley and Nancy, along with Munroe and two prison guards, stood in the middle of a spacious thirty-foot-square room filled with a Nautilus machine and exercise equipment.

"Not like I remember it." O'Riley pointed toward the far corner. "The chamber was over there. We sat in chairs right about where we're standing."

"Sorry I missed it," the warden said. "I always did like fireworks. This area's been a lot of things over the years. We had to quit using the three cells down that hallway near the door for solitary confinement back in 1962 when the government started what I call its be nice to prisoners policy. We've had boilers in this area, then it was a prison library, and now it's the inmate gym."

O'Riley motioned the entourage into a small hallway adjacent to the three old solitary-confinement cells, one of which had been Jimmy Seabold's. A single light bulb still hung from the ceiling. Same bulb. O'Riley asked a guard for a flashlight.

Gripping the barrel firmly, he shined the beam into the last cell down the hall and peered into the musty four-foot by eight-foot cell. The thin metal bed was still bolted to the wall and two metal pails stood side by side in the cell's far corner.

"This part hasn't changed at all," said O'Riley. He aimed the beam at the wall, illuminating the crudely-carved still visible message left by Jimmy Seabold. Closing his eyes, he recited the words from memory as the others looked on, their eyes riveted to the decades-old threat.

"With eyes of red
My actions are blue,
When your time comes, O'Riley,
I'll be waiting for you."

No one spoke. Finally Nancy broke the silence.

"Let's get out of here," she whispered to O'Riley, tugging at his sleeve.

He glanced at Munroe and winked.

The warden escorted them to the front entrance. After handing over the promised whiskey and thanking him for his hospitality, they drove down the access road to the highway.

Daylight soon faded to night as the car weaved its way toward Knoxville.

"You worn out?" O'Riley asked, wondering why Nancy had been so quiet since leaving Brushy Mountain.

She just stared out the window into the darkness.

"What's the matter? Cat got your tongue?"

Nancy turned her head, eyes glaring. "How could you?" she asked, her tone sharp and angry.

"What?"

"Don't *what* me. How could you take me to that godforsaken place? Those inmates tried to see right through my clothes."

"Maybe they got good taste."

"Don't joke," Nancy snapped. "It's not funny. You bring me up here for a holiday and we go to a prison. But not just *any* prison. The one where a serial killer, who just so happened to murder your wife, scrawled a threat as he went off to die—a threat to you."

"But it—"

"How's that supposed to make me feel?"

"It didn't enter my mind you'd be upset," O'Riley replied, apologizing.

"That's the problem. You just thought about yourself." She buried her eyes in her palms.

"And why not? It is *my* problem," he answered curtly, his voice rising. "I hid my feelings pretty damn well. Know what I saw in that cell? I saw my wife lying in a pool of blood, her chest split open like a melon."

The corners of Nancy's eyes crinkled tightly.

"I saw her murderer, smug and unrepentant, taunting me—telling me how much he enjoyed killing her." O'Riley drew a deep breath and puffed out forcefully, lightly fogging the windshield. A vein bulged on the right side of his forehead. "I saw his ass get fried in the electric chair again. And I remembered wanting to pull that switch myself!"

Nancy flinched.

O'Riley shook his head. "He caused my nightmares. He caused my loneliness. It wasn't her time to go. She was too young—I was too young. He made it her time to go. That filthy son of a bitch. . . ."

Then, gazing at the passing flash of headlights in the opposing lanes, he realized how selfish he had been, thinking only of his own feelings. All the pain and suffering he endured after his wife's death compounded with the anger and loathing he felt for her killer had been thrust back into his life. She was there to help him forget the past, not dwell on it. She was there to help him be strong, to look to the future.

Nancy reached over, taking O'Riley's hand in hers.

"I'm sorry," O'Riley said, squeezing her hand. "Sometimes I get all wound up. Can't help but snap."

"I guess we'll just have to hold each other together to keep that from happening, won't we?"

He squeezed her hand more tightly.

"You know," Nancy said, "I really would like you to plan a nice vacation for next summer. Hmmm, let's see. Where should we go?" She touched a forefinger to her chin as if in deep thought. "Attica in New York might be nice while the weather's hot. Or maybe California. I hear San Quentin is real quiet these days, unless, of course, there's an earthquake. But it is nice and warm there year-round. And don't forget Leavenworth. . . ."

24

That night during dinner at the elegant Regas Restaurant they talked and teased each other like high school sweethearts as the aroma of steaks char-broiled over mesquite wood wafted around them. But they also delighted in long periods of silence, comfortable in their mutual trust.

"Open up," O'Riley said. The last bite of his dessert teetered on the tip of his spoon.

Nancy shook her head, smiling. "I can't. Got to watch my weight."

"C'mon, it won't kill ya," he urged. "Couldn't be more than three, four hundred calories."

She gave in with a shrug and he slipped the spoon cradling rich, dark brown chocolate cake into her mouth. She closed her eyes and sighed, savoring the now rare taste of sweets.

Her eyes slowly opened and she asked, "What if we were both younger? In our twenties. Would we have met?"

O'Riley put his coffee cup down and leaned toward her, smiling slightly. "Not unless I went back to high school or you got arrested."

"I'm serious. Let's pretend I wasn't a teacher. Maybe then we would have met. And if you hadn't been a policeman, what would you have been?"

"Can't imagine being anything else," O'Riley replied, shaking his head. "I used to ride my tricycle up and down the street wearing a tiny policeman's cap. Always wanted to be like my dad. And you?"

"I would have started a restaurant. With me as chef. A quiet little romantic place—seven or eight tables." She paused. "I'd even give a free meal now and then to any policeman who'd keep an eye on the place." She winked.

"You answered your own question . . . that'd have been me." He leaned even closer. "You are so beautiful."

The flickering flames from the nearby open-hearth fireplace lit Nancy's face, reflecting in the depth of her eyes. She reached out and touched his cheek with a fingertip, moving slowly to his chin and then upward, tracing his lips.

O'Riley gently kissed her hand, searching her face and she his, enthralled by the delicious comprehension of what soon would be.

Upon returning to their room at the Hyatt Regency, they sat on the edge of the king-sized bed, gazing ten stories down at twinkling lights on the meandering Tennessee River below.

O'Riley began to speak in a hushed, soft tone. The prison visit had brought back those painful memories of his wife's death, and his sense of responsibility for it.

"Joe, it wasn't your fault," Nancy said softly.

"It *was* my fault. Nine people murdered, five in Memphis. The ninth on that Tuesday afternoon. It was November twelfth. I'll never forget that godforsaken day."

Nancy grasped his hand. He looked down at the floor as he uncontrollably relived the most tragic period of his life.

"Evelyn loved the movies. Jimmy Stewart, Cary Grant, Gregory Peck, Clark Gable, Gene Kelly. That damn Gene Kelly. She had to go see him in *The Happy Road.* 'Go ahead,' I told her. 'The crazy son of a bitch has already met his quota today,' I said."

His eyes glazed as the corners of his mouth quivered with emotion.

"'Don't worry,' I said, 'the Guild's not two blocks from home. You walk to the 7 o'clock show and I'll break away from the investigation to pick you up at 9.' She was *so* excited. I hadn't let her go to the movies for two weeks because of that goddam lunatic. I told her I loved her as we hung up. Just like I always did. That was the last time I talked to her. . . ."

O'Riley buried his face in Nancy's shoulder.

"It's all right," she said, holding him, her eyes glistening. She gently patted the back of his head and then kissed his cheek, wet with tears.

"Ever since then, I've kept my emotions all closed in. Never even much thought of another woman. Got all wrapped up in my work. Became chief of police. Never thought about breaking this barrier I'd built around me. Until now," he said softly, gazing into her eyes, his right hand cradling her chin. "Until you."

Then, with eyes gleaming, he pulled her toward him, smiling slightly as their lips met. His hands slid down to her hips and held her firmly against him.

O'Riley's heart was racing. "I feel like a bridegroom," he whispered.

In no time their clothes were strewn about the room, and their pent-up passion consummated. They collapsed into each other's arms, filling the room with the sounds of laughter and tears and love once again found.

25

On Monday the rain started at dawn. Initially a heavy downpour, then a slow, constant drizzle. All the way home from Knoxville.

But there was something about overcast skies that relaxed O'Riley. Some people are depressed by the dark, cloudy chill of fall and winter days. Not him. Especially not with Nancy at his side.

By the time they hit the outskirts of Memphis, the drizzle had subsided. To the west, the sun was kissing the horizon, turning the parting clouds pink in the emerging powder-blue sky.

He took Nancy home, holding open the wrought-iron security grate as she unlocked the front door.

"Always the gentleman," she observed.

"Always," replied O'Riley. "Some things never change."

He left her with a kiss, lingering for a moment to enjoy the sensation before promising to call later.

Then O'Riley dashed through snarled traffic to be on time for his appointment with Dr. Peter Morgan at St. Jude. After wheeling his car into a spot in the adjacent parking garage, he hurried inside the pink-stone hospital's research tower, finding his way to the doctor's fourth-floor office.

Peering through the open door, O'Riley spotted the wiry doctor scribbling notes, surrounded by thick file folders on his desk. "Knock, knock?" he announced.

Morgan looked up. "Come in, Mr. O'Riley. Have a seat." He brushed his brown pony tail back behind his head with a quick motion of his hand and pushed his black-frame glasses up the bridge of his long nose.

"Thanks for staying around to see me, Doc. I wasn't sure if I'd catch you when I called this morning."

"It's the least I can do," replied Morgan. "You're the one who had to drive six hours to get here."

"In the rain, no less."

"A lot has happened since I last spoke with you what, five weeks ago?" the doctor said, his cheerful demeanor turning serious.

"Almost six. David Lancaster *did* murder his wife. And it looks like four more women, the last one here at the Orpheum this past Friday night."

"I know," said the doctor, shaking his head and staring blankly at the floor. "I've been keeping up with it in the news."

"I'm hoping you can help me out."

Morgan looked up. "What can I do?"

"I need your opinion. Say a guy knows of somebody or has studied somebody's behavior. Could the combination of that memory drug and radiation or chemotherapy trigger a personality shift where a person thinks he actually *is* the person he was so familiar with?"

The doctor sat thoughtful for a moment, then said, "What are you getting at?"

"Take a classic example. There's always some kook in the looney bin who thinks he's Napoleon, right?"

Morgan nodded.

"If somebody who's studied Napoleon or, at least, somebody who's familiar with him were to take your memory drug *and* get a healthy dose of radiation or chemotherapy, do you think there's a chance it might trigger a reaction in his brain where he believes he's the ruler of France and starts acting like it?"

"I'm no psychiatrist," the doctor replied after another pause, "but I think it's highly improbable. I've seen no evidence in any of my patients. It seems to me you're looking for something that would trigger a multiple personality disorder. Something which has made David Lancaster *think* he's a killer he's heard of or has read about at some point in his life."

"Have you noticed any side effects from your Alzheimerzone?"

Morgan frowned. "Alzheimerone," he corrected. "No second z."

"Sorry. Any side effects?"

"Some patients say they seem to have visions in which they remember places and things which they *think* they may have experienced in a previous life."

O'Riley leaned forward. "What percentage?"

"Statistically, it's fairly significant. About three in every ten patients."

"Do you think it's possible? I mean, that they really *are* remembering past lives?"

"I have to admit, that's an intriguing possibility but I'm discounting it for now. The memory drug is most likely enabling some of the patients to become more creative as it stimulates portions of their brain tissue. Some of the locales and remembrances in those reporting visions have been out of the ordinary. Some quite exotic. Probably wishful thinking."

"Did Lancaster mention any visions of a past life?"

"Never," replied Morgan.

O'Riley then stood up, thanking the doctor again for seeing him on such short notice. "Two last questions. How many patients have taken your experimental drug in conjunction with chemotherapy?"

"That's tough to say off the top of my head. Maybe twelve. Sixteen tops."

"And how many have taken the drug along with radiation?"

"That's easy," answered Morgan as he leaned his slight frame back against his chair. "One. David Lancaster."

That night, after a half-hour talk on the phone with Nancy, O'Riley settled down into his old green-tweed recliner in the corner of his den, clad only in white boxer shorts and undershirt. At his feet on the left lay his German shepherd, sound asleep. To his right was a small table holding a nearly full bottle of Bushmills, along with a full shot glass and a tumbler of ice water. The local 10 P.M. newscast blared on a console television set against the wall.

He downed a sip of water to chill his throat, then slowly lifted the shot glass to his lips and gulped the contents. Wincing for a split-second at the bitterness, he relaxed as the warm, soothing sensation spread down his throat.

He muted the volume but continued to stare at the screen, the images far off dances of light and shadows. He pored over details of the five murders, comparing similarities and differences.

He slugged down a second shot.

The killings resembled Jimmy Seabold's in a number of ways. Movie theater locales. Similar weapons plus the same attack technique. Hearts cut out and missing. And the playing card, left only at Memphis murder sites in the past, taking up where Seabold's grisly body count had ended over forty years ago.

Perplexed, he ran his right hand through his hair and finished off a third and final whiskey as a slight buzz spread over him.

A giant jigsaw puzzle loomed with too many pieces and more than a few missing. But some things were certain. This puzzle he had been pulled into was far from being solved. And, it was deadly.

26

The radio played softly as Lancaster whipped his car across the Poplar Avenue bridge over Interstate 240 heading west. He tried to stay close to the speeding red Mustang. Close, but not too close. He couldn't risk losing the advantage of surprise. Even if she slipped from sight in traffic, he knew her destination.

Excitement surged within him. He wiped the sweat from his forehead. This time would be even better than the last.

The mother had been a nice touch. It was over for her the day she bought those tickets at the Orpheum box office. All he had to do was quietly enjoy the show from the row behind her until the opportunity to work his magic presented itself. Work his magic with not one of two thousand people the wiser, least of all the mother.

This one would be even more delightful. Having kept an eye on her for a few days, he now knew her routine. He could take his time with this one. Create a masterpiece. He'd even throw in a special added touch for an old friend.

The Mustang suddenly raced through a yellow light just as it turned red, holding him at an intersection on Park Avenue near the Dixon Gallery. A minor inconvenience. A police cruiser in the opposing lanes ignored the speeding Mustang. Perhaps he wouldn't have been so lucky. Even better this way. She could settle in at work before he made his appearance.

"What do you think of her car?" he asked himself, gnawing on his thumbnail.

"Why do you ask?" he replied.

"Just curious."

He paused for a moment, then a sneer crossed his face. "I like it. Especially the color."

"Figures," he responded. "Red was always your favorite."

His heart began pounding. The urge had to be dealt with. It was almost time to strike.

A shapely receptionist at the Park Studio stared intently at the computer screen, proof-reading a customer invoice as she lifted a steaming coffee mug to her lips. She glanced up to see an attractive young man with a short-cropped beard pulling open the side delivery door and crossing the narrow lobby toward her desk. A black leather briefcase dangled from his right hand.

Her eyes widened. "What happened to you last night? I looked all *over* the bar," she said.

"Sorry," he replied, "I wasn't feeling too good. Upset stomach. Didn't want to make a big deal out of it. Thought I better get home. This'll be a killer of a day for me. I've got about twenty accounts to call on."

"I forgive you," she said, running a hand through her light brown hair. "I'm glad you stopped by. Maybe tonight?"

"Maybe sooner."

"Do you know you came in the delivery door? You don't look much like a delivery man," she teased.

"I can be," he replied. His intense, penetrating eyes focused on her alluring figure, traveling across her without hesitation, noticing every feature. The smell of her cheap perfume filled the air. His pulse quickened as he breathed in her scent.

The receptionist squinted in the nearly blinding glare of the morning sun streaming through the delivery door. She tilted her head for refuge in his shadow. Her large breasts strained against a sheer cotton blouse. "What is it you deliver?" she asked.

"I think you might like this," he answered with an engaging grin, his right eye twitching slightly. He placed the briefcase on her desk, unzipped it, and slowly reached inside.

O'Riley slammed down the phone, cursed under his breath, and bolted out the back door, adrenaline hitting his system like an I.V. of black coffee. He arrived at the old Park Theater at 11:45 A.M., just twenty minutes after the call from Mills.

The neighborhood movie house, its facade painted gray but the red-brick side walls unchanged from its glory days as a premier film showcase, had been transformed into a studio and production site for filming commercials and music videos. On this day it could pass for a three-tenor concert.

Patrolmen furiously directed traffic at the gridlocked Highland Street and Park Avenue intersection. The former theater and its adjacent parking lot were ringed by yellow crime-scene tape holding back gawking lunchtime crowds. Over a dozen squad cars and unmarked detective cruisers encircled the studio property, their blue lights flashing non-stop.

All four local news stations had their mobile broadcast vans at the site, preparing live reports for their upcoming noontime news shows. Death was palpable, casting a pall on the sunny, crisp, fifty-five-degree day. Soon everyone would get the chance to experience it firsthand from the comfort of their own homes.

Mills had pulled his gold Cross pen from his coat pocket and was taking notes as O'Riley walked up. From the old ticket booth near the front door they immediately proceeded inside. The former concession area, converted into the studio's reception lobby, was painted gray with matching gray furniture and dark gray carpets.

"What do you know so far?" O'Riley huffed, out of breath.

"The victim was the receptionist. Twenty-five. Single. Name's Sally Vance. A brunette with the face of a model and the body of a strip-joint dancer. She don't look so good right now. Has a long brown-haired wig on. And bright red lipstick."

"A note with a name next to her?"

"Yeah. Lauren."

"Lauren Bacall?"

"That's who I think she's supposed to look like. Give or take a few years."

"What's the time frame?" O'Riley asked.

"The owner tried to call in at 9:45. Got no answer. Called a direct line to the editing studio upstairs. The tape editor said she was there at 8:30 when he came in. He went downstairs and looked around. Saw some small dark stains on the carpet leading to a stairwell. Felt it. His finger came up red. He opens a door on the stairwell and finds the body on the floor near a sink. Sound familiar?"

O'Riley nodded.

"The guy's clean," Mills continued. "We checked him out."

Instinctively, O'Riley eyed all doors, looking first at the front entrances and then glancing at the side doorway. "This place open all the time or do you have to be buzzed in?"

"The front doors have to be buzzed open for access. The side door is always open during business hours. Mainly for deliveries. United Parcel, FedEx, whatever. I'd say that's how he got in."

Detectives and uniformed officers scurried about the lobby and throughout the rest of the complex.

Mills motioned toward an open door off a short landing on the third step of the stairwell. It was just inside the front entrance. "That's the storage closet where she was found. Come take a look. Some friends of yours are just finishing up."

O'Riley peered in to discover the medical examiner, Brian Davenport, and a forensic anthropologist, Stan Sims, hovering over the bloody corpse. Bright halogen lamps bathed the scene in a blanket of white light.

"Long time no see, Davenport," said O'Riley.

The crew-cut doctor, covered in blue Tyvek protective gear, looked up and squinted in instant recognition. "Pleasure's mine," he replied. "I'd shake your hand but . . ."

"It's the thought that counts. I see you brought Dracula along." He nodded to tall, lanky Sims, calling him by the nickname given for his skill at bloodstain pattern analysis. "You become one of us yet or are you still way out there, Sims?"

The anthropologist cocked his long neck to the right, shook his already disheveled brown hair, bared his eyeballs, and twisted his face into a grotesque contortion exaggerating his bony extremities. "They try to kill Igor by hanging but rope broke," he replied, pretending to knock on a bone protruding from his neck. Those within earshot smiled for the first time all morning.

"I thought bodies long dead were your specialty," remarked O'Riley.

"They are," Sims responded. "But they're getting hard to find. I figured I'd become expert on other stuff like bloodstains and bone cuts. Crime-scene photography, too. Always some action there, especially in this town."

"Anything you don't specialize in?"

"Yeah, matter of fact. I'm not too good at tracking down serial killers. But give me the aftermath and I'm hell on wheels!"

"I'll keep that in mind." O'Riley glanced at Davenport. "What's your verdict here?"

"Same song. Almost like the Orpheum. Mills fill you in on that one?"

"Every gory detail."

"Well this one'll give you a first-hand look for yourself. A virtual carbon copy. Evidence of a blow to the head. Blunt trauma. I'll know more when I get her to autopsy. The contusion pattern will jump out after I shave her head."

Sims joined in. "Manubrium sternum fractured. It's a full thickness chest wall defect." He stood over Davenport and aimed his camera, taking shots from every angle.

"No apparent sexual overtones," continued the medical examiner. "No defensive wounds on the hands, either. A surprise attack. Knocked her out, dragged her in here, and left her. Like Sims said, her sternum was fractured." He slightly pulled open the sternum. "Heart's gone. Just like before."

Mills and O'Riley flinched.

"At the Center I'll have better light. We can check on any traces left in the wound, like rust from a blade."

"What kind of instrument did he use?" asked O'Riley.

"Funny you should ask." Davenport smiled. "That's one thing I'm *totally* sure of. A small axe. About yea big." He held his gloved forefingers about four inches apart.

"How can you be so damn certain?" Mills asked.

"See for yourself." Davenport pointed to a bloody spot near the base of the sheet-metal mop sink. A red impression of the side of the axe and the crescent of the blade stained the concrete floor.

O'Riley's eyes narrowed. The outline seemed to be the exact size as the one used by Jimmy Seabold.

"I think he cracked open the sternum," Davenport observed, "wedged the axe in sideways to keep the sternum pried apart while he excised the heart, then walked over to the sink to wash it off. He put the bloody axe down and that left us the transfer pattern." He beamed. "Sherlock Holmes ain't got *nothing* on me."

"Compare it to the one last Friday," suggested Mills.

"Similarities are the weapon type, cut marks, and the position of the body with the victims' legs close together and arms at their side. The main difference is he was standing over this one rather than on his knees when he used the axe. Made him lose a little accuracy. He missed the center of the sternum. Hit the costal cartilage. Cut right through it. Everything else is the same. The square end indention on one side between two ribs and the sharp cut in the breastbone show where the axe blade was lodged as he went for the heart."

"Forensics aside, anything else different?" O'Riley asked.

"Plenty," replied Mills, nodding at a pair of bloody khakis, a blood-stained white pinpoint shirt, and a pair of shoes piled in the corner against the unpainted cinder-block wall. "He wore a different color shirt and different type of shoes this time. White instead of blue. Topsiders instead of Rockports. Same sizes. Just wanted to look a little different. In case we were looking."

"Also the time of day," O'Riley said.

"Hell, yes. I was right about Tuesday. So, he hits in the morning instead of night. Changes his M.O."

"Any notes besides the movie star name?"

"Hey, Harris! C'mere with those notes."

Harris handed Mills two baggies, each with a note enclosed.

"This one would be first," Mills said, "the other one second."

O'Riley and Mills then walked into the lobby, leaving Davenport and Sims to pack the body and the discarded clothes for the Medic ambulance trip to the morgue.

O'Riley silently read the notes, written in the same hand as the message left on his newspaper.

With eyes of red
My actions are blue,
Funny I should show up
"Cross Town" from you.

Worrying, fretting,
Guessing what I'm next to do,
Seems I'm gone with the wind
What a shame for you.

"You think any of this is aimed at me or just the police in general?" O'Riley asked.

Mills shook his head. "I think he meant it for all of us. The bastard's taunting us with that first one. I've had over a dozen cops virtually *living* at the Jehovah's Witnesses Assembly Hall where Seabold's second murder took place."

"The old Crosstown theater."

"Exactly," he snarled. "He knew about it."

"So he changes his M.O. and goes to a place where nobody got murdered in 1957."

"But a place that *was* a theater back then," Mills added.

"What do you make of the second note?"

"Friday night the Orpheum's showing *Gone With The Wind* at their classic film series. The son of a bitch is gonna hit there again."

"What? You think he's gonna go for a repeat at the same site?" O'Riley asked, eyebrows raised.

"Why not?" Mills replied. "He feels safe there. Got by with it once. Why not try again?"

O'Riley shook his head. Sound reasoning but he didn't agree with it. "Why not do something to throw everybody off course? Make 'em think you're gonna do one thing, then catch 'em off-guard. Don't you see? I don't think he'd hit the same place twice. Too dangerous."

Mills grunted, his tone remaining serious. "Let me tell you about this guy. He's meticulous, neat, and driven to kill. There's a logical selection of each crime scene."

"And he does a lot of planning so he has control of his operating area," O'Riley was quick to add.

"This is his work and he's *damn* proud of it." Mills paused thoughtfully, checking the knot of his tie. "Sex, race, and a general age similarity are all present in his murders but that's not the overriding factor. It's not just a *victim* thing but a *location* thing as well. Here's what I'm gonna do for Friday night at the Orpheum."

O'Riley listened intently.

"We set up constant surveillance of the theater up until the screening with a thorough search of every nook and cranny in the place. We'll have the manager look around with some detectives taking pictures—he'll be able to tell if anything's been disturbed. During the show we'll saturate the theater with both concealed and undercover officers in specific locations. Plus we'll bring out the infrared cameras."

O'Riley appeared skeptical. "And what if you're wrong?"

"I'll cover my ass there, too. I'm ordering still-watches around the clock at all theaters, past or present, that were in operation in the late 1950s no matter what they're being used for now. He's getting pretty brazen. Let's hope he's also getting sloppy."

O'Riley nodded. "I'm impressed."

"Oh, there's one other thing. I'm surprised you haven't asked." The detective called Harris back over and asked for the third bag.

O'Riley reached for it, staring at the eight of hearts. "Keeping count, just like before. Six plus two equals eight."

"Flip it over," Mills said.

O'Riley froze, his face turning pale.

The smiling visage of W.C. Fields wearing a velvet-trimmed chesterfield top coat, a black top hat, and an ascot was centered on the card. A black and gold border framed the oval around the comedian's image.

O'Riley felt dizzy, his arms sweeping up to grab something, anything, to hold on to. The room tilted wildly, like a bridge collapsing under him.

"You okay?" Harris asked, grabbing O'Riley.

"Just a little hypoglycemic," he mumbled, waving off help with his hand.

"I got just what you need," responded Harris, reaching into his pocket. He unwrapped a peppermint, handed it to O'Riley, and walked away.

"Since when did you become hypoglycemic?" Mills whispered in his ear.

"Since about one minute ago." He looked at Mills with unwavering eyes. "That card—it's Seabold's."

"Resembled it?"

"Hell, no! *Just like it!* From the same goddam deck."

"How can you be so sure?"

"Believe me. I know. I'll prove it to you." O'Riley paused and his eyes narrowed. "You ever been on a bird dog hunt?"

"Not recently," Mills replied.

"Well, if you're gonna keep up with me, you better put on your waders. I got a plan in mind."

The shadowy figure moved about the dark, dingy room as if it had been his haunt for decades. Reaching into a clear plastic bag, he pulled the pinkish-red contents out with his right hand. After effortlessly lifting the glass lid from a large specimen jar, he slowly eased the soft, shiny mass into the pungent formaldehyde and replaced the lid tightly. His face glowed, pulsing with the heat of satisfied pleasure.

Pulling a black Sharpie marker from his pants pocket, he wrote SALLY VANCE on a thin strip of adhesive tape affixed to the middle of the jar. Glancing at the shelf-lined wall, he excitedly counted the jars on the top row, numbering ten in all. His gaze then fell to the shelf below. He placed his newest acquisition in its appropriate sixth spot on the row.

Serenity filled his thoughts as the names printed on the other five containers brought pleasant memories: JEAN LANCASTER, MARGARET TISDALE, MELISSA MURDOCH, PAM MILLER, LISA HOWARD.

He knew what the police would do. They were all the same. The state didn't matter. Neither did the city. Charlottesville, Roanoke, Knoxville, Nashville, Memphis. New York City or Los Angeles for that matter. Strategic, tireless, but so very predictable. With cunning flair, he would outplay them all.

He then pulled the axe and knife from his pockets and began his daily sharpening ritual. The raspy cadence of metal scraping against the hone brought an arrogant smile to his face. His Memphis fun was just getting started.

27

At eight-thirty the next morning, O'Riley's car weaved through the thinning rush-hour traffic near the midtown medical center, pulling to a stop in the parking lot of the Regional Forensic Center on Madison Avenue. As he entered the building, he spied the slightly built yet muscular form of Davenport walking toward the examination room.

"Sorry about the smell," apologized the medical examiner. "We've had a few decomposed this week."

They walked through the examination room past two bodies in white plastic bags resting on gurneys.

"What's with those two?" O'Riley asked.

"A couple of easy ones. On the left is a stab victim from last night. He beat up his girlfriend. Then he started doing the same to her fifteen-year-old daughter. The kid picked up a butcher knife and stuck it in his gut. The guy bled to death."

"And the other one?"

"Older man, dead four days, just starting to decompose."

"Ugh." O'Riley winced. "Never could stand those."

"This one's not so bad. The old guy evidently had a heart attack and just checked out. Hadn't lit his pilot light so the house was pretty chilly. Not too far off from the temp in our storage room behind you." He flipped a thumb at the large stainless-steel door through which the heart attack victim would soon pass for safekeeping until the funeral home arrived. "The estranged wife just came to identify him."

"It's always hard on the relatives," O'Riley said with a shake of his head.

"You'd be surprised. Some of the people walking out of here after an I.D. are smiling *big time*. Insurance policy dollars dancing in their heads."

Davenport moved quickly up a flight of stairs to the second floor with O'Riley trudging behind. An antiseptic odor hung in the air, a constant companion to the study of death and its causes. They came to a door marked *Medical Examiner* in the middle of the long hallway.

"Go on inside," Davenport directed. "I'll round up Sims. He's probably stroking a skull or a femur. You know how it is," he called out from down the corridor, "anthropologists love their bones."

Pushing open the wooden door, O'Riley felt he had entered another world, an oasis of eclectic tastes in the otherwise spartan building.

Dimly lit by three lamps and inviting, it had the feel of a cozy den, totally unlike what he had expected. The maroon walls exuded warmth accentuated by elegant ceiling-to-floor golden-yellow draperies, their valences swagged with cascades. Three oriental rugs and antique furniture divided the large room into a suite consisting of a sitting area, a desk area, and a lounge area for stealing sleep made scarce by the long hours.

Framed landscapes and etchings hung on the walls in an area peppered with military memorabilia including bullets, shell art, and helmets, one of which showed evidence of a fatal bullet hole.

The couch in the sitting area, covered in floral chintz, faced a floor-to-ceiling twelve-foot-long bookcase filled with not only hundreds of medical, military, and forensic volumes but macabre mementos of death and torture.

The desk was piled high with files, journals, notepads, clipboards, and correspondences delayed by the constant crush of unexpected, violent death. A recliner, sitting in the corner of the lounge area, shared quarters with a personal computer and a small table filled with a mix of vitamin bottles, deodorant, foot powder, 35MM slides, scalpels, hemostats, and a change of boxer shorts.

O'Riley smiled at the clutter and took a seat in an antique captain's chair facing the couch. The door soon swung open. The medical examiner and Sims slouched down on the couch opposite the former chief.

O'Riley spotted a small keloid scar on Davenport's chest near the border of his blue v-neck scrub shirt. "How'd you get the scar? I never noticed it before."

Davenport shifted the v of his shirt to the right, revealing a second scar. "Which one?"

O'Riley's eyes widened. "Both."

"First one was a bayonet. Second one, shrapnel. You haven't seen the ones in my side from the bullets."

"Bullets?"

Davenport lifted his shirt, revealing three circular scars in a neat row near his right rib cage. "From a machine gun. Even had a flak jacket on. They snapped right on through."

"Did you get the guy?"

"Never saw him. A sniper. It was night."

"What about the guy with the bayonet?"

"Suffice it to say I was the last person he ever stuck." He motioned with his eyes to a framed Iraqi battle flag on the wall. "Didn't think he'd need it anymore."

"When the hell did all this happen?" O'Riley asked.

"I had a life before I became a doctor, you know. Once you're in the military, you can't quite seem to get out. Even if you get out physically, you can't shake it mentally. That's where I learned about weapons and violent behavior."

"You still in?"

"Captain o-six in the U.S. Naval Reserves Medical Corps. The next level up is the admiral series."

"That accounts for those," O'Riley said, eyeing the black military combat boots on the medical examiner's feet.

"Became a habit. I never leave home without 'em. Besides, they're easy to clean off if things get messy in autopsy."

O'Riley continued. "The scars—where'd you get 'em? Vietnam? Desert Storm?"

"I was a little too young for Vietnam. Got lucky in Desert Storm, though. Stepped on a land mine. It malfunctioned."

Sims eased back into the couch.

"Where then?"pressed O'Riley.

"I got my scars in dirty little wars you never heard of. Sometimes you get caught in the scramble."

"You mean like covert operations? Black-record ops like in the movies? Were you a Navy Seal or something?"

"Yeah," Davenport deadpanned. "Something."

O'Riley frowned at the runaround.

"Some were Mil to Mil operations," Davenport said, humoring O'Riley. "Our military helping their military. Had an occasional hostage-rescue situation. Your standard Sunday walk in the park fare."

O'Riley realized there would be no more answers.

"I don't imagine you drove all the way down here to chit-chat about my past. What's on your mind?"

"I know you're both gonna think I'm crazy but . . ." O'Riley paused, fighting to spit out the words.

"But what?" Davenport asked anxiously, popping his knuckles.

"What if we tried a little experiment?" O'Riley replied as he stood and paced in front of the bookcase, his back to the medical examiner. Then he turned to face him. "I can get the weapons originally used by Jimmy Seabold out of police storage."

"Why aren't they in the state property room like the other evidence from old trials?" responded Davenport.

"They were. The state lent them to the police department for display at the police museum down on Beale Street a few years ago. The brass thought it would make a nice crime curiosity display since it was the most famous serial-killing spree ever in the three-state area. You never seen it?"

Davenport shook his head.

O'Riley turned to Sims. "How 'bout you?"

"Sorry," he replied. "Didn't even know it was down there. I don't get out much—among the living, that is."

"The display's getting refurbished during the museum renovation. The stuff's been sent to the police property room for safekeeping. We didn't tell the state. They might want it back and it was hell getting them to lend it in the first place."

"How you gonna get your hands on it?" Davenport asked.

"I'll handle it." His face hardened. "The big question is, can *you* get us a real body to experiment on?"

He scratched his freshly-buzzed scalp. "If you don't mind me asking a stupid question, exactly what in hell are you trying to prove?"

"I can't prove anything, but I can come damn close. You forensics guys can figure it out after you get the results. I want you to use the axe from the Seabold case to re-enact what we think Lancaster is doing. I think the weapons are the exact same type."

Davenport stared wide-eyed at the older man, then rolled his eyes at Sims. "C'mon, you got to be kidding me."

"I'm serious," shot back O'Riley. "Dead serious. How about one of the stiffs from the freezer?"

"I can't do that. They all belong to somebody." Davenport paused for a moment. "All except one."

"Male or female?" O'Riley asked.

"Female. A caucasian in her forties. We figured she was homeless. Froze to death during that cold snap last February. We've kept her on ice ever since. She's about due to take up residence down the street in the University of Tennessee Medical School anatomy lab."

"Would anybody miss her if she didn't show?"

"O'Riley, nobody cared about her when she was alive. Do you think being dead has changed things?"

"I guess not."

Davenport continued, "We haven't had one inquiry about her. She didn't match up to any missing person reports on the local or national wires."

"How long would it take her to thaw out?"

"She not frozen. Just cold. Look, I know what you're getting at. It's just not ethical."

"Let me get this straight," O'Riley said, his voice strong and unruffled. "It's not ethical to whack on this nameless lady's chest with an axe in hopes of finding out if we have a match to our killer's weapon. This, of course, might help save the lives of a few innocent females yet to be attacked."

"Yeah, but—"

"Yet it *is* ethical for you, on an everyday basis, to cut open skulls, pull out brains, weigh them. Use a little power saw to cut open chestbones so you can take out and examine livers, hearts, lungs, intestines, stomachs, maybe a kidney or pancreas here and there. Even a gall bladder on a lucky day."

Davenport shook his head. "Sorry. No way. We'd be accused of experimenting. The victims coming to us come unwillingly. They never agreed to get experimented on."

O'Riley shifted gears. "What about cadavers at the med school? They're donated."

Sims spoke up. "They're donated but the problem is they've been processed in such a way that it alters the biomechanics of bone fracture. Their sternums are too brittle. Besides, the tissue won't react like fresh flesh."

"What about a dip pack?" Davenport said, holding aloft a small block of man-made material that resembled a bar of Neutrogena soap.

"Nah, it's a synthetic," Sims answered. "Doesn't react like bone to a fracture. We're interested in overall gross characteristics of the chop mark, not tool mark striations."

"How about a chestplate from a cadaver?" the medical examiner asked, tapping a forefinger to his temple with eyes tightly shut.

Sims shook his head. "Won't work. The chest is a dynamic structure with tissue, flexible bone, cartilage, stabilizing vertebra. We can't just fracture a sternum on a table. I'd be afraid it wouldn't react the same to the weapon."

The three sat in silence. Davenport flexed his jaw muscles, avoiding O'Riley's stare.

O'Riley turned to Sims. "Can't you come up with *something*, Dr. Frankenstein?"

Sims looked down at the oriental rug and squinted. His head suddenly jerked up. "The Body Farm!" A wild-eyed expression of glee swept across his face.

Davenport's blue eyes lit up.

"The *what*?" O'Riley asked.

"The Body Farm. In Knoxville. We anthropologists don't usually call it that—everybody else does. Technically it's the Anthropological Research Facility. Started by Dr. Battle at UT. I was his graduate teaching assistant for five years in the early eighties. I helped him build it."

O'Riley was confused. "What is it?"

Sims smiled. "Its main purpose was and still is to help scientists and forensic specialists learn more about determining time of death. Donated corpses are placed out in a wooded area and allowed to decompose under various sets of circumstances. Shallow graves, underwater, out in the open in direct sunlight, others in shade, whatever a graduate student deems appropriate for a study. The bodies are regularly examined at timed intervals to check the decomposition of the bodies being monitored. Since Dr. Battle founded the place, we think of it as Battle's Anthropological Research Facility. BARF for short."

O'Riley's confusion, followed by repulsion, quickly turned into intrigue.

"It's worth a try," Davenport remarked. "If we have to have a fresh body."

"I'll give Dr. Battle a call." Sims grinned. "A favor for an old student."

O'Riley then stood up and headed for the door.

"Where you goin'?" Davenport asked.

O'Riley winked. "To keep my end of the bargain."

28

After a brief stop at a Wendy's drive-thru, the former chief walked through the ornate marble lobby of the downtown police headquarters on Adams, two bulging sacks from the fast-food restaurant under his arms. For the first time he avoided the marble staircase up to the second floor Homicide Squad room. Instead, he continued straight down the corridor past the Vice Squad entry to a narrow, seldom-used staircase. Descending two flights at a fast pace, his footsteps sent hollow echoes upward.

He opened the stairway exit door and stepped into the dim light of the basement. The air was stale, thick with an odor like an old antiques store.

Backing up what he had in mind without proof would be hard. And proof he was determined to get.

He approached a massive precinct desk, its aged wooden surfaces scratched and scarred from nearly a century of use. Slouched behind the desk was the ample figure of Captain John Schmidt, his fat waist that of a man in late middle age who never said no to a second helping. Strands of gray hair brushed back from his forehead clung to the top of a balding head. A forty-plus years veteran, he was playing out his string until forced retirement. Behind the captain gray file cabinets lined the wall. To his right was a cage that served as the police property room.

"Chief Joe O'Riley," bellowed Schmidt with a wide smile on his pudgy face as the outline of his former colleague emerged from the hallway shadows. "To what do I owe the honor?"

"Whatcha got planned for lunch today, Smitty?" O'Riley asked.

"I was just *thinking* about that." He patted his imposing stomach. The buttons on his light blue shirt strained to keep the girth contained.

O'Riley placed the two bags on the desk. "How about three burgers with the works and two fries?"

"Singles or doubles?"

"Doubles."

Schmidt beamed. "Milkshakes?"

O'Riley nodded.

"Chocolate?"

"Two of them."

"You must need a favor," the policeman remarked, retrieving the food with the fervor of a man who hadn't eaten in days. An empty box of dough-nuts lay in the morning trash at his feet.

"I need three favors." The tone in O'Riley's voice was urgent. "Are we dutch?"

"Name 'em," Schmidt said as he began to eat.

"Remember the Seabold case?"

"Remember it? I was there! If you hadn't had me stationed in the men's room, I'd have been in on more of the action when he was caught. What's up with it now?"

"I need the artifacts we've had on display down at the police museum on Beale."

"The axe and the knife?"

"And the cards. That's favor number one."

"Two?" Schmidt asked.

"I need to see the Seabold case file from the cabinets." He nodded to the officer's left. "Have to look up a few details."

"And last?"

"The old homicide log book. The big one. Covering the case."

"You got it," replied Schmidt. After dabbing ketchup from his mouth with a napkin, he stepped down from behind the old desk and led O'Riley to a table catty-cornered to the wall at the far end of the file cabinets. A small lamp, like those illuminating condolence books at a mortuary, provided the only light.

Quickly locating the homicide log, the captain dropped the thick, cumbersome book onto the table with a loud thud that echoed throughout the cavernous room. In a few minutes, the case folder was located.

"You got something I can write on?" asked O'Riley, taking a seat on a wooden stool.

Schmidt handed him a yellow legal pad and smiled. "Keep it. Compliments of the city."

O'Riley winked. "They'll never miss it. Thanks."

Schmidt unlocked the property room gate. It screeched loudly as it swung open. "This might take a few minutes." He disappeared into the bins and shelves.

Only the sound of O'Riley's scribbling broke the silence. The wheels in his head were spinning furiously as names and dates in the log book and case file backed up his suspicions. The striking parallels with the murders from decades ago jolted him.

Schmidt returned and laid the axe, knife, and cards on the table.

O'Riley picked up the axe by its ten-inch-long wooden handle and examined the slightly rusted head before placing it in his left hand. The four and a half-inch length of the head from poll to blade edge easily fit in his palm.

Next he zeroed in on the folding hunter knife, its closed length the same as the axe head, about four and a half inches. Picking up the cordovan jigged-bone handle, he opened the steel blade and ran a page of the legal pad across the edge. It sliced the paper like a surgeon's scalpel on human flesh. He closed the knife with a loud click.

Then he reached for the playing cards, the ace through the seven of hearts, representing Seabold's six successful murders in Memphis and his ill-fated seventh attempt when he was captured at the Luciann theater.

As he had expected, the cards not only bore the same W.C. Fields image as the one left at the Park Studio but also the same scuff marks from use.

He stared over at the file cabinets, absorbed in thought. *No way* could this be Seabold. "Impossible," he muttered. "It can't be."

Schmidt's brow wrinkled. "You all right?"

"I'm fine," assured O'Riley, placing the weapons, cards, and the legal pad into a brown grocery sack. He thanked Schmidt and stood up to leave, promising to return the articles in a few days.

"What do you need that old stuff for anyway, Joe? Going camping?" He displayed a toothy grin as he attacked the french fries.

"Going hunting, Smitty, going hunting," he replied as he walked away, vanishing into the shadows.

At three o'clock that afternoon, O'Riley was back in the medical examiner's office, along with Davenport, Sims, and, at O'Riley's request, Trevor Mills.

"You heard from the folks in Knoxville yet?" O'Riley asked Davenport, dressed in blue surgical scrubs.

"Don't look at me," Davenport replied, pointing at Sims. "It's his show."

"Nothing yet," said Sims, his long fingers tapping on the cluttered ledge of Davenport's bookcase. "We should know something soon. Dr. Battle was pretty receptive to the idea. I think he really wants me to come up there and see how much progress he's made at the research facility in the last few years."

Davenport turned to O'Riley. "How'd you come out?"

O'Riley pulled the cards from the bag.

"I'll be damned!" Mills exclaimed. "Just like the one from yesterday." He examined the cards closely, then passed them around the room.

O'Riley's eyes crinkled into a smile. He lifted the axe out next and handed it to Sims.

"Give it to Davenport," Sims said. "He's the weapons expert."

Davenport's eyes lit up as he gripped the handle. "Haven't seen one of these in a while. An old Marble's pocket axe."

"What's the scoop on it?" Mills asked.

"They were real popular with outdoorsmen in the 1920s to the late 1950s. Then they went out of production. You could find 'em in flea markets in the 1960s and later—scarce as hell now." He handed it to Mills.

"What's this for?" inquired the detective, pointing to a metal device imbedded in the wooden handle.

"Pull it out," urged the medical examiner.

A metal sheath folded out to cover the small cutting edge.

"Pretty nifty," Mills marveled.

"Fits right into the hip pocket of your pants without the danger of cutting yourself to ribbons," Sims said.

O'Riley reached into the sack again. "The perfect size to conceal on your person, then use for a sneak attack. Just like Jimmy Seabold. And maybe David Lancaster." He passed the knife to Davenport. "What's the diagnosis here, Doc?"

"Classic folding hunter knife. Popular from the mid-1800s until the mid-1900s." He opened the blade. "The swing guard between the handle and blade is characteristic of this type. Like the famous Schatt and Morgan version."

"For ornamentation?" Mills asked.

"Functional. If you're cutting something, the swing guard will keep your hand from slipping down the handle onto the blade. The edge on this thing is every bit as sharp as any scalpel I've got here."

"Good for cutting hearts out of bodies?" ventured Mills, pursing his lips slowly.

"Was for Seabold," O'Riley answered.

Suddenly a female voice over the intercom announced, "Doctor Sims, there's a long distance call for you on two. From Knoxville."

Sims bolted from his chair. Picking up the receiver, his stoic expression transformed to one of elation as he listened. He gave O'Riley a thumbs-up. "Great. We'll be there tomorrow between noon and one." He hung up and rubbed his hands together excitedly. "We're good to go. They have two options. The first is a seventy-seven-year-old female cancer victim. Died yesterday."

Davenport frowned. "The dynamics of the chest wouldn't be right. We need somebody under fifty."

"Option two is a woman on life support. Thirty-eight. Car accident. Head-on collision. The air bag protected her upper body but her pelvis and legs were crushed. Had to have bilateral BKA's."

"What's that?" O'Riley asked.

"Below the knee amputations," Sims replied. "She's heading south fast. In irreversible shock. Anoxic brain injury. Her brain's dead and her body is playing out. The plug's getting pulled in the morning between six and eight. If she lasts that long. She was a nurse at the UT Hospital. Her husband said she'd devoted herself to medicine. He's donating her remains for any studies they see fit. That would include ours."

Silence filled the room.

"She's in DIC now," continued Sims. Noticing looks of bewilderment, he translated. "Disseminated intravascular coagulation. The body's used up all its clotting ability."

"Also known as Death Is Coming," joked Davenport.

No one smiled except Sims.

"We need to leave by six in the morning to get there on time," Sims directed. "We lose an hour to the eastern time zone. They're going to notify the Knoxville medical examiner, Casey Corliss, that we're coming."

"I'll drive," volunteered Mills. "Official police business."

"Be my guest," replied Sims. "I can stare out the window and wonder where missing bodies have been buried as the scenery flashes by."

O'Riley turned to Davenport. "You sure *he* needs to go?"

"*He's* in charge of the experiment," came the laughing reply.

O'Riley shook his head. "You know something? I hadn't been to Knox-ville in forty years and now I'm going up there for the second time in three days."

"It'll be fun," Davenport promised. "But you better bring your Bushmills."

"You gonna need it?" asked O'Riley.

"No," the medical examiner responded dryly, "but before we're fin-ished at The Body Farm, you will."

29

The next day at mid-morning, as a thunderstorm pelted downtown Memphis, a hollow double-knock at the door marked 2B echoed through the second floor hallway of the Porter Building.

"Just a minute," Annie said, her shuffling footsteps accompanied by the light tapping of her cane. "Who is it?"

"A friend," the female voice replied. "A friend of Joe O'Riley's. I could come back if it's not convenient."

Annie's face took on a warm, knowing glow. She clicked the deadbolt and opened the door. "Come in, Nancy. It's nice to meet you." She held out a sinewy hand, gripping Nancy's in a firm handshake. "I've been expecting you."

Nancy's face tightened with curiosity. "Even I didn't know I was coming until last night. How could you?"

"I didn't know you'd be here today," Annie replied, ushering her guest into the living room with a wave of her hand. "Just someday. I could feel it whenever I talked to Joe. Have a seat."

A brown paper grocery sack rustled. Nancy placed it on the hardwood floor. Slipping off her tan raincoat, she laid it beside her as she eased down onto the billowy cushions of the couch and then glanced around the room.

White plantation shutters thrown open to the overcast sky framed the two windows in the uncluttered, clean room. A pastel floral design covered the couch and two matching chairs, all facing a spotless, never-blackened pink marble fireplace. A floor-to-ceiling bookcase packed tightly with volumes covered the wall behind the couch. Paintings, mainly portraits, dotted the remaining walls. A scent of roses lingered in the air from a crystal bowl filled with potpourri on the fireplace mantle.

Nancy eyed the only recognizable painting. "Why the portrait of Ronald Reagan?"

Annie sat next to her on the couch and brushed her long, gray-streaked brown hair back behind her shoulders with her slender fingers. "He was here for a campaign trip in 1980. The motorcade stopped and he sat for what seemed like all of about forty-five seconds. Good PR, I guess. Made all the newspapers. My fifteen minutes of fame." She paused a moment. "I guess Joe told you how he and I first met?"

Nancy nodded. Annie took the silence to mean yes.

"Then I imagine you could say I've had thirty minutes of fame." A beaded turquoise necklace dangled from her neck, coming to rest against her ivory caftan as she leaned back on the couch. "Can I get you something to drink? Coffee? A Coke?"

"No thanks," Nancy replied, "I'm fine. I did bring *you* something, though."

"An apple pie," Annie said, as Nancy reached for the bag.

Nancy hesitated, squinting, before placing the pie on the glass-topped coffee table in front of them. "You *can* read minds, just like Joe said, can't you?"

"Joe's a little bit off base. I can't read minds, but I do have a sensitive sniffer," Annie replied. She tapped her nose twice with a forefinger. "I hear the mind compensates for the loss of one sense by enhancing the others. You and I have a lot in common—we're both artists."

Nancy frowned, tilting her head slightly to one side.

"Your canvas just happens to be in the kitchen. And the classroom."

The wrinkles in Nancy's forehead vanished as her thin lips broke into a smile. "I expected to find you by the fountain but—"

"The rain took care of that. It's about the only thing that keeps me away. Heat. Cold. Not a problem. But water and paint just don't mix." She moistened her lips with a quick flick of her tongue and said, "I understand you're an English teacher. What grade?"

"Tenth."

"Why is it you're not at *your* normal spot today?"

"I took a personal day off. Doctor's appointment. Second one this week—day off, I mean. Today's was planned for a while. Monday's wasn't. I went for an extended week-end trip with Joe. To Knoxville."

Annie nodded. "A fact-finding trip. Did he find what he was looking for?"

Nancy blushed. "I know he found one thing he needed." She hesitated a moment, then added, "He's going back up there today. More police business." Her gaze shifted from Annie to the bookcase. "You have quite a collection of books."

"All in Braille. Largest collection in the city. Probably this part of the country. What books do you have your students read?"

Nancy touched a finger to her cheek. "*The Great Gatsby. The Sun Also Rises.*"

Annie stood and deftly maneuvered around the furniture toward the bookcase. She pulled a book bound in black leather from the third shelf on the left side and then a tan clothbound volume from the bottom shelf on the right. She handed them to Nancy and sat back down.

"I'll be," Nancy said, taking a deep breath and placing a hand to her mouth in one quick motion. "And I thought *I* had it together." She thumbed through the Braille copies of the two books she had just mentioned.

"Don't feel bad. It's a gift I have. These books of mine are all connected—like a network in my mind. I know just where to go for whatever I need. Like you."

Nancy again looked over at her hostess.

"Think about it," Annie urged, sensing Nancy's confusion. "Why did you come to see me today?"

"I . . . I don't really know. I just felt drawn to meet you. Does that sound strange?" she asked, seeing her own reflection in Annie's dark glasses.

"Not at all. You came because you needed something. Just like my books are connected in my mind, so is everything in the world connected. There's a link between all of us, present and absent, living and dead, those we know and those we don't." She reached out, cupping Nancy's hands in her own.

Nancy's eyes glistened. Her throat throbbed as she held back tears. She thought of her sister, two years older, whose death at twenty had robbed her of her confidante. She felt her sister's presence, as if through Annie's touch. "My sister would be about your age," she said, lips quivering. "I feel her now, her memory, and I haven't for the longest time." Her face crumpled and she began to cry.

Annie pulled her close, cradling Nancy's head in the small of her shoulder. "What I think is you were drawn to me through your link to Joe and, because of that link, you found your sister." She gently patted Nancy's back. "I've never met your sister, nor has Joe. I don't even know her name. Yet here we are—me, you, Joe, and your sister—all here together right now."

"Elizabeth," Nancy said. "Her name was Elizabeth." She took a deep breath and righted herself on the couch. "I'm sorry. I'm usually not this emotional." She fished a tissue from the bottom of her brown leather purse, dabbed her eyes, then softly blew her nose.

"You have nothing to be sorry about. You now have your sister, at least in spirit, and you have Joe. What are your feelings for him?"

"I was confused when I first met him. A strange, wonderful confusion. I never thought I could love again after losing my husband to cancer. We were always too busy with our careers to think about children. Thought we'd have each other forever. Forever ended over ten years ago."

Annie nodded. "I know the feeling. My husband was killed in a car accident. Five years after we were married. I saw the world through his eyes. When they closed, so did mine."

"I threw myself into teaching by day and tutoring by night. Just to keep busy."

"And I began painting. All day, every day. For Joe, it was police work. We all deal with pain differently, yet the same."

Nancy's eyes glistened again, this time with tears of gratitude. She reached over, clasping Annie's right hand in hers. "You have such a comforting way about you, the way you look at life. And you could be so bitter after what's happened to you."

"Bitterness serves no purpose. It chokes off the soul and destroys creativity. If I had embraced bitterness and self-pity, I could never have painted these portraits and the hundreds you don't see. Or read every book on that wall." Annie waved her left hand about the room.

"That's what I realized about Joe. My confusion. I was holding back when I should have been letting myself go. I finally let my heart take over. He can be so inconsiderate at times. Running around like he's still a policeman. I worry." She paused, gazing out the window into the muted light, her brown eyes soft and dreamy. "But he has a gentle side that nobody knows. Nobody but me."

"He's a good man," Annie said. "A strong man. You're lucky to have him. He doesn't mean to be inconsiderate. But there's evil in the world. We can choose how we deal with it. Some people become religious. Others chase after evil physically, trying to overcome the mental anguish and scars it leaves behind. Joe is dealing with that evil now and he needs your help, your love to pull him through." She squeezed Nancy's hand. "*Now* do you know why you came here today?"

Nancy smiled.

The two women talked for almost an hour. Then Nancy glanced at her watch. "Will you join me for lunch? My umbrella is big enough for two."

"I'd like that a lot," Annie replied. "Do you mind if we stop by the park so I can scatter some nuts and birdseed for the squirrels and pigeons?"

"They have to eat, too." Nancy slipped her raincoat over her narrow shoulders. "You know, this may sound trite, but I feel like I've known you my whole life."

Annie clutched her mahogany cane and closed the door behind them. "Never can tell," she replied, the corners of her mouth drawing up in a grin, "maybe you have."

30

The quartet of O'Riley, Mills, Davenport, and Sims reached the University of Tennessee Medical Center not long after noon. They met with Casey Corliss in her fourth-floor office and were soon joined by the head anthropologist, Murray Marcum, and two graduate students. Marcum informed them of the accident victim's death at seven-thirty that morning. Her remains were waiting at the Anthropological Research Facility.

Soon the entourage stood on the fringe of the hospital's back parking lot, adjacent to a heavily wooded area. A chain-link fence loomed before them.

"Who's the lucky man?" asked Corliss. The trim medical examiner's searing blue eyes glanced first at her former mentor, Davenport, and then at Sims.

"I'm the winner," replied Sims. "An all-expense paid trip to the beautiful, bucolic . . ." Looking quickly at the others with crazed eyes, he lowered his voice to a whisper as if uttering an obscenity, ". . . Body Farm high on a ridge overlooking the winding Tennessee River in Knoxville, Tennessee!"

Davenport joined in, imitating the deep voice of an announcer. "And what else do we have for our winner, Casey?"

"A one-day supply of Tyvek disposable clothing!" Corliss announced with a flick of her short, shag-cut blond hair. "Suitable for crime scenes, autopsies, excavation of remains, and even human experimentation!" She tossed a grocery sack at Sims.

Marcum and the anthropology students grinned. Mills looked on stone-faced.

"You people who deal with dead bodies for a living have a strange sense of humor," O'Riley commented.

Marcum, a balding, barrel-chested doctor in his fifties, shrugged. "Have to. It's the nature of our business. If we want to keep our sanity, that is." He took a deep breath. A serious expression crossed his face. "Our plan here is one we all strictly adhere to. That being the respectful study of bones. We tolerate the slings and arrows of those who have nicknamed our facility The Body Farm but they have no real idea of the important work performed here."

A cool breeze whipped through the bare trees as he spoke, rustling limbs that swayed to and fro, as if the departed spirits were gathering around the group, echoing their approval.

Marcum continued, "The express purpose in founding the Anthropological Research Facility was to create an environment where students, scientists, phyicians, and forensic personnel who study bones could conduct research which would ultimately help us learn more about the elusive art of determining time of death. As the years have passed, we have branched out to help law-enforcement agencies in any way possible in regards to providing information useful in the apprehension and conviction of criminal elements. *That* is our purpose here today."

Corliss tossed Davenport a second bag of clothing. "I brought one for you, too. In case Sims needs some back-up."

"A woman after my own heart," he said, opening the sack.

Both men began to slip on the white, plasticized paper clothing, first the jumpsuits, then hair covers, followed by masks with built-in eye shields, shoe covers, and finally gloves.

"This is it?" asked O'Riley, as Marcum unlocked the chain-link entrance gate to the unimposing compound.

"We don't want to be too obvious near the entrance," Marcum replied. "Don't want to disrupt the neighbors any more than we have to. You'll understand in a few minutes."

They walked through the gate single file, then passed through another gated fence, a tall wooden one weathered by the elements. It separated the prying eyes of the curious from this unique world of the dead.

A covering of leaves and branches crunched and cracked as the caravan plodded through the forested area, home to many human corpses in various degrees of decomposition.

O'Riley sniffed lightly, turning up his nose. "It don't smell so good around here."

A putrefied stench tinged the air, somewhat diminished by the chill of the season.

"Ah, the lovely aroma of research," Sims replied, inhaling deeply. "This is nothing. You should be here in August when it's ninety degrees outside. I remember back when we built the place. Things got so bad that first month we had hospital employees puking in the parking lot."

"You are lucky," Marcum added. "Yours is the first body we've had in three weeks, other than the older lady you declined. The smell won't be too bad on either of them for a few days."

They continued through the woods, passing uneven mounds of dirt, grim evidence of where bodies had been buried and dug up.

"Looks like an exhumed cemetery," commented Mills softly.

"In a way, that's exactly what it is," Corliss replied.

An old, rusting Buick Electra 225 sedan, late sixties vintage, sat parked to their left with one skeleton at the wheel and another with its feet poking out of a burlap bag in the open trunk. Three bathtubs filled with murky water were nearby, holding bodies submerged, tethered to weights in two of the three. Ligatures hung randomly from assorted sturdy tree limbs.

"I can just *imagine* what those are used for," O'Riley said. "What's the deal on that big winch?" He nodded at a rusted, discarded piece of scrap metal partially hidden in the underbrush.

"It was going to be used a few years ago for a moving water decomposition experiment in the river below us," Marcum answered. "We were all set to hook the winch to an auto, strap a body into it, and monitor its decomposition. Had to abandon the project due to public concerns. Translated, that means pleasure boaters weren't too thrilled with the idea."

"Don't guess anybody wanted to run the risk of picking up a stranger, or parts of one, on their way up the river for a UT football game at Neyland Stadium," joked Sims.

"Who in hell thinks up all this weird shit?" Mills blurted out.

Marcum chuckled. "Any number of graduate students who endlessly parade through the UT Anthropology Department." He suddenly grabbed O'Riley by the collar and yanked him to the right, almost knocking the former chief off-balance.

O'Riley righted himself and shot a puzzled look at Marcum.

"You step there," the anthropologist warned, "and your friends will have you walking back to Memphis."

"Yeeech," gagged O'Riley. The heavy odor of decomposition seemed to stick on his tongue.

A skeleton lay nestled in a pool of tannish goo at his feet. A small hank of brown hair was tangled and matted next to a row of pearly-white teeth.

"What on earth is this one's story?" Mills asked, his face contorted.

"This is why *they're* here," replied Marcum, pointing at the two anthropology students. "It's their baby."

The two students, one male and one female, donned aprons and popped on latex gloves.

"This is our stop," the woman said, smiling. "We're *always* open for volunteers if someone wants to give us a hand."

Davenport, Sims, and Corliss mockingly gave them a polite round of golf-course applause.

"Like I said, strange sense of humor," repeated O'Riley. "How long's this one been here?" He and Mills backed away from the body.

"Six weeks, maybe seven."

"Why's it stink so much?" O'Riley asked.

Marcum motioned toward the students. "They were out here yester-day poking around. Got it all stirred up. They'll finish today." He turned to the male student. "What's the experiment called?"

"Effects of Decomposition on Bullet Striations."

"Translation?" O'Riley asked.

"They took five types of bullets," began Marcum. "Lead, copper-jack-eted, aluminum-jacketed, nickel-plated, and nylon-coated. Then they fired them into a cotton stopbox to engrave rifling marks on them. After taking magnified photographs of each one, they implanted a series of bullets into a fresh cadaver's brain, chest, abdomen, muscle tissue and, lastly, fatty tissue to determine the effect of the microenvironment of the decomposing body on the rifling marks for each bullet type."

"What's that gonna tell ya?" asked O'Riley, squinting in disgust as the students raked through the remains with their gloved fingers and excitedly held aloft each bullet they found as if it were the prize in a box of Cracker Jack.

"You want to get an estimate of the quality of rifling marks in bullets recovered from decomposed bodies at crime scenes. Some people don't try to recover the bullets because they think they won't be readable. We're prov-ing them wrong. It might help solve a murder if we can trace a bullet found in a decomposed body to a gun in the possession of a suspect."

The group, minus the graduate students, then walked fifty yards down a dirt path strewn with dead leaves.

"Omigod." O'Riley placed a hand to his mouth. A musty, moldy odor laced the air. "Looks like what's left of another human and . . ."

Two mounds lay in the underbrush off to one side of the path, spaced some twenty feet apart. The human remains were nearly identical in appear-ance to the body in the bullet experiment. A mummified shell that looked like furry, dried parchment with ribs clearly outlined under the skin lay nearby, its underside gone, eaten away by bugs.

"Yes, human remains," Marcum said. "Any guesses about the other?"

O'Riley shook his head as Sims began to sing. "Old MacDonald had a farm, E-I-E-I-O. And on the farm he had some—"

"Pigs!" shouted Davenport and Corliss.

"E-I-E-I-O."

The three then sang in unison. "With an oink-oink here and an oink-oink there, here an oink, there an oink, everywhere an oink-oink—"

"Awright, already!" O'Riley bellowed, bringing the impromptu sing-along to an end. "I get the picture."

The trio plus Marcum all laughed, Sims a little louder than the others. Mills and O'Riley exchanged unamused glances.

Okay," O'Riley said. "Now that we've all gotten our daily quota of yuks at my expense, what's a pig doing here? I thought this place was just for humans."

"*Mainly* for humans," Marcum replied. "We make exceptions now and then, in this case, for a forensic entomology experiment."

O'Riley's frown exposed his ignorance of the term.

"Entomology," Marcum explained, "is the branch of zoology that deals with insects."

"I take it forensic entomology ain't the study of dead bugs," Mills said.

"Correct. It's actually one of the newer up-and-coming fields in forensic sciences. Until the last couple of decades or so, homicide investigators and forensic personnel would see insects on a corpse and brush them off in their search for cause of and time since death. That's not the case anymore. Now we collect surface insects, burrowing insects, even insects flying around the corpse. We've realized that the insects help in determining the post-mortem interval, that is, how long a body has been deceased."

O'Riley put a hand to his nose as the smell shifted his way.

Marcum pointed at the animal carcass, drew in a deep breath, and exhaled, unfazed by the odor. "Our friend Porky over there and his human cohort are examples of faunal succession, which is the succession of different species of insects on decomposing remains."

"You up for some pork chops tonight?" Sims asked O'Riley. He arched an eyebrow.

O'Riley curled his lip in disgust.

"Pigs have often been used for testing since they're in the one-twenty to a hundred fifty-pound range that easily mimics the size of a human," Marcum said. "One noted forensic entomologist at a California university voiced the opinion that pigs shouldn't be relied upon for data because faunal succession would be different for animals compared to humans. Our students began this experiment eight weeks ago in an attempt to show that a correlation exists between the progression of insects on decomposing human remains and that on a pig or, for that matter, any other animal about the same size as a human."

"When you say progression, you mean like maggots, then flies?" O'Riley asked.

"It's a bit more complex than that. The maggots are responsible for the dramatic consumption of a corpse's tissues. But later, when a corpse has dried out to a great extent, other insect species, most notably beetles, move in to continue the process. Numerous types of beetles become members of the host corpse community, feeding and rearing their offspring while various types of flies set up colonization. The corpse eventually comes to support a very diverse community of insects numbering hundreds of species and thousands of individuals. They fly, crawl, and scurry about in the remains and in the soil beneath it."

"This is all well and good," Mills said, "but say we find some stiff who's been out in a field for no telling how long. Four weeks, six weeks, three months, whatever. How do you figure it out precisely?"

"We're not talking precise," Marcum replied. "We're talking ballpark. The progressive nature of the colonization process enables the entomologist, when supplied with a representative sample of the insects found with the remains, to develop meaningful information concerning the timing of the individual's death."

O'Riley thought for a second, then said, "I get it. By determining what players are on the field when a body's found, you can figure out what inning you're in." He puffed out his chest like a winning game show contestant and added, "I just wish the uniforms didn't stink so much."

The tour then continued, snaking back in view of the river.

Marcum peered at O'Riley. "This one might be more to your liking. It's a little more antiseptic."

Before them were three bronze-colored metal coffins set individually on short concrete platforms. Two clear plastic tubes, one at the head, the other at the foot, protruded from each coffin and were attached to battery-powered, gray metal measuring equipment boxes about the size of grocery sacks.

"I feel like I'm in a coffin showroom," Mills remarked.

"You're almost right," replied Marcum. "The Smoky Mountain Coffin Company is paying us to set up and monitor an experiment for them." He banged on the lid of the coffin closest to him with his knuckles three times as if it were a car fender. "Don't worry," he said reassuringly, "the three we've sealed inside are *not* light sleepers."

"At least they don't smell," O'Riley murmured to Mills.

"The purpose of their experiment is two-fold," Marcum continued. "On the one hand they want to visually see how well their coffins hold up to the external elements in comparison to others we have buried directly into the ground that we'll dig up one at a time annually for the next ten years. On the other hand, these three containing cadavers are measuring the dynamic effects of decomposing bodies on a coffin's interior."

Mills' gaze shifted back toward O'Riley. "This place is like Disneyland for the Dead," he said under his breath.

Marcum tapped a finger on one of the tubes. "That process is accomplished by using one hose to test the air inside for humidity while the other checks for moisture, fluids, and pH levels to try to predict the amount of corrosiveness associated with decomposing bodies."

"Will this be on the final exam in Intermediate Coffin Interactions 202?" Sims asked, but he got no response.

Continuing up a short incline, they approached a white vinyl body bag lying on a concrete slab enclosed by wire mesh.

"Here's our subject," announced Marcum.

"What's the wire for?" O'Riley asked.

"Didn't want any predators getting to her before you did," he said, pointing to a buzzard circling overhead. "They're pretty smart. They know something's up when they see us in here."

"Like pigeons in a park," Sims said with a laugh.

"Exactly," Marcum replied. "Just more to go around." He lifted the mesh and unzipped the bag.

A standard white hospital gown with UT Hospital stamped in orange lettering on the front draped loosely over her pale torso, still dotted with monitor pads from EKG equipment. With her partially-amputated legs heavily wrapped in gauze, she resembled a half-prepared mummy. The left side of her mouth was slightly depressed where an air tube had been only hours before and her brown hair was stringy and disheveled.

"She don't look so hot," O'Riley remarked, wondering if he looked as queasy as he felt.

"Nobody *ever* looks good dead, not even after a funeral home gets finished with them," Sims said, as he pulled the Seabold axe from a navy blue workout bag along with an indelible marker. Then he gently lifted the gown, exposing the woman's chest and outlined the manubrium sternum in black ink. "I'm going for a straight line between the sternal notch and the xiphoid tip."

Mills and O'Riley stood a body length back as the others crowded around for a closer view.

"They look like a bunch of kids making cookies," the detective whispered.

O'Riley nodded.

Sims took a deep breath and raised the axe. "Here goes nothing."

A muted hollow thump followed.

O'Riley grimaced, shoulders flinching at the sound. He turned the other way.

"C'mon," Davenport chided, "you look like a school girl playing pat-a-cake. Give it a good whack. Put some mustard in your swing."

"Look," replied Sims, glancing over his shoulder. "It's not like I've ever done this before." He shook his head, muttering, "Or ever will again, I hope."

His second attempt was more forceful. He followed with a third. And then a fourth.

"This is where *I* take a hike," O'Riley announced, moving away from the scene as he cautiously watched where he stepped, avoiding any tell-tale mounds.

Davenport, Sims, and Corliss then compared crime scene photos from Memphis and Knoxville to the sight before them.

"How's it look?" asked Sims.

"About right," Davenport replied. "Let's wedge in the axe head." The sternum creaked, but held tight under the forceful prying. "*Definitely* wide enough to get the heart out."

O'Riley stared at them from a distance, his stomach flipping at the creaking sound that carried through the wooded area. He bowed his head, closed his eyes, and massaged his graying temples with quick, short strokes.

In his mind he saw Evelyn reclining in her favorite floral dress, eyes closed in a deep sleep, her shoulder-length brunette hair flawlessly styled. But she wasn't alone.

The stocky body of Jimmy Seabold hulked over her. His thick fingers held an axe above his head. He swung down. Thud after thud resounded in O'Riley's ears. The yellow dress turned red.

Seabold wedged the axe into her open chest and pulled Evelyn's still-beating heart into the air.

O'Riley's jaw ached from the pressure of his tightly clenched teeth. His fingers gripped the trunk of a sapling so hard they turned white, his short nails imbedded in the bark. He gagged at the rush of liquid in his throat and, bending over, vomited into a clump of twisted vines and leaves.

After righting himself, he pried his fingers from the tree and wiped cold sweat from his forehead with a sleeve.

The medical examiner began excising the chestplate for comparison processing. Within fifteen minutes, his work was done.

He placed it into a red biohazard bag and stored that in a white, eight-inch square specimen box. Both men then took off their bloody coveralls and other clothing, throwing it all into a larger biohazard bag before cleansing their hands with antimicrobial wipes.

"Let's get the hell out of here," Sims boomed.

At 6 P.M. Davenport, Sims, Corliss, Mills, and O'Riley stood around one of two stainless-steel autopsy tables in the Knoxville morgue, which was tucked in the basement of the University of Tennessee Medical Center, two floors below the main lobby of the hospital. They stared at the creamy-white chestplate, soaked first in bleach and then simmered in soapy water for almost three hours. It seemed to glow under the glare of the bright flourescents. To its side were the two other chestplates and photos from the Park Studio murder victim autopsy.

Sims took his time peering intensely at the bones through an operating microscope as the others looked on. The walls of the dated, 1950s-era examination room were stark white and pictureless with no charts or signs of any kind for decoration.

Sims glanced up. "Looking at the limits of the defects in the bone, this is definitely the same class of tool." He pulled out his ever-present six-inch stainless-steel ruler and took a measurement. "The breadth of the tool is the same. Class characteristics are identical. The kicker is, not only do we have dimensions of the tool replicated, we've got evidence indicating *how* the killer used the tool. He spread the ribs with it as evidenced by the indention on one side of the sternum by the back of the axe and the wedged cut marks of the blade on the other side. Pretty convincing."

"We thought it was the same type," Davenport remarked. "Now we know. That's as close a match as we could ever hope to find. I wonder where the hell he got one of those old-time axes? Maybe he frequents flea markets."

O'Riley stared at the bones on the table, fighting with himself over his own determination, not daring to mention it aloud. Not yet.

Corliss motioned Davenport over into the corner. His jogging shoes squeaked against the gray linoleum floor, a surface mopped countless times, washing away the blood of hundreds of murder and accident victims.

"Think you might be able to stay an extra day?" she whispered.

He toyed with the sleeve of the white lab coat covering her green surgical scrubs. "What do you have in mind?"

"Oh, thought I might show you some sights," she answered. "For old time's sake."

"I'd like to," he replied, trying to figure out a way to say yes, "but I'm riding back with the guys in a couple of hours."

"I'll make it worth the cost of a plane ticket tomorrow," she promised.

"Let's load things up," Sims said. "We can stop for a burger at the Old College Inn on the strip. I'm so hungry my stomach thinks my jaw's been wired shut. Then we'll hit the road. We got a long ride ahead of us."

"I'm gonna stay an extra day and look over a few things with Casey," Davenport called out. "I'll catch a flight tomorrow afternoon."

A few minutes later Mills, O'Riley, and Sims headed into the cold of the Knoxville night.

"I think he'd rather jump some bones instead of studying them," Mills observed.

"Yeah," laughed Sims, nodding vigorously, "live female ones!"

"Don't know what it is about this town," remarked O'Riley. "Brings out the romance in a man."

Sims and Mills shot perplexed looks at him.

The older man just smiled, staring at the distant bright lights of the Hyatt Regency Hotel cutting through the darkness.

31

Fear shrouded Memphis the next day as the afternoon warmth blended into the cool of the evening.

News accounts of the murders and speculation on when and where the killer might next strike had the city in an uproar. Graphic descriptions leaked by witnesses about the Memphis deaths and those across Tennessee and in Virginia as well, went far beyond warning the city's citizens of possible danger. Sensationalism was rampant in newspapers, tabloids, and local television coverage.

Women were gripped in terror, many purchasing handguns. Cans of pepper gas sold like flashlights and batteries during a power outage.

Meanwhile, according to plan, over fifty police officers and detectives were positioned in the Orpheum theater as the house lights dimmed for the screening of *Gone With The Wind* that evening. All were either concealed from public view or undercover, posing as concession workers, maintenance personnel, ushers, and moviegoers. Those concealed throughout the ornate showplace panned the darkened auditorium with infrared night vision equipment, paying particular attention to anyone in lightly hued slacks and a solid shirt.

At the other old theater buildings, single patrol cars stood guard with one officer behind the wheel and another on foot at the entrance, carefully scrutinizing every person who entered. At the Book World bookstore on Poplar Avenue, site of the old Plaza theater, two units kept watch in deference to the murder that occurred at its sister store in Nashville at the former Belle Meade Theater.

As the lengthy movie entered its final hour, the situation at the Orpheum and the other spots under surveillance appeared calm and problem-free.

✳

He silently eased down the ladder from the trap door in the ceiling until he felt the concrete floor beneath his feet. Everything was going as planned. Better, in fact.

At first he thought it might be her night off. She didn't arrive at her normal time. She was never late. The dread of disappointment sent adrenaline racing through his system. Then she showed up. Such worry for nothing.

Now his task would be easier. Much easier. And much more fun. It was time to make her acquaintance. After all, he felt as if he already knew her.

He slowly opened the door and proceeded toward the end of the long hallway, lightly tapping his fingers on the wall along the way.

His temples pounded furiously, throbbing as if they would explode. His quarry was cornered.

The Book World manager sat quietly at her second floor desk, sipping a Diet Coke and looking out through a large viewing window at the nearly deserted sales floor below. What was once the cavernous auditorium of the Plaza movie theater was now filled with row upon row of shelves packed with thousands of hardcover and paperback volumes.

Strange tapping sounds from the hallway broke the silence. She curiously eyed the open door, then eased from her chair to investigate.

"Shit!" she shrieked, jumping back as a man suddenly appeared.

"Sorry," apologized the young man wearing thick, black-framed glasses. "I didn't mean to scare you. I wanted to apply for a job. The assistant manager unlocked the door downstairs and told me to come up here. I know you're closing soon—I could come back."

She managed a faint smile. With medium-length reddish hair and freckles dotting his cheeks, he looked innocent and impressive, clad in pressed khaki slacks and a white dress shirt with an over-stuffed briefcase at his side. A plastic pocket protector stuck in his shirt along with a pencil, a pen, and markers of various colors.

"No problem," she assured him. "I didn't mean to scream. Everybody's a little skittish around here. Women, at any rate. You know," she said, walking back to her desk and shuffling papers in search of an application, "that crazy killer on the loose. At least we get a policeman near the front door. Being an old theater and all."

He nodded politely and sat down in an old lopsided chair next to her desk. He stuck his right thumbnail just inside his mouth and began to gnaw.

"I'm surprised my assistant manager didn't handle you," she went on, finally finding an application. "He's trying to do everything else to get my job."

He said nothing.

"Full-time or part-time?" she asked.

"Part-time." He paused. "During the day. I'm busy at night. Usually."

"In school?"

"The University of Memphis. Engineering."

"That's what I figured."

His eyes silently asked why she would think that.

"All the stuff in your pocket," she said. "The only thing missing is a slide rule. Have you had any experience in bookstores?"

He unzipped his briefcase and stood up, staring at the attractive woman's straight, shoulder-length blond hair. His right eye began to twitch. "Oh, yes," he replied. "Lots. In fact, I just finished up a job a few weeks ago. In Nashville. Let me give you my résumé."

He reached into the briefcase. He felt exhilarated. On top of the world.

The telephone rang at 11:45 P.M., rousing O'Riley from a deep sleep. By 11:55 he was up, dressed, and in his Lincoln, leaving for Book World. Mills would be waiting for him. As would another victim.

O'Riley jammed the pedal. The car abruptly accelerated, its tires squealing down North Avalon toward Poplar. As Friday night faded into Saturday morning, traffic on the streets had faded as well. He clutched the wheel, staring straight ahead, watching the white beams of his headlights cut through the darkness.

The drive at almost sixty miles an hour took less than six minutes. The moon was just coming out from behind passing clouds when he arrived.

Mills met the former chief as he approached the yellow police tape surrounding the entrance and escorted him inside. A sea of flashing police lights had turned the building's beige facade blue.

Walking past book-filled displays in the lobby, the detective recapped the details. Female. Twenty-five. The manager. Blow to the head. Chest hacked open. Heart missing.

A policeman guarded a door near the center of the lobby.

"This leads up to the offices," Mills said. "It's always locked. You have to know the combination to get in."

"I thought you had this place under watch. With *two* cars."

"We did."

"Then how the hell—"

"You'll see."

O'Riley frowned, struggling up the long, winding flight of steps to the second floor. At the top they exited into a long hallway with numerous doors leading off each side.

O'Riley felt like he was living the same bad dream over again. Detectives were almost tripping over one another while forensic personnel dusted for prints, searched for hair and clothes fibers, and performed their other tasks.

Mills pointed to small dark stains on the carpet with the toe of his Gucci shoes. "She evidently got whacked in her office where the trail of blood starts. Then he dragged her past the accounting office to the mop closet."

Halfway down the hall, a pine door was propped open. They peered inside to find Davenport hovering over the blood-soaked body. She lay face-up, partially under an old porcelain wash basin. Cardboard boxes, cans of paint, and a roll of toilet paper filled a corner near the victim's head in the cramped four-by-six-foot room.

The medical examiner glanced up at O'Riley. "This is one helluva welcome-home present, don't you think?"

O'Riley nodded, trying to keep his eyes off the gruesome sight. "How'd it go in Knoxville? Did you work her over, uh, I mean, did you get your work over?" He did his damndest to keep a straight face.

Davenport nodded.

"Where's your running mate?"

"Sims? He had to fly up to South Dakota to see his mother unexpect-edly. He'll be back Sunday."

"Guess it's time for another one of his electric shock treatments," O'Riley said, smiling. "How come nobody's filled in for you so you can catch a break?"

"The office tries to keep the same M.E. on cases that seem linked. Makes testifying more unified."

"I hope you get your chance," responded O'Riley. "You guys ready to fill me in?"

Mills sighed and began, "The place has six employees on duty at night. Three on the sales floor, two handling the cafe plus the manager or assistant manager. Tonight they both worked. The manager, Barbara Murphy's her name, was supposed to be off but she filled in when somebody called in sick."

"Her lucky night," Davenport remarked under his breath.

"Normally she comes down from her office at around 10:30 or so to start closing the joint down," continued Mills. "When she was late, the assistant manager went up to look for her. Found her gutted here on the floor."

"How's he doing?" O'Riley asked.

"That's him you hear. Crosby's trying to calm him down in the break room. It's an understatement to call the guy a basket case. He keeps saying he'll never set foot in here again."

O'Riley turned to Davenport. "Same class of weapons?"

"Yep."

"Calling cards?"

"Nine of hearts. W.C. Fields deck," replied Mills. "And, of course, a name printed on his same three-by-five slip of paper in black marker. Harris has 'em in evidence bags. Who's she look like to you?"

"Not a very good likeness this time," O'Riley answered. "He's slipping. But I'd say the paper is marked Ava. For Ava Gardner."

Mills was astounded. He turned to Davenport, who shrugged, then back to O'Riley. "How'd you know?"

"Just a hunch."

"Notice anything else?" Mills asked.

"Yeah. Her hair's spray-painted brown instead of a wig."

"Looks like he took his time. Didn't want any roots to show."

"I guess he figured most of the cops were down at the Orpheum. What about your *Gone With The Wind* notion?" O'Riley asked.

"He was partially right," Davenport replied. "In place of her heart, I found a paperback copy of *Gone With The Wind* stuffed in her chest cavity. Harris has that, too."

They stood in silence for a few moments before O'Riley turned and walked across the hallway. He fought to bridle his anger, to keep his feelings in check.

Images flashed back into his mind of Evelyn's blood-soaked body on

218

that cold tan concrete floor, surrounded by detectives as he burst through the doors of the Guild theater. Sweet Evelyn. Hacked like a piece of meat at the butcher shop.

His breath quickened and he choked bile back down his throat. His face reddened and his teeth gritted involuntarily as his fists opened and closed. It couldn't happen again. Not ever.

O'Riley returned to the doorway. "Okay, now how the hell did that scum get in here if we had two patrol cars watching the entrance?"

"By changing his M.O.," Mills answered. He pointed up at a narrow metal ladder bolted to the wall. It led to a three-foot-square trap door in the mop closet ceiling. The lock on the door had been snapped off. "Go through that opening and you're on the roof in no time. It's supposed to be the access to the air conditioning units. No way we'd see him coming or going. Unless we were using helicopters."

O'Riley calmed down, letting out a deep breath. The redness faded from his face. "Think he's trying out for a circus act?"

"Hardly. But he does seem to be promoting reading awareness week." Mills motioned at Harris who was walking by with the blood-stained book in the evidence bag.

"A play on words?" guessed O'Riley.

"No doubt," Mills agreed. "He's gone with the wind."

"Is there anything else Harris has that I should know about?"

"I was saving the best for last. There's the usual rhyme. I hope you can make some sense out of it." He recited it from memory:

> *"With eyes of red*
> *My actions are blue,*
> *If I'm normal*
> *Then you better be too."*

O'Riley squinted. "What's that supposed to mean?"

Mills didn't have a clue. Neither did Davenport.

"Anything different with this one?" O'Riley asked, sighing heavily.

"She was *definitely* alive when he cut out her heart," noted Davenport. "Unconscious but very alive."

Mills pointed at the wall near the victim's head. It was splashed with blood. "You figure that out from looking at the wall?"

"You're getting good at this forensics stuff, Sergeant. We might have to sign you up someday," Davenport kidded. "The cast-off trails resemble those at the other scenes. Looks like four blows to open up the chest cavity. But see that zig-zag blood distribution?"

Mills and O'Riley studied the wall.

"Arterial gushing. He cut a major heart artery while the heart was pumping at a good clip. It zig-zags on the wall from the fluctuation of pressure in the breached artery as a result of the systolic and diastolic pressure." He turned to O'Riley. "What do you remember about the Seabold murders? Clean, concise cuts like these?"

"Hell, no. It was awful," he responded, his face tightening. "He ripped out a few of the early ones. Getting out his frustrations, I guess. By the time he hit his stride on the second or third one in Memphis, he was getting pretty good with the knife."

"What about his M.O.?" Mills asked.

"Hit and run. After an attack he split right away. Didn't seem to be a whole lot of planning involved. Location was the determining factor."

"This guy Lancaster takes time to meticulously clean himself up." The detective eyed a towel, stained deep red, lying in a clump inside the old wash basin. He rubbed his sculpted chin with the palm of his hand. "So much alike, yet so different."

"What about those?" O'Riley pointed to a pile of blood-spattered clothing in the far corner. "Any different than last time?"

"Same stance as at the Orpheum," Davenport answered. "Kneeling over the body as he struck with the axe. Blood stains on the back calves of the pant legs."

"The clothing itself," Mills added, "is the *exact* same as at the Park Studio. Khakis, white pinpoint shirt, topsiders." Anger rose in his voice. "The sonuvabitch is taunting us. Wearing the same damn thing we would have been on the lookout for."

"Temper, temper," cautioned Davenport.

Mills closed his eyes, drew a deep breath, then slowly exhaled. Upon opening his eyes, he was the poster boy of serenity.

O'Riley glanced from Mills to Davenport and back. "I think *I* need to try that meditation crap sometime."

The detective turned to the medical examiner. "We'll leave it with you. When you need Medic for removal, just tell Harris or Crosby."

They poked around upstairs for a half hour, then headed down. Another half hour later, the ambulance crew wheeled the morgue-bound corpse past them on a gurney, its wheels squeaking loudly.

Mills leaned against the curved wall near the entrance to the rest rooms in the lobby. For once even he looked fatigued. He clutched the coat of his suit in his right hand, letting it hang loosely behind his broad shoulder. O'Riley slouched against the wall next to him.

"This guy is something," Mills remarked. "He's the very definition of a psychopath. When a psychopath sees that you've figured out his M.O., he changes his manner. We realize he's hitting Seabold theater murder sites so he hits a theater Seabold didn't use. Next we cover the entrances to all the places that *were* theaters during Seabold's time and he uses the goddam roof to get in. We look for somebody concealing a wig and he switches to a can of spray paint."

O'Riley listened as intently as he could for a tired older man at two in the morning.

"We've forced him to change," Mills continued. "He's having to choose new locations. He knows we're looking for disguises; he sees our officers at the old theaters. It's taking him more time—he's getting his way but he's getting pissed. Mark my words," Mills vowed, "he's going to step up his pace. Expect another attempt in three days or less."

O'Riley shut his eyes and faintly mumbled. "I think you're right," he suddenly replied, opening his eyes. "The next one will be in three days. Monday night. November fifteenth."

The detective looked at him curiously, tilting his square jaw. "What aren't you telling me?"

O'Riley glanced at his gold watch, eyes dull, his face hollowed and drained. "I think we better call it a night. I'll get with you tomorrow," he promised as he shuffled toward one of the heavy glass doors and into the night brightened by flashing blue lights.

Less than a half hour later he was sitting on the side of his bed, dressed in navy-striped pajamas with Bullet asleep at his feet. He rubbed his temples to stifle a throbbing headache. The muscles in his lower back ached and burned. The two shots he had gulped down had done nothing to allay his discomfort.

His physical pain would go away with a bit of sleep. His mental anxiety would not be so easy to dispel. The time had come to share what he had uncovered, what he believed, with someone he could trust. Someone who wouldn't write him off as crazy or obsessed. Someone who would believe the unbelievable.

O'Riley pounded his pillow into shape and clicked off the bedside lamp, plunging the bedroom into darkness. He slid under the cool covers, trying to get more comfortable by turning from his side onto his back. He tossed fitfully, drifting in and out of consciousness. Finally he relaxed.

Soon he was dreaming. He stood on the steps of a church, dressed in a tuxedo, surrounded by hundreds of policemen cheering wildly. He felt someone grasp his hand and he looked to his side, expecting to see the radiant face of his new bride, Nancy Summerfield. The face he saw was that of Evelyn O'Riley.

32

Late Saturday afternoon, slightly ragged from lack of sleep, Mills had mobilized the Memphis Police Department in a plan of attack unprecedented in the city's history. Joining the officers already assigned to the entrances of the theater locations were additional policemen stationed on each building's rooftop. Squad cars were also cruising every new theater multiplex. As a precaution, law-enforcement personnel in the bordering suburban communities of Bartlett, Germantown, and Collierville did the same.

In his recliner at home, O'Riley sat for a long time, warily eyeing the axe, knife, and playing cards before him, oblivious to the Tennessee-UCLA college football game blaring on the television. He picked up the objects, one by one, reviewing the many pieces of the puzzle playing in his mind. The one face he saw floating in the hazy mist within his head was Jimmy Seabold, not David Lancaster.

O'Riley was soon out the door and headed for police headquarters. Within twenty minutes he was entering Homicide, clutching a one-foot-long Federal Express shipping box under his right arm.

After exchanging pleasantries with all the detectives except Driscoll, he motioned to Mills.

"Got a few minutes?" O'Riley asked.

Mills nodded, his eye on the box.

"Let's go in here," O'Riley said, pointing to the interrogation room. "For some privacy."

The small, sparsely furnished space contained only a cheap conference table, three folding metal chairs, a phone, a black chalkboard mounted on one wall, and a big, round, black and white electric clock on the opposite wall. The less distractions when interrogating a suspect, the better. O'Riley wanted the same. No distractions when he confided in Mills.

The heavy wooden door shut quietly, unnoticed by the detectives amid the constant clicking of their computer keyboards.

"Have a seat," O'Riley offered, as he sat down. "I got something I been meaning to ask you for a while." He leaned forward, elbows on the table. "Why'd you become a detective?"

Mills gazed down at the gray floor. His eyes had a faraway look. "It goes back to my childhood. Hide and seek. I'd *always* win. It got to be not if I'd find the other kids but how long it would take me. I'd offer two-to-one odds if it took me more than five minutes; four-to-one if it took me more than fifteen. I never had to pay out four-to-one. Ever." He grinned triumphantly. "Made a lot of money."

"Okay, so you're good at it. Why do you like it?"

Mills looked up, his blue eyes sparkling. "The thing about being a detective is, each day you wake up to endless possibilities. What's behind *this* door, how about *that* one? It's like this sixth sense I think I have. I always wonder what I might find before I go in. What was in the room or who had been there before me? What was he or she doing in there? What kind of person were they? It's a fascination. One that never ends."

O'Riley saw in Mills the same excitement he had felt in his own days on the force. "You love it," he said.

"Yeah," replied Mills, adjusting the knot on his tie and again grinning broadly. "I guess I do."

O'Riley liked the thirty-five-year-old detective's manner and spirit.

"How about you?" Mills countered. "What did you like most about it?"

"It was a feeling I got inside," he replied, pounding his chest twice with his fist. "A sense of what's right and wrong. Seems justice is skewed to the rights of the criminals these days. It's the other way around with me. I'm from the old school. Back then it was honorable to be a cop. I'm gonna uphold that high standard until the day I die." He let out a deep breath. "You know something else? I know it's old hat to say this, but murdered people have rights. So do the families and friends who loved them. I've been there. I know. Murder's not something you let people get away with, especially if you're in authority to do something about it. You search and you search until you find out who's responsible."

Mills considered O'Riley's words. "At least we got a big advantage in this case. We know who our killer is."

"That's what worries me. Do we *really* know who he is?"

The detective cocked his head to the side. "I'm not sure I follow you."

"You'll think I'm nuts . . ."

"There's a reason we have only one mouth and two ears," Mills answered. "Make your point."

"You've got to understand some things." O'Riley held Mills in his stare. "These murders. The circumstances and weapons. It's just what Jimmy Seabold would have done."

"But we *know* the killer is David Lancaster. He's just trying, for some godforsaken reason, to get under your skin by making it look like he's Jimmy Seabold come back from the dead. Why, I have no idea."

"Unless . . ."

"Unless what?"

"Unless he *really is* Jimmy Seabold."

Mills shook his head in disbelief.

"Listen to me," O'Riley said. "When you watch an old movie filled with deceased actors, you can see the dead walk and talk again. They've essentially become immortal. Our guy's got some kind of connection with movies from the fifties. He gets comfort from older actresses somehow. Makes him remember happier times. Maybe even reminds him of his mother."

"Lancaster's mother is still alive. Hell, she's not *that* old. She probably didn't even start watching movies until the 1960s."

"I know," replied O'Riley. "But Jimmy Seabold's mother isn't."

"What are you gettin' at?"

"Seabold's mother died when he was twelve. She *loved* the movies. Passed that love on to her son. She'd put make-up on right in front of Jimmy for hours on end. Won all sorts of look-alike contests. That could explain the make-up on the victims."

"You think Lancaster was Seabold? In some previous life?" Mills scoffed, shaking his head.

"Listen to me. What if death's door is an entrance, not an exit? An entrance to another life. We're just not aware of it. There's books on that stuff."

"Look, I'd *love* to believe in reincarnation," Mills replied, "but it's a tough pill for me to swallow."

O'Riley went on. "When he's with a victim, he's acting out his rage. Something from his childhood."

"You mean being pissed off having to deal with his Hodgkin's?"

O'Riley frowned. "I ain't talking about Lancaster. I'm talking about Seabold. He saw a woman stab his mother to death. He goes into a rage and kills the woman. Let your mind wander for a minute, all right? Take Lancaster. A classic *organized* serial killer. Above-average intelligence, obsessive-compulsive, meticulous as hell. Ritual-oriented so he can maintain his sense of control. Real neat. Real clean. But something sets him off. In a movie theater. Or a place that used to be a movie theater. In Seabold's time."

"I know where you're going with this," Mills remarked, "and I don't like it."

"The stars on the screen reminded Seabold of his mother. How she used to get all dolled up before she was snatched from him." O'Riley gritted his teeth and clenched a fist, shaking it with wild, threatening eyes in the detective's face. "Then the rage took over. He killed to vent his anger. It was his only relief."

"And now?"

"Now we've got a hybrid. A present-day obsessive-compulsive with the psyche of a killer from the past. How else is he gonna know all the things he seems to?" O'Riley asked. "I've been doing a little investigating on my own."

He opened the box he had placed on the table revealing a shiny new pocket axe, an exact duplicate of the one used in the Knoxville experiment.

"Where'd you get *that*?" Mills asked.

"Same place I got this," replied O'Riley, pulling out a piece of brown shipping paper and unraveling it. The folding hunter knife he held in his hand, complete with its swing guard, was identical to Seabold's.

"I thought those weren't made anymore."

"They weren't. Until a couple of years ago. A knife and hunting gear company in Arkansas, A.G. Russell, had a limited number of them made as collector's items. I found their catalog when I was nosing around at Bronson's Sporting Goods. I had these FedExed."

Mills' face shined. "I'm impressed."

"That's not the half of it," O'Riley said. "David Lancaster bought these same two items. The company records showed they were sent out FedEx on Thursday, September 23rd. That's five days before his wife's death." He paused momentarily, clearing his throat. "There's more. Dates."

"Dates?"

"Yeah, dates. I looked up some information in the old Seabold file and the homicide log book from the 1950s."

"Been snooping around in the dungeon with Schmidt, I guess," Mills said.

"Found some interesting stuff to back up my *crazy* idea."

"Such as?"

"Seabold's first murder in 1957 was on Tuesday, September 24th. Lancaster's was on Tuesday, September 28th. The second for both was *exactly* one week later, October 1st and 5th respectively. In Roanoke. The third, in Knoxville, two weeks after that on Tuesday October 15th and 19th. The fourth, one week later in Nashville on the 22nd and 26th."

227

Mills stood and placed a foot on his chair. He leaned forward with his arms resting on his knee.

"The first murder in Memphis for both was a Friday, exactly ten days after the Nashville attacks," continued O'Riley. "Four days later, on Tuesday, November 5th and 9th, we get the second Memphis murders. The third three days later, Friday, November 8th in 1957 and last night, November 12th, for us. *That's* why I'm so sure he'll strike next in three days. On November 15th. A Monday. That's the way it was last time. In 1957."

"And after that?"

"The next day. Tuesday. Twice. Once in the afternoon. The second at night." O'Riley's eyes became slits, his voice husky. "That one was my wife."

"So the intervals are all identical."

"Hold on, I ain't finished. Remember what else I amazed you with?"

"Ava," Mills quickly answered. "At Book World. How did you figure that out?"

"Can you name the stars, in order, from each of the murder sites? From the beginning in Charlottesville?"

"I think so," replied Mills. "Marilyn Monroe, Elizabeth Taylor, Jayne Mansfield, Debbie Reynolds, Sophia Loren, Lauren Bacall, and Ava Gardner."

"Look deeper and he's left a clue that links his past to the present."

The detective threw his arms up in exasperation. "I give up! What is it?"

"The names of Seabold's first seven victims were *Marilyn* Larson, *Elizabeth* Nolan, *Jayne* Greer, *Debbie* Raines, *Sophia* Locke, *Lauren* Travis, and *Ava* Malone. Plus, the hair color of each original murder victim is the same as the altered hair color on the corresponding new movie star victims. If I'm right, our killer's next victim will either have on a blond wig or have hair spray-painted a blond shade. And the name on the note will be Janet. I'm thinking for Janet Leigh."

"The original victim's name was?"

"Janet Baker. A blond."

Mills stared at the former chief. "This isn't just a game of *What If* is it, O'Riley? You really believe it's him."

O'Riley nodded slowly. "I'm retired. I can believe anything I damn well please."

"So you're telling me that Lancaster is a come-back-from-the-dead, can't-be-killed zombie hell-bent on wreaking havoc on you for getting him fried in the first place. And, along the way, he'll slice and dice some victims just like in 1957."

"Almost. But I never said anything about a zombie who can't be killed. Or a guy who came back from the dead. There's a big difference in that and reincarnation. Jimmy Seabold died in 1959. That's a fact. David Lancaster has lived his own life since he was born. That is, until his radiation treatments and the experimental memory drug."

The detective's eyes widened.

"Somehow after that, I think a previous life surfaced. Probably as flashbacks, maybe voices in his head. I don't know. Maybe the radiation mutated the memory drug. It's Lancaster doing the killing but his actions are being influenced by Jimmy Seabold." He let out a deep sigh. "He's different this time, like I mentioned. More sophisticated and more efficient. With the help of a smarter brain, he's evolved into a smarter killer."

"I don't know." Mills shook his head. "This is *too* bizarre."

"See what Lisa Howard has to say about it. Or Sally Vance. Or Barbara Murphy. Try the dead women in Nashville, Knoxville, Roanoke, and Charlottesville."

Mills then sat on the edge of the table and stared at the blank chalkboard for a few seconds. "One problem I know he's got is a repetition compulsion. By continuing to kill women and physically cutting out their hearts, he's battling some unresolved conflict."

"Now *you* sound like a shrink," remarked O'Riley.

The detective smiled, again adjusting his tie. "I had a double major in college. History and psychology. I'd have to opt for Lancaster having a multiple personality disorder. I can't quite accept the reincarnation thing. I *could* see him being taken over by some evil personality. Maybe after studying Seabold's murder spree, he's allowed the perpetrator into his mind. That would explain Lancaster's toying with you even though you've never met him. His alter-ego could feel compelled to get revenge on you since you put him away."

O'Riley shrugged. "Think whatever you want. Did his alter-ego tell him where to find the original deck of W. C. Fields playing cards?"

"Hey, I can't explain everything. I don't care if the guy has come back from the dead or just *thinks* he has. No matter what, I'd say you're standing on some pretty thin ice."

"I'd say we all are." After a pause, he continued in a subdued tone, "Years ago, my wife was the sixth Memphis victim."

"I know," acknowledged Mills, his expression somber.

"At three and counting, I'm not taking any chances this time. I've already talked to the chief about having protection put in place on Nancy Summerfield. You know Alex Milligan?"

Mills nodded. "Used to be on the county S.W.A.T. unit?"

"That's him. She don't know about it yet. I'll tell her tonight. He starts tomorrow morning."

"Twenty-four-hour?"

"Not quite. He'll watch her house while she's home. Tail her to school and back on weekdays. I told him he could go home and sleep between eight and three while she's teaching. He'll check out the house every time they return from school or running errands."

"I'd say she's in good hands."

"I'm not worried. She has a state-of-the-art home alarm system and her tutoring after school keeps a steady stream of kids flowing in and out of her house all afternoon and into the night sometimes. Plus, I told Milligan he might even see me going in occasionally for dinner."

"I can imagine," Mills chuckled. "And staying for breakfast."

33

"Come on in," Nancy said with a smile, opening her front door and flicking on the entrance hall light. "Had a busy week, haven't you? Two murders and another trip to Knoxville."

"Wasn't as much fun as ours." O'Riley grinned, pecking her lips with a light kiss.

"I should hope not!" She laughed, leading him inside. "I know you've got your hands full when I don't see you on a Saturday until after dinnertime."

They walked into the elegant living room. An ebony baby grand piano stood in the corner opposite a polished, white marble fireplace. A rose-colored velvet couch was flanked by two wing chairs, all centered around a leaded-glass coffee table. Dominating the wall opposite the fireplace was a gold-framed Rembrandt etching.

O'Riley took a seat on the couch. Nancy crossed the room, her eyes on the not-quite-centered fresh-cut flower arrangement on the dining room table. She caught a glimpse of herself in the mirror above the antique sideboard and gently fluffed her hair with her right hand.

He couldn't take his eyes off her. Thoughts swirled in his head. He was finally in love again.

Nancy sat down beside him. The soft sounds of James Taylor filled the room. "Earth to Joe," she said. "Off somewhere?" She gently touched his face. "Mind if I join you?"

"I was just thinking."

They held hands, saying nothing, enjoying the silence.

"What's the matter?" she finally asked.

"We're not having any luck slowing this guy down," he replied, his voice filling with concern. "To be honest, I'm worried about your safety. How about moving in with me until all this blows over?"

"How long will that be?"

He shrugged. "I just don't know."

She shook her head. "If you're that concerned, *you* move in with *me* for a while."

"Then you'd know what I really look like first thing in the morning."

She laughed, poking his stomach. "It's not like I haven't seen it before."

"Yeah, I know, but you haven't seen it on a regular basis. It ain't a pretty sight. Besides," he continued, "Bullet would get jealous if he couldn't come too. I know you don't want any extra fertilizer in your garden."

"You have never been more correct," she countered with a laugh. "Not that kind."

O'Riley then explained that he had arranged protection starting the next day.

"You think I need that?" she asked. The lines around her almond-shaped eyes tightened. "This house is like a fortress with my alarm system. Plus, I have more pepper gas around here, thanks to you, than they've got down at the police station." She laughed again.

Stone-faced, O'Riley insisted. "Just in case, all right? It'd make *me* feel better."

Their eyes met and held, the way they had the first time they met. The lines on Nancy's face loosened like a hundred pieces of twine come undone. She nodded.

O'Riley glanced at the miniature ornamental clock on the table beside the couch. It was nine o'clock. "I better be going. Sorry I'm so edgy." He leaned forward, about to stand.

"Why don't you stay tonight?"

His eyes grew soft, lingering on the woman before him. A boyish grin crept over his face.

She took him by the hand and led him to her bedroom.

Later, their love spent, they lay quietly in the warmth of the bed and each other's arms. They smiled as their eyes locked.

Then Nancy broke the silence with a hushed whisper. "We both have happy memories of our loved ones. They'll always be special. What the future will bring, no one can ever tell. We hope certain things will happen according to plan—that dreams we have deep inside will be fulfilled. One thing we do know for sure, one thing we *must* appreciate is how precious the time we share with each other is." She gently stroked the side of his face. "Whenever we're together from now on, let's cherish that time. Think of it as the gift of today." Her eyes sparkled as she spoke.

O'Riley nodded, enjoying the comfort in her words.

"After all," she smiled, "that's why it's called *the present*."

34

On Sunday O'Riley helped Nancy adjust to the strain of police protection, attending morning services with her at Second Presbyterian Church in East Memphis and going to lunch afterwards at The Cupboard on Union Avenue. The rest of the afternoon was spent watching NFL football and helping with Nancy's late-season backyard gardening.

Forty-two-year-old Alex Milligan, a sturdy six-foot-one with medium-length auburn hair, cut an imposing figure as he shadowed the couple, alternating between sitting behind the wheel of his unmarked navy police cruiser and leisurely strolling around the yard on North Avalon, becoming familiar with the surroundings. With a white Notre Dame sweatshirt tightly stretched across his muscular chest, he looked more like a weightlifter than a former county S.W.A.T. team member.

As Monday dawned cold and bright, Milligan sat wide-awake in his vehicle, noticing everything and everyone who passed down the street. After tailing Nancy to Memphis University School at seven-thirty, he went home to sleep, returning at three-thirty to follow her home. After a brief stop at a Seessel's supermarket, he helped carry her groceries inside, carefully checking the house.

He watched from the street as students to be tutored paraded in and out of the house on the hour from six until nine. At ten-thirty her bedroom light flicked off, leaving the house dark except for a bright porch light cutting through the night.

Scanning the street, he noted every parked car, jotting down makes, models, and license plates. His solitude was broken at midnight when he caught a glimpse of a man taking a dog on a late-night stroll in his rearview mirror.

∗

Fear still hung like a heavy mist over Memphis and the surrounding communities. One group urged all females to stay in their homes as much as possible, venturing out only when absolutely necessary. Another faction made light of the situation, preferring to cast caution to the wind by throwing "killer costume parties," going so far as to openly invite the murderer to attend.

But it was business as usual at Newby's on the Highland strip near the University of Memphis campus. Billing itself as the South's largest cozy neighborhood bar and grill, it had become the preferred hangout for students over the years, boasting something for anyone needing a break from the stresses of academia.

The main dining room, dark and comfortable, displayed a diverse mix of decor including mounted bear, deer, and moose heads. An array of obsolete metal beverage signs advertising defunct soda pop brands PopKola, Zesto, Stone Fizz, and Mil-Kay Orange adorned the aged, red-brick walls. Wood beams and columns accented the maroon ceiling. The matching maroon carpet was stained almost black, disguising countless dropped sandwiches and spilled drinks.

A game room with pool tables and pinball machines offered an alternative to dining, while an outdoor patio provided a seasonal option to eating and drinking in the restaurant's dark confines.

The main draw was the music room, located in an adjacent space occupied originally in the forties and fifties by the Normal theater. By knocking an entrance through a brick wall into the former movie house's cramped lobby, the restaurant had come up with a profitable source of added income. The stage had been preserved but the auditorium seats had been ripped out, leaving a dance hall perfect for regional touring band performances.

An appearance by Mel and the Party Hats, a local favorite from Nashville, had swelled the standing-room-only crowd to over six hundred by the time the band took the stage at 10 P.M.

Red and green spotlights flashed across a black cloth backdrop behind the performers, illuminating the lead singer, dressed in a black cowboy hat, and his four band members as they played pounding, raucous hits from the 1980s.

Two undercover policemen stationed inside the building kept their eyes on the crowd, searching for anyone wearing tan khakis with solid white or blue shirts. Nearly fifty customers fit the description.

Moving along the bar, one of the policemen suddenly lunged to avoid being doused by a young woman hurrying by with a sloshing pitcher of beer. He bumped into a man in a red plaid shirt sitting at the bar with his back toward him.

"Sorry," the officer said. "Didn't want to take a beer bath."

"No problem," replied the man with a humorless smile as the officer moved away. He had more important things to worry about.

If only she would sit on the vacant stool next to him before someone else grabbed it. He scratched his goatee, flicked his black pony-tail behind his shoulder, and signaled to the bartender for another Perrier.

He pretended not to see her sit down next to him, keeping his eyes fixed on the old cook taking a break from the kitchen. He bit down on a thumbnail. His pulse quickened. Tonight would be her night.

"How ya doing?" she yelled, competing with the band's thundering beat.

He glanced over with a half-smile, trying not to appear overly interested. Better that way at first. Get her to take the bait. Make her commit.

"You a student?"

He nodded.

"What's your major?"

He then turned and grinned. "I'm in grad school. Engineering."

"A smart one," she remarked, smiling. "You come here much?" Her stale breath smelled of cigarettes.

"Every now and then. Can I buy you a drink?"

"That'd be real nice." She ran a hand through her long brown hair.

He motioned to the bartender.

"He knows what I drink. Bourbon and Coke. Come on, have one yourself," she urged. "You can drink that ole water anytime."

"Sorry, can't do it," he replied. "It might mess up my plans."

Her hand slid across the bar and began toying playfully with his. He gave it a squeeze, then dropped his hand onto her knee.

"What plans?" she asked breathlessly.

He pointed at the navy canvas backpack at his feet, barely visible in the darkness under the bar.

"Whatcha got in the bag?" she asked as his fingers gently massaged her thigh.

"Gym clothes. I was planning on working out tonight."

She leaned over, kissed him lightly on the cheek, and whispered seductively into his ear, "Maybe I could join you. I'll give you a work-out you'll *never* forget."

His heart began pounding. Everything was falling perfectly into place.

By midnight the frenzied audience had driven the temperature in the seven hundred fifty-square-foot music hall to over eighty degrees. Oblivious to the heat, the wildly gyrating revelers continued dancing. The officers wandered into the cooler restaurant area to catch some air.

About then, a crew-cut young man rushed out of the men's room into the dark lobby and slipped on the wet concrete near a closet. Picking himself up, the seat and leg of his pants felt soaked. Thinking he had slipped on beer leaking from a keg behind the door, he decided to investigate. He gripped the doorknob, yanking it firmly. His loud, startled scream was drowned by the reverberating music.

In the bright light of a single bulb, a young woman was hanging upside down, her legs bent through the rungs of a metal ladder bolted to the wall. Her yellow knit top, soaked in blood, was ripped open revealing a gaping chest wound. Her hair had been awkwardly cut and spray-painted a light cream color. A piece of paper with the name JANET printed in black protruded from her mouth. Resting on her chin, propped against her neck, was a playing card—the ten of hearts. The floor of the tiny room was covered by blood that had seeped out into the lobby.

Others in the crowd soon noticed the grisly sight. People screamed, running in every direction like ants whose hill had suddenly been leveled. The music abruptly fell silent leaving the room echoing with cries and yells as the masses shoved their way toward the nearest exit. Some were fascinated, craning their necks for a better view.

The Highland strip soon rocked with sirens. Policemen tried to restore order as back-up arrived, including O'Riley, who came with Mills.

Mills ordered the detectives to cordon off the remaining patrons, hoping the killer might still be among them. Deep down he knew better.

Two hours later, Newby's was empty except for detectives, uniformed police, ambulance personnel, and Davenport and Sims.

Davenport stood inside the tiny room, his blue shoe covers turned dark red, finishing his initial examination as Sims, Mills, and O'Riley looked on. He flashed a grin at the three, shaking his head in awe. "He's good. Split sternum. This one's even cleaner than the last. A regular kitchen magician."

Sims smiled, stroking his chin with long fingers. "We better catch him before he takes a step up to a Cuisinart."

"You were right about the name," Mills said to O'Riley, "and the hair color."

"He's toying with you guys," Davenport said. "He wanted this one found quickly. Left her hanging for two reasons. One, shock effect. The blood and all. Plus the fact he whacked off her long hair and left it soaking in blood on the floor while he played hairdresser to make her look like Janet Leigh."

"What's the other reason?" Mills asked.

"To get you two over here in a hurry." He arched his eyebrows. "Might be outside right now observing."

"Hmph," scoffed O'Riley. "I doubt it. He ain't that stupid. What about clothes? He leave any this time? And a note?"

"Might be up there," replied Davenport, shining a flashlight up the ladder to the loft. "He's been upstairs for sure." He aimed the beam at bloody handprints down the wall.

"What in hell's up there?" O'Riley asked.

Mills spoke up. "The cook, an old guy named Willie, said it's storage. Used to be the old projection booth in the movie theater days. They only go up there twice a year. To get Christmas decorations down and put 'em back."

"We can check it out after Sims and I unhook the body and get her wrapped for the morgue," Davenport said. He motioned to his colleague to call in the ambulance crew.

O'Riley backed away with Mills. "Anybody see anything fishy?"

"The cook did," Mills replied. "Remembers seeing a guy come on to the victim at the bar in the main room. The bartender saw it too."

"What'd he look like?"

"About five-ten. Muscular build. Long black hair pulled back in a pony tail. Mustache and goatee. Dressed in olive pants and a red-plaid shirt. It was a *Polo*. They remembered the pony logo. It was him."

O'Riley frowned. "How can you be so damn sure?" He began jingling the keychain in his pocket.

"His right eye. They both noticed a bad twitch." Mills paused momentarily. "The girl was all over him. Sounds like she was pretty willing. Six hundred frigging people in here and not one of them saw the two go through that door."

They wandered around for a few minutes while the corpse was taken out.

"Ready for some climbing?" Davenport called out, slipping on a new pair of shoe covers. "We soaked up the blood as best we could."

"Mind if I go up alone for a couple of minutes?" Mills asked, his question more of a statement.

"Be my guest," the medical examiner replied.

The detective clambered up the rusting metal ladder, his gray herringbone suit coat flapping behind him, and carefully stepped off onto the loft's dirty wooden floor. A high-beam flashlight was clutched in his right hand.

Closing his eyes, he called on his senses in an effort to share the external world that Lancaster had experienced in this killing chamber for twenty-one-year-old Sue Lowry. He drew a breath in through his nose.

A musty, mildewy odor pervaded the space, reminiscent of an unventilated attic on a hot summer's day. With his mouth open he again breathed in deeply, tasting the stale air. Dust particles coated his throat. He visualized Lancaster inhaling great amounts of air as he feverishly hacked, while choking and coughing.

Eyes still tightly closed, he filtered out the muffled sounds of the voices at the foot of the ladder and instead imagined how the throbbing, pulsating sounds of the music and the roars of the crowd had freed Lancaster to make as much noise as needed.

He then opened his eyes and scanned the room with his flashlight, revealing shelves cluttered with old movie equipment unused for decades. Opaque garbage bags with unknown contents lay strewn across the floor along with boxes and broken chairs, all covered by a thick layer of gray dust. In a small booth at the far end of the room stood a floor-to-ceiling black Simplex movie projector, a relic from the 1950s.

Across the room, in the only uncluttered spot on the entire floor, were a pair of olive slacks, a red-plaid Polo sport shirt, and a pair of tan Wallabees, all spattered with blood and clumped in a heap next to a large, wet, crimson stain on the floor. A clear bag loaded with bright red plastic Christmas poinsettias lay nestled near the clothes like flowers marking the scene of a death on the highway.

The depraved animal had a well-thought-out plan, Mills realized. The tricky part remained. Figuring it out.

Mills called for the others to join him. "We need some halogens," he ordered, "and the photographer. Harris needs to come up, too."

One by one they scaled the rungs to join him, each armed with a flashlight. The floor creaked and moaned under their weight as they huddled together, trying not to disturb anything.

"Charming," remarked Sims, his flashlight's beam reflecting off huge spider webs clinging to the rafters and corners of the ceiling. "Just like at home." He began snapping photos for the medical examiner's file with a 35MM Canon.

With the lights soon in place and the police shots taken, the men inched their way toward the tell-tale murder spot.

"The bastard's strong as an ox to have carried her up that ladder," Harris said.

"Maybe he didn't," remarked Mills. "The bartender said she was hot to trot. She may have led the way."

"Well, he had to be pretty damn strong to get her back down," Harris replied.

"Could have dropped her," added O'Riley. "If the music was as loud as they say it gets in this place, a loud thump wouldn't be noticed."

"She would have sustained some evidence of injury—a gash or at least some mild abrasion," Davenport countered. "All I saw was a blow to the head and the chopping wound that opened her chest. I think he excised the heart up here, then carried her down. And he *is* strong as an ox to get her to hang upside down from that ladder. That's a hundred and ten pounds of dead weight. Would have gotten him damn messy though. Not like his previous jobs."

Mills examined the discarded clothes. "Polo shirt could've come from anywhere. Everything's a lot bloodier than before."

"What about the pants?" O'Riley asked. "Any store label?"

"Nope. Looks like it was cut out." Mills pulled a folded note from the shirt pocket, opened it, and began to read, silently mouthing the words.

"See the cast-off on the wall," Sims commented, "and the blood spattered everywhere in the dust? Just like at the other murders."

Davenport nodded. "Drag marks in the dust show what happened next. She did have dust all over the back of her clothes. He carried her down, climbed back up, changed his clothes, then climbed down again. *Carefully* to avoid getting blood on himself. That accounts for the contact stains on the clothes in addition to the spatter."

"He better have brought some handi-wipes—no sink this time. A first," O'Riley said.

"Like I told you before, he's having to change his M.O.," Mills said. "What's the note say?"

Mills handed it to the former chief. Davenport, Sims, and Harris gathered around to read over his shoulder.

With eyes of red
My actions are blue,
Your time has come
It's now me and you.

O'Riley bristled. "These goddam notes. They've all been for me. I shoulda picked up on that last one. Talking about *normal*. It wasn't about his state of mind. It was where he was gonna hit. Here at the old Normal theater. They're all about where he's gonna hit next." His lips pressed into a thin line. He adjusted his pants, weighted down by his keychain and gun, back up on his hips.

Davenport again arched his eyebrows. "I'd say you're next on the menu. I'd watch my back if I were you."

"Let him come," O'Riley said softly, patting his right pants pocket concealing his ever-present Walther.

"Attaboy, Chief," encouraged Harris. "You'd kick his butt. Just like in the old days." The stocky detective touched his chin with a beefy forefinger, tilted his head to one side and asked, "How do you think he'd try to come after you?"

Suddenly O'Riley's eyes glazed with fear, his heart pounding.

"Nancy!" exploded from his lips.

35

The traffic was light, almost nonexistent at 3 A.M. as Mills' unmarked cruiser barreled at eighty miles an hour down Poplar Avenue.

O'Riley stared out the windshield, right foot nervously thumping the floorboard. A call to Nancy's house got the message on her answering machine. And there was no response on the radio from Alex Milligan.

Voices crackled across the detective's hand-held radio resting on the front seat between the two men.

The car veered north down Angelus, its tires screeching loudly, then made a quick left onto Overton Park Avenue and another left onto North Avalon. Mills flicked off the headlights, slowed, and inched down the street, approaching Milligan's car from behind.

The parked car glistened in the misty, luminescent haze of an old street lamp. A wave of relief swept over O'Riley when he spotted the silhouette of the officer's head above the car seat.

After easing to a stop at the curb, both men jumped from the car and ran over to the driver's side.

The night air was cold, cold enough to see their breath. Not a sign of light came from any of the neighbors' windows.

Both men staggered back in unison. Milligan's head was tilted slightly downward, eyes wide open. His once-white sweatshirt was soaked red from blood that had flowed from a gaping wound in his neck.

Mills whipped his .40-caliber Smith and Wesson automatic from his shoulder holster, spinning in a three hundred sixty-degree turn. O'Riley pulled his pistol from his pocket and bolted up the shadowy driveway.

The detective depressed the transmit button on his radio. "Need back-up at 267 North Avalon and an ambulance," he barked. "Officer down."

"Copy," came the reply. "On the way."

The front door was ajar. "Nancy!" O'Riley frantically screamed over and over as he rushed from room to room.

He dreaded what he might find, but she was nowhere to be found. A sinking feeling punched him in the gut.

Then he saw it. Propped up on her bedside table.

> *With eyes of red*
> *My actions are blue,*
> *Tucked away in Hollywood Armageddon,*
> *You'll find one close to you.*

In no time the scene was the same as at Newby's. Same vehicles. Same flashing lights. Same faces.

Mills watched from a few feet away as Davenport and Sims examined the fallen officer. O'Riley returned after a search of his own house turned up nothing.

"Something's not right here. This ain't the way he operates. He strikes and leaves. He never abducts," said O'Riley, squinting in the blue lights blazing in his face.

"Nancy's not the one he wants," Mills grimly replied, staring into O'Riley's weary eyes.

"Well, the sonuvabitch is gonna get his goddam wish!" O'Riley's face darkened.

"What do you make of the note?"

The former chief edged toward the medical examiner. "I don't know. There was a theater named the Hollywood but it's long gone. Probably a vacant lot now. As for the Armageddon part, maybe he's gone biblical on us—who knows? I can hardly think straight," he admitted.

Mills turned to Davenport and Sims. "What's the verdict, guys?"

"No sign of a struggle," Davenport replied. "Tomahawked in the back of the neck. His head must have been out the window. Like he was looking at something or giving directions."

Mills bit his lip to stem the anger welling up inside.

"The blow fractured through the spinous process of the cervical vertebrae allowing the blade into the spinal canal. Paralyzed him instantaneously. Probably had fifteen seconds of consciousness," Davenport concluded.

Sims jumped in, pointing. "Look at that drip pattern down the side of the car door and in the street here. Appears he got shoved back in and propped up real fast. That's the only way to account for the arterial gush on the inside of the back left passenger window."

Harris approached. "The canvassing officers haven't turned up any witnesses on either side of the street from Poplar down to Overton Park Avenue."

"Well tell them to keep looking—the guy had to get here and leave somehow." Mills' hands balled into fists, his blood pressure rising. "A man gets his neck chopped open *right* in the street and a woman gets abducted from her *own* home and nobody sees or hears a thing? Not the next-door neighbors, the people across the street—nobody?" His right fist smacked his left palm with a loud pop.

They continued talking but O'Riley only pretended to listen. He was a thousand miles away.

✳

Two and a half hours later, the mob who had gathered around the crime scene had, for the most part, dispersed—detectives, patrol officers, medical examiner and forensic experts, ambulance personnel, newspaper reporters, television film crews, neighbors, and, again, the thrill-seekers always attracted by flashing emergency lights.

O'Riley and Mills stood at the curb where Milligan's car, towed to the

246

police lot, had been parked only an hour before. Harris walked slowly down the sidewalk, aiming his flashlight in neighboring yards, looking for any clue that may have eluded the earlier investigators.

The former chief, with fear and uneasiness showing in his bloodshot, darkly-ringed eyes, massaged his temples. "It's not like Milligan, not what I heard about him," he said. "He was always cautious as hell."

"I heard the same thing," replied Mills. "Always on the lookout for the least little thing."

"Maybe he fell asleep and Lancaster snuck up on him."

Mills shook his head. "I don't think so. Something made him drop his guard. He didn't even reach for his gun. Still tucked in his waist."

Suddenly Harris' voice broke the morning silence. He stood in a bed of thick ivy two houses down the street. "Hey, guys—take a look at this," he shouted. Dangling from a ball-point pen in his left hand, a silver dog leash gleamed in the light of a street lamp.

The two men quickly headed over.

"It's making sense now," Mills said. "That woman who saw the stray Sheltie. Milligan had a weakness for dogs. Loved 'em. They loved him, too. I remember right after I came to Memphis. There was this pit bull. His owner had been shot six or seven times. A drug dealer. The animal wouldn't let us near the body—growling and snapping like a rabid wolf. Thought we were gonna have to shoot him. Milligan walks up to the goddam dog, sweet talks him for about five minutes and, before you know it, he has the son of a bitch eating out of his hand. He just had a way with 'em."

"So you think Lancaster walked up with that Sheltie on a leash?" O'Riley said.

"Had to. No doubt. Stuck his head out the window to see the dog. Got hit in the neck."

"Then he got to Nancy, posing as Milligan." O'Riley slapped a palm to his forehead. "How can we be so *stupid*? The bastard can disguise himself to look like anybody."

Mills nodded, chewing his inner cheek.

O'Riley yawned in spite of himself and rolled his head across his shoulders, trying to work the stiffness from his neck. "I got to lay down, at least for a little while," he said, fatigued. "I'm about to drop."

"How 'bout I crash at your place?" Mills asked. "We can catch a couple hours sleep and then go hard at it. When we're thinking straight."

"Take your pick—living room couch or extra bedroom. I'll set the alarm for ten."

"I'll be in after a while," Mills called out. "Lock up that dog of yours, will ya? I don't need any more surprises."

O'Riley nodded, then disappeared into the darkness.

A black cruiser pulled up minutes later with a fresh two-man detective crew to go through Nancy's house for clues, closely followed by Chief Charlie Perry in his burgundy Buick Park Avenue, checking out the situation on his way to work.

Mills filled him in.

"You stick on the old man's ass. Just in case," Perry directed. "This lunatic wants him. I want someone with him who knows what to do."

Mills nodded.

"Don't let him know I ordered it. Just tell him you want to be with him as a friend."

"I'd planned to anyway," smiled the detective, "as a friend."

"I should have known," Perry acknowledged with a wink. "He's got you under his spell, too."

Upstairs in his bedroom, O'Riley stripped and stepped into the shower, a bottle of Bushmills in hand. He turned it up, taking three stiff gulps, wincing at the bitterness. After screwing the cap on, he placed the bottle in the corner of the stall and deeply inhaled the steam as he closed his eyes.

Dear God, how could it be happening again? The feelings came crashing back—the loneliness, the fear, the guilt. Standing under the torrent of hot water, he shut his mind off, losing himself in a trance-like state.

A few minutes later, after drying himself, he slipped under the coolness of his bed covers, clicking off the bedside lamp. He stared up at the darkened ceiling, starting to lighten from dawn's first glow.

He squinted, his tired eyes filling with an anger tempered by resolve and determination. He clenched his teeth, jaw firm. Death would end his quest—either the killer's or his own.

36

O'Riley let out a moan as he slowly opened his eyes and caught sight of the green-lit numerals on his bedside clock radio. 9:30.

He had been in bed for almost three hours. Had he fallen asleep? Probably not. At least not completely. His deep anxiety about Nancy had made sleep almost impossible.

Where was she? How could he find her? Had Lancaster already killed her? He was drawing blanks.

Overcome with unbearable fear, his eyelids slowly closed. In his mind he gently stroked her brunette hair and massaged the small of her neck. Her skin felt smooth to his touch, like silk. He breathed in deeply, then began to pray out loud, an act of desperation by a man who had been a stranger in churches for years.

"Dear God, please keep my Nancy safe. I'd be lost if anything happened to her. I don't know where to turn. Give me a sign. Anything. Please. I'll be more charitable to others. I promise. Amen."

His eyes flicked open and he bolted upright in bed.

"Annie! Maybe she can help. I shoulda thought of that." He glanced upward. "Thanks, God."

He threw back his covers and rushed into the bathroom, startling his near-deaf dog from a sound sleep. Looking in the mirror, weariness stared back at him. His puffy face was covered with stubble and dark circles clung under eyes that felt filled with sand.

After brushing his teeth, he splashed water on his face and sprayed Right Guard under his arms. His eyes then panned the bedroom and found his khaki pants hanging on a chair. He quickly dressed, pulling a navy cotton sweater over his green-plaid shirt, topping it with a dark green wind-breaker.

Downstairs the house was quiet except for slight snoring coming from behind the door to the extra bedroom where Mills lay sleeping. O'Riley scribbled a note telling him to meet back at the house at one o'clock and left it at the base of the doorway.

He then quietly left by the back door, amused at the sight of his aged, hard-of-hearing German shepherd staring at Mills' door, inquisitively crooking his neck from side to side at the unfamiliar noises.

At 10:15 O'Riley walked briskly into Court Square from Second Street. Annie sat in her usual spot beside the Hebe Fountain, a loosely woven postman's blue mohair shawl draped over her sloping shoulders.

A sliver of sunlight leaked from behind a tall building and through the bare trees, illuminating the blind artist. She smiled and turned.

"You give free sittings on Tuesdays?" O'Riley called out, his arrival announced by leaves crunching beneath his feet.

"I give free sittings *every* day," replied Annie. "But the portrait's gonna cost you." She placed her palette on the taboret at her side.

O'Riley sat down on the short stone wall next to the artist's chair. A squirrel foraging for food scampered between them.

"I knew you were coming," she said quietly. "I just wasn't sure when."

"Did a squirrel tell you?"

Her tone was serious. "I sensed it. You have a habit of coming to see me when something's on your mind."

"You been keeping up with the murders on T.V.?"

"Hard not to."

"And the policeman killed last night on North Avalon?"

She nodded.

"He was guarding Nancy's house. Trying to protect her. Just in case . . ." His voice cracked as tears welled up in his eyes.

He was proud of the strength he had shown in front of Mills and the

251

others. Tough as nails. Strong and steadfast as a rock. Now, in front of a woman, his invincible facade had cracked.

"I'm sorry," he said, swallowing hard.

"Sometimes it takes tears to renew strength." She reached out with her right hand, patting him on the shoulder.

O'Riley stared at the gray concrete walkway. "Nancy's been abducted by the killer. The same guy responsible for the murders." He looked up into Annie's face, seeing only his reflection in her dark glasses. "You've got to help me."

Annie cupped his hands in hers. The only sound heard above the rushing waters of the fountain was the clanging bell of the trolley rumbling down Main Street.

"She's alive," came the reply after a few moments.

"Is she hurt?"

"I don't think so."

"How can you be sure?" he asked, desperation in his voice.

"I feel it strongly. Think of life as a plane, a continuum of existence, with people linked by feelings and emotions."

"It's hard for me to understand," responded O'Riley, frowning.

"Take the death of Princess Diana," she replied softly, still clutching his hands. "Or John Kennedy Jr. There was a tremendous outpouring of love and affection not only from their families and loved ones but from strangers around the world—people they never met. This affection was there, invisible, even before their deaths. Just because you can't see something doesn't mean it's not there. Remember?"

O'Riley nodded to himself as he squeezed her hands.

She continued, "You and Nancy are linked together by your love. I can feel that attachment through you. That love is still alive and vibrant. If she were gone, I'd be filled with emptiness." She smiled, her iridescent lipstick sparkling in the sunlight. Suddenly she frowned and placed her hands to her mouth.

252

"What?" O'Riley asked, alarmed.

"I sense fear and peril," she replied. "You must find her quickly."

He threw his arms in the air. "Where?"

She covered her face with her hands for a few moments. "I see a building. An old one. It starts with the letter L. That's all I can see." She put her hands on her knees.

"What's the building look like? Can you describe it?"

She shook her head. "It's gone. I just remember the L." She let out a deep sigh.

"If anything comes to you, please call me day or night. You still got my number?"

She nodded.

O'Riley kissed her on the cheek, promising to check back with her the next day as he rushed toward Second Street, following his instinct.

Annie sat quietly, pulling her shawl tightly to ward off a sudden breeze, contemplating what she had seen in the depths of her darkened thoughts. He must hurry.

Once before she had felt this same overwhelming sense of danger. Just seconds before she had lost her sight. In 1957. At the hands of Jimmy Seabold.

37

Every muscle in O'Riley's body ached as he finally returned home a few minutes before two o'clock. Mills stood glaring at him from the sidewalk as the Lincoln pulled to a stop at the curb. Three squad cars and two detective cruisers were parked down the street in front of Nancy's house. A few neighbors milled about.

"Where the hell have *you* been?" asked Mills, looking rested in a fresh suit after a trip to his house for a shower. "I started to worry when I couldn't get you on the radio."

"Sorry. Went to see a friend," O'Riley replied, slamming the car door shut.

The detective crooked his neck. "Want to give me a hint?"

"A blind artist in Court Square. Annie Shepherd. Has this gift. Kinda like a psychic. She senses things."

"And?"

"She saw an old building with an L on it. So I hauled ass to where the old Loew's Palace used to be."

"Now a parking garage and Cafe Samovar?"

"Yeah. Checked every parking level. And the restaurant. Including the bathrooms and kitchen. Not a sign of her."

"There's no L on the building, is there?" Mills asked.

"Nah. I figured I'd check. Just in case. Then I went to the former Luciann theater on Summer. Now the Versailles adult bookstore. The old name's still on the top of that one."

Mills shook his head, frowning. "You shouldn't have gone without me."

"I was all right—I had my pistol."

A grin eased across the detective's face. "I ain't worried about you—I haven't been to a girlie store since I got to town!"

"You didn't miss nothing." O'Riley laughed. "The scumbags running the joint looked at me like *I* was an old pervert. You know, having to check out every one of those goddam private viewing booths. Good thing it was a slow day."

"Any more bright ideas?"

"Matter of fact, yeah. You driving?"

Mills nodded, thumping the hood of his navy Chevy cruiser with his knuckles.

They got into the unmarked car and pulled away. Heading west down Poplar they quickly passed fast-food restaurants and a Kroger supermarket before turning left onto Cleveland.

"Hang a right up here on Peabody and go down to Somerville," O'Riley directed.

Five minutes later an abandoned strip of three storefronts at the curved juncture of Somerville Street and Linden Avenue came into view.

"Pull over, right there," O'Riley commanded, pointing to the broken, battered sign of the Linden Circle Lounge, mounted on the marquee of the old Linden Circle theater.

Both men stared at the weathered tan siding covering the front of the once-handsome red-brick-facaded neighborhood movie house, a remnant of its conversion into a failed nightspot long out of business. Years of neglect had left the buildings on the strip, all with boarded-up windows, looking like a bombed-out war zone.

"This just might be the place," O'Riley said. "Hollywood Armageddon. Maybe that's what he meant. A seedy old movie theater. A perfect hideout for a wigged-out psychopath who loves the movies."

"I ain't taking any chances," responded Mills, calling for back-up on his radio.

They got out of the sedan as the afternoon shadows slid across Linden

255

Avenue. The front entrance was secured with a padlock. The two men circled around back, hoping for an open window or door. No luck. They returned to the front of the building.

"Screw this shit!" O'Riley barked in frustration. "Let's cut the damn lock."

Mills placed his radio to his mouth. "2150 here," he said, identifying himself, "need a Crime Scene unit on Somerville Street across from the Salvation Army house at Vance and Somerville."

"Check, 2150," crackled the response from the dispatcher.

Moments later Harris arrived, followed shortly by detectives Harvey and Norton. O'Riley filled them in, finishing up just as the crime scene squad car pulled up.

The two-man crew opened their trunk and handed a bolt cutter to Mills.

"Mind if we keep this one?" Mills asked.

"Fine by me," replied the officer.

The squad car officers and Norton spread out around the building to keep watch as the detectives and O'Riley prepared to go in.

"Why wasn't this one of the places under surveillance before?" O'Riley whispered to Mills.

"Manpower. We put our men anywhere there was an old theater site still in use. Didn't have enough to stake out abandoned buildings. Didn't think they posed much of a risk. Not that many of 'em around anyway."

"What ever happened to overtime?"

"Ask the mayor."

Mills gripped the lock bolt firmly with the cutter. It snapped with a crack and clunked onto the cold concrete. The wooden door slowly creaked open.

O'Riley's heart raced. He pulled his blue-steel Walther from his pocket and flipped the safety forward, ready to fire.

Armed with flashlights and their own pistols, Mills, Harris, and Harvey cautiously peered inside, shining their beams around the dusty, deserted room.

Then they entered, followed by the former chief.

The only thing left that resembled an old theater was the shape of the long, rectangular room and its twenty-four-foot-high ceiling. A worn parquet-wood dance floor stretched from wall to wall with a bar on one side and a stage on the other.

Broken bottles of cheap wine littered a burned area on the floor piled high with the remnants of charred bar stools that at one time provided warmth to winos on a cold night. The mirror behind the empty bar was shattered, probably the result of a night of drunken target practice.

The detectives then combed the upstairs offices, finding nothing. They quickly returned to the main room, ending their hour-long investigation.

"Looks like we came up empty—nobody home," Harris said to O'Riley.

Suddenly a voice came over the police radio sharp and clear. "2150, call office."

Mills pressed the send button on his radio. "Okay, 2150."

"Something's up," Harvey said. "Anderson lays off the radio unless there's a *big* problem."

Mills turned to Harris. "Gimme your cell phone a sec, will ya?" He was quickly connected to Lieutenant Anderson and his face instantly turned ashen.

The men said nothing as Mills slowly handed the phone back to Harris, his expression grim. "Anderson said they found another body. At the Landers Shoppe in Eastgate Shopping Center."

O'Riley's heart skipped a beat. A building with the letter L. He held his breath.

"Crosby and Driscoll made the scene. Female. Middle-aged. Same M.O. No I.D. yet."

O'Riley took a breath. "Any other physical description?"

Mills reply was soft, too soft. "A light brunette."

"Let's go," shouted O'Riley. He could feel the arteries pounding in his neck. They rushed to their vehicles and screeched off, engines roaring and blue lights flashing.

Mills led the way, stepping hard on the accelerator, zooming past cars, weaving in and out of traffic wildly like a child in a dodgem car. After two sharp turns he was back on Poplar Avenue, racing toward East Memphis at almost ninety miles an hour.

38

The entire perimeter of the sixty thousand-square-foot discount clothing store anchoring the northeast corner of the shopping center was already ringed in yellow crime-scene tape when the detectives' cruisers came to a screeching halt.

This murder, unlike the others, coming in broad daylight in a public place during a busy pre-Christmas-season sale, informed an already-fearful public that no place offered safety from the killer. Just as Lancaster must have planned.

A throng of onlookers gathering in the parking lot and in front of the adjacent Rite-Aid Drug Store increased by the minute as passersby on White Station Road swerved into the shopping center, attracted by the fleet of flashing blue lights. Dark clouds were forming overhead, muting the late afternoon light.

Detective Driscoll, respectful of the former chief's concerns for once, met the men outside the front entrance. "We identified the woman," he said loudly in an effort to be heard over the blaring horn of a passing freight train. "She's forty-eight. Name's Meredith Morgan. Widowed. Shopping for her grandbabies."

O'Riley and Mills looked at each other in relief.

Driscoll ushered them inside. "Davenport's examining the body," he continued. "Found in a small storage room under the southwest stairwell. Near the rear emergency exit."

"Does it have a sink?" O'Riley asked.

Driscoll nodded.

"Bloody?"

He nodded again.

"Back to his old ways," Mills added.

"Don't think so," countered Driscoll. "We got tape of him this time."

"Finally!" Mills blurted, eyeing the dark security camera domes dotting the ceiling of the enormous, warehouse-like selling floor.

"Come on up to the manager's office. See for yourselves. This place has a high-tech system you won't believe. Can focus in on a wristwatch fifty feet away. Color, too."

Harris, Harvey, and Norton fanned out into the aisles while Mills and O'Riley went with Driscoll. They passed four gray formica check-out counters and a sea of chrome four-way racks and rounders, finally reaching the secluded office in the back of the store.

Driscoll inserted a tape into the recorder. It clicked and whirred until he found the right spot and pushed the play button. "That's Lancaster and the victim in the toddler department. There's a door marked employees only in the corner. Leads to the stairwell. The storage room's underneath the stairs. That door's also the way to the rear emergency exit. The escape door he used."

The television screen filled with the image of a man as the camera zoomed in. Driscoll hit the freeze-frame button.

"I'll be damned," Mills said. "Minimal make-up. Only a mustache. But more fashionable clothes. Black and white tick-weave slacks. Black sport shirt. Dress loafers."

"If you want a closer look, they're piled in the storage room. Not so fashionable now," Driscoll added.

Mills ran a hand through his neatly layered blond hair and fidgeted with his tie. "I don't think most of our guys would have recognized him in that get-up. Even if they knew he was coming."

Driscoll resumed playing the tape, zooming out to show the entire department. "When the camera scans around again, about forty-five seconds later, they're gone. Don't know if he dragged her or lured her through the door for sure. I suspect he lured her somehow. There's no blood on the carpet outside the door but there are a few drops on the concrete leading to the storage entrance."

"Any more shots of him?" O'Riley asked.

"You'll *love* this one," replied Driscoll, fast-forwarding the tape and punching up a different camera. "It's the one outside the emergency exit."

Lancaster, now with no mustache or disguise, wearing navy slacks and a navy-plaid shirt layered under a tan sweater and tan windbreaker, sticks his face so close to the camera that his eyes, the left one blue and the right one green, are easily discernible. Then he holds a can of spray paint in front of the lens and the image turns black.

"That brazen sonuvabitch," said O'Riley, his voice thick with disgust. "He knew where every camera was."

"The paint on the camera was the same color he used on the woman's hair. Light brown," Driscoll said.

"Did he leave a name?" Mills asked.

Driscoll nodded. "Audrey. Crosby said she looked like an actress. I never heard of—"

"Audrey Hepburn," O'Riley said.

"Yeah. Audrey Hepburn."

Mills turned to O'Riley. "Who was the fifth murder victim here in 1957?"

"Audrey Hall. A brunette."

"What about a card?" Mills asked.

"Jack of hearts," came the reply.

O'Riley shot a knowing glance at Mills. "Seabold's next victim was my wife. The next card in his deck is the *Queen* of hearts. My queen of hearts. That must make me the *King* of hearts—I'm the last heart in his deck."

Mills nodded. "But there's something I can't figure out. There wasn't a theater here in the late fifties."

261

"There was in the mid-sixties. Opened with *The Sound of Music*. Played for over a year. Maybe he's been doing a little research.'"

"Would that theater happen to have been the Paramount?" Driscoll asked.

"Yeah," replied O'Riley, surprised. "How the hell would you know? You didn't even know who Audrey Hepburn was."

"There's *one* last thing I haven't told you two about."

O'Riley felt like he knew the answer. "A verse?" he guessed.

"A number of them," Driscoll replied, staring directly into O'Riley's tired eyes. "And they're all for you."

Five minutes later O'Riley and Mills stood under a small green awning that covered the rear emergency exit from the building, surveying the secluded parking lot and the likely escape route.

"He had it all planned," O'Riley said, catching a glimpse of the spray-painted camera aimed at the doorway. "A quick exit to a waiting car and he's history."

They ducked back inside and headed toward the door to the storage room under the stairs. Suddenly the medical examiner emerged, dressed in blood-stained white scrubs, and peeled off his gloves. A popping sound echoed in the stairwell. He smiled at the sight of his two friends.

"Making a fashion statement?" Mills kidded.

"You guessed it," Davenport replied. "Got tired of the blues. Hoped the whites might change our luck. Didn't work."

"Sims inside?"

"Nope. Didn't make it. He's at the office comparing bone cuts from one of Milligan's vertebrae to specimens from the victims' sternums. He said to call if we need him."

"I don't suppose you noticed any difference with this one?" Mills asked.

"Not much," replied Davenport, scratching his bristly scalp. "This one's older. Late forties. You think he's exploring new territory or it's just random?"

Mills thought for a moment, glanced at O'Riley, then looked back at Davenport. "Both. He took what was available but he's telling us older women are fair game."

O'Riley's lips pressed together. His face tightened.

"Other than that, it was status quo," continued Davenport. "Blow to the head fractured her skull. Left temple. From the trail of blood drops and drag marks it looks like it happened just a few steps inside the stairwell entry door from the sales floor. Dragged her into the storage room. Pulled his Lizzie Borden routine and gave her five whacks to the sternum. Then the same stuff."

"Just like a butcher at the grocery," added Mills.

Davenport nodded. "Then he cleaned up. This one's more like the Orpheum than the last three. He had more space." He paused a moment. "It was bloodier than all the others in that one respect."

Mills and O'Riley stared at the medical examiner, sharing confused expressions.

"Didn't Driscoll tell you?" Davenport asked. "He left a verse in blood. The fourth one."

"Hell, we haven't even seen the first three yet. Harris!" bellowed Mills. "Where are the notes?"

Harris nodded to Crosby who handed an eight-by-eleven sheet to Mills.

"Changed his paper of choice," observed O'Riley. "Still prefers a black marker, though."

"He used his regular paper for the name," Davenport said.

O'Riley nodded. "We know. Audrey."

Mills held up the plastic-wrapped note as he and O'Riley read.

> With eyes of red
> My actions are blue,
> The public's safety
> Should have been "Paramount" to you.

You wouldn't believe
The lengths I go to.
I've done my homework,
That's how I knew.

She twists in the air
Not knowing what to do.
Think hard, O'Riley,
Your "wife" is waiting for you.

O'Riley's blood boiled. "He knew *all* about the damn theater being here," he said, his voice rising. "And if any harm comes to Nancy, I'm gonna kill the bastard. I'll rip his own goddam heart out!"

Mills placed a hand on O'Riley's shoulder to calm him down. After a few moments they walked over to the storage room.

The bloody body of Meredith Morgan, dressed in black slacks with a pink silk sweater pulled up over her shoulders, lay on the gray concrete floor. Lancaster's blood-stained clothes were piled in the corner near a wash basin.

"The slacks and shirt were made in Italy," Davenport said. "Just like a well-dressed detective."

Mills acknowledged with a slight smile.

Then the three turned toward the cinder block wall.

The bloody writing was skillful—the letters almost perfectly formed:

But first a mind game,
A deadly one, too,
There's some unfinished business
I've long needed to do.

O'Riley closed his eyes, rolling the message over and over in his mind, mumbling repeatedly, "Unfinished business, unfinished business."

"What'd he use to get the writing so neat?" Mills asked.

"It's already bagged," Davenport replied. "An artist's paintbrush."

O'Riley's eyes widened in horror.

39

A fading light hovered over the horizon as Annie Shepherd sat quietly in her chair, the last person remaining in the park. She reached into her bag and pulled out a handful of birdseed and flung it over her shoulder, a treat for the pigeons keeping her company. Their cooing and the rush of flapping wings was soothing music to her ears.

Suddenly there was an urgent tapping of shoes on pavement.

"Time for one more painting?" asked a man with a husky voice.

A slight chill ran through her. She answered the question with a question. "Are you asking if it's too late for a portrait or just getting too dark to do it?"

"Take your pick," the voice replied.

"Time is something I have plenty of," she answered, pausing a moment, "so it's never too late for one more effort. As for the darkness, to me, night is day and day is night. The light of day and I have been at odds for a long time. You could say that darkness is my best friend." Receiving no response she said, "Have a seat."

He eased down on the knee-high wall and faced the artist. "How much will it cost me?"

"Fifty dollars. But you get two portraits. One as you are now. The other as I think you looked years ago."

"How long will it take?"

"Depends. I can do a rush job in twenty minutes. You in a hurry?" She knew the answer.

"Yeah, you could say that. I got a lady friend hanging around at my place. She can't wait for me to get back."

"Where do you live?" Annie asked nonchalantly.

"Right off Lamar. Not too far from Southern Avenue," he replied, his voice agitated. "What's with the questions? I heard you're a psychic. You must not have your *on* button activated or something. You shouldn't have to ask so much."

"It doesn't work that way. It takes a little time to get a feel for someone, both inside and out."

"What can you tell about me?"

"Some people are harder than others."

"With me, what do you see?"

"Right now, only darkness," came her reply. "Lean forward so I can feel your face. And let me feel your hands. That'll get me started."

He stuck his neck forward and held out his hands, elbows resting on his knees.

"You certainly are a handsome young man," Annie said, hoping to defuse some of the anger she felt in him as her touch glided across his face. She felt something else. A sadness and despair. She could see a scared boy crying out for his mother.

Then she ran her fingers across his hands, noticing the more muscular right one, balled in a fist.

"What's with the hand bit?" he asked.

"You're right-handed. And you bite your nails, especially your right thumb."

"So?"

"Everything I learn about you makes for a more realistic portrait," she answered. "Sit back now and take it easy."

He relaxed, facing the back of her easel.

Annie's loaded brush flicked across the linen surface, soon rendering the contour of the man's face. She slowly blocked in the shadow areas with the darker colors from her palette, leaving a thickening impasto on the canvas.

Twenty minutes later, the Court Square area was deserted and dark, lit only by a few antique street lamps in the park and the glow of lights from the Main Street trolley line.

"C'mon, c'mon, how much longer?" he asked, fidgeting. He rubbed a knuckle across his lips. His right eye began to twitch.

"Just a few finishing touches," she replied, trying to buy more time, feeling his building rage. She knew screaming would do no good.

His mind abruptly flashed years back to the Luciann theater. Remembering the thrill of the attack, his heart pounded, vibrating like a drum. He slowly stood, easing the axe from his pocket. This time he would not fail.

Just as he swung, Annie sensed his movement and jerked her body away.

The blunt end of the axe clipped her on the side of the head and she fell sprawling to the concrete, unconscious. The canvas toppled over at her side.

Suddenly a figure appeared from the murky darkness. "Police! Drop your weapon or I'll shoot!" echoed through the park as an officer took aim.

But Lancaster lifted the axe above his head, eyes locked on his victim's chest.

The policeman's gun jumped twice, accompanied by booming shots. The first pierced the flesh under Lancaster's right shoulder blade with a dull thud. The second missed.

Lancaster let out an anguished yell and the axe clanged to the pavement. He lunged to pick up his weapon, then ran down the sidewalk to Second Street amid a fluttering cloud of startled pigeons taking flight.

Without looking he stumbled into the street. Tires screeched and horns blared as he dodged one car, then another. A white Volvo sedan swerved to avoid him, sideswiping a parked black Mercedes, then demolished a fire hydrant with a crash. Water spewed two stories into the air, flooding the street.

Lancaster ducked through a small parking lot, cut down an alley and, turning the corner, spotted his car parked on Third Street. In a split-second he was in the sedan, pressing an old McDonald's sack against the flesh wound under his shoulder. With a turn of his key, the engine ignited and he vanished into the night.

✳

Trying to keep up with Mills, O'Riley sprinted into Court Square, his heart pounding painfully, his throat dry from sucking cold air through his mouth as he ran.

"Did you get a chance to shoot?" Mills asked the policeman.

"Twice. I hit him at least once. There's blood on the pavement."

"Much?"

"Just a few drops. He let out a yell and dropped his weapon. Then picked it back up."

O'Riley rushed to Annie's side. A passerby had placed a wool scarf under her head. O'Riley peeled off his green jacket and placed it over her chest.

"Help's on the way," he said, grasping her hands as the siren of an approaching ambulance wailed. "You're gonna be just fine."

Her dark glasses lay at her side and, for the first time, O'Riley gazed into her unseeing eyes. They were the bluest he had ever seen.

Annie squeezed his hand, attempting a smile.

Glimpsing the canvas, O'Riley felt like he had seen a ghost.

The larger portrait was blond-haired David Lancaster. In the upper left corner, in dark tones of gray and black, the image of Jimmy Seabold stared out at him. The only similarity was the color of the eyes—the left one blue, the right one green. How could she have known?

"I could sense it was him, Joe," Annie whispered. "I knew it from the moment he walked up. I could never forget that face. . . ." She took a deep breath. "I held him as long as I could. I knew you'd come. I felt it."

He rubbed her hands to warm them. "You are one brave lady, let me tell ya."

"It's not bravery—it's a matter of faith," she said, before quoting one of her favorite sayings, her voice becoming stronger. "'He who is consumed by fear at the sight of Death will not have the strength to withstand Death's might. Yet he who holds his ground against Death's darkness will live to embrace another day's light.'"

O'Riley gripped her hands tightly. "You've got plenty of days, you hear me? Years of 'em. Know something else? You were right. He *was* at a place with an L. The Landers Shoppe."

Annie shook her head feebly. "Not him. I saw . . . her."

O'Riley placed his ear close to her mouth.

"Hunt . . ." she whispered, "on Lamar. Lamar . . ."

An ambulance crew rushed up with a stretcher.

Within minutes she had been examined and loaded into the ambulance, destined for the trauma center at The Med in midtown. With red lights flashing and siren screaming, it roared off into the night.

Mills walked over to O'Riley, asking with his eyes how Annie was.

"They think a concussion. Said she'd get a Catscan and an MRI and be held for observation for at least a couple of days. She's tough. She'll be okay. This ain't near as bad as last time." He paused. "You find anything?"

"No notes," replied Mills.

"I guess we're screwing up his game plan. The S.O.B. didn't figure he'd get shot."

"He planned on one thing. Us finding this." Mills handed him the W.C. Fields card. It was a joker.

"Annie Shepherd was his wild card, a freebie he didn't want to waste a heart on. It's time we put an end to this bullshit. C'mon," motioned O'Riley, "let's me and you go for a ride. I got a hunch."

"You had a hunch about the Linden Circle and you were way off base."

"This time I might be, too. But at least we already got bolt cutters."

40

"Think about it," O'Riley said as they sped past dilapidated storefronts dotting the low-income Lamar Heights neighborhood on Lamar Avenue near Southern. "Hollywood Armageddon. Like I said earlier, an old movie theater fallen into disrepair. Run-down, decaying, locked up for as long as anybody can remember."

An aging yellow and orange sign, its dark brown letters rising vertically above a rusting, shattered marquee, caught the car's headlights.

"The Lamar!" the detective blurted out, making a sharp turn onto Felix and pulling to a stop on the quiet residential street.

"They don't fall any harder than this one—unless it's under a wrecking ball."

In a couple of minutes they were at the entrance, Mills clutching the bolt cutter.

The broken and cracked tubes spelling out the theater's name hadn't felt the warmth of neon for decades. Wires hung down from the marquee that had once beckoned theatergoers into a world of escape. The wooden triple-entry doors, originally dark brown and shiny, now stood scuffed, faded, and deteriorating behind iron-barred door guards tightly fastened with chains. White and tan paint peeled from the stucco facade.

Taking their flashlights, they quickly walked the perimeter in search of an open window or door but found none, ending up in a narrow alley on the building's east side.

O'Riley gripped a chain meant to keep trespassers from entering through the former side exit, rattling it slightly. "Probable cause, I'd say."

Mills grasped the chain with the cutter. It broke with a brittle snap.

Mills' hand slid under his jacket, gently pulling a .40-caliber from his shoulder holster. He checked the magazine, making sure it was firmly in place. O'Riley eased his pistol from his pocket and clicked off the safety.

The door creaked as they pushed it open and entered.

Their footsteps barely echoed in the eerie quiet of the old auditorium as they shined their flashlights down row upon row of grungy, deteriorated theater seats. The air was cold, like outside, but stale and thick with the smell of mildew.

They stepped cautiously down the center aisle to the stage and followed a narrow passageway behind its left side to a small storage room. Old metal movie reels, splicing equipment, and movie projector parts lay scattered across the floor.

O'Riley aimed his flashlight at the dusty, aged wooden beams that criss-crossed the ceiling. Webs glistened in the darkness of the spider-infested building.

A sudden shuffling startled both men. They whirled around, pointing their guns and flashlights up in the direction of the noise just as a rat slipped down, its claws clinging to O'Riley's shoulder.

"Get it off!" he yelled, his arms flailing, the flashlight beam gyrating wildly around the room.

Mills swatted the terrified rodent, sending it scurrying for cover behind an old crate. "If I had a leash, I coulda walked that one," he whispered. "Looked as big as a Yorkie."

"Spiders don't bother me but I *hate* rats." O'Riley shuddered.

"Wait a sec," said Mills, shining his light into a corner.

Their flashlights revealed the faint outline of a trap door.

"Reminds me of an old bomb-shelter entry. They built a lot of 'em in the late fifties and early sixties during the cold war years with Russia."

The door squeaked as they pulled it open to reveal a steep set of ten steps leading to another door.

Mills went down first, sweat forming on his brow. Then they eased toward the door.

O'Riley reached for the tarnished brass knob and, holding his breath, twisted it slowly then yanked the door open. Mills, gripping his gun firmly with both hands, took aim by the beam of O'Riley's flashlight.

"Oh my God," O'Riley whispered.

Mills' eyes narrowed, his gun dropping to his side.

Two rows of large Mason jars lined plywood shelves crudely built into the wall. Each jar on the top row contained a human heart, dark brown and hardened with age, soaking in a bronze-shaded formaldehyde solution. Faded strips of yellowed adhesive tape stuck to the front of the bottles bearing the names and dates of death of Jimmy Seabold's victims, all written in thick black marker.

O'Riley slowly examined the neatly labeled jars on the top shelf as his mind peeled away four decades of memories. MARILYN LARSON, ELIZABETH NOLAN, JAYNE GREER, DEBBIE RAINES, SOPHIA LOCKE, LAUREN TRAVIS, AVA MALONE, JANET BAKER, and AUDREY HALL. His gaze lingered on the last one. EVELYN O'RILEY.

He reached out, touching the dust-covered container as if he had found a long-lost keepsake. Tears clouded his vision. Evelyn could finally rest in peace.

Both men then scanned the lower shelf. New adhesive tape clung to identical Mason jars lettered in black Sharpie with the names of Lancaster's victims. JEAN LANCASTER, MARGARET TISDALE, MELISSA MURDOCH, PAM MILLER, LISA HOWARD, SALLY VANCE, BARBARA MURPHY, SUE LOWRY, and MEREDITH MORGAN.

The liquid in Morgan's jar, unlike the others, still displayed a bloody tint. Two jars next to it were empty. They were marked ANN MORRISON/ANNIE SHEPHERD and NANCY SUMMERFIELD.

Then he saw it. There on the shelf beside the last bottle they sat—the very deck of W.C. Fields cards Jimmy Seabold used so many years ago.

273

O'Riley picked it up and fanned it open. Neatly arranged in ascending order were the Ace, number cards, and picture cards for clubs, diamonds, and spades. The hearts were all missing.

"I swear I'll never doubt you again," whispered Mills, noticing the identical style of writing on both the older and newer jars. "This Lancaster . . . he *must be* Seabold."

"Better call for back-up," O'Riley replied, his voice hardly audible.

"I'm one step ahead of you," replied Mills.

But just as his finger reached for the button on his radio, there was a loud metallic clanging and Mills crumpled, his gun and radio clattering onto the floor.

O'Riley whirled around and fired a booming shot into the darkness. The flash of the gun gave off just enough light to see the glint of a shovel blade aimed at his head. He fell hard.

Lancaster quickly clicked on an overhead bulb and glanced up at the shelves, relieved that his trophies were intact. Then he scowled at the unconscious intruders at his feet. "I don't imagine it would hurt to trade one joker for another," he muttered, as he ripped the tape off the jar marked ANN MORRISON/ANNIE SHEPHERD and replaced it with a blank label. He carefully printed a new name.

JOE O'RILEY.

41

O'Riley winced, fighting the throbbing pain in his head. Trying to reach up and rub his sore skull, he found his hands tied behind him. A drying stream of blood snaked its way down his face, pulling at his cheek.

What had happened to him? Where was Mills? He shook his head to clear his thoughts. Then he remembered.

"Nice of you to join us, O'Riley. Welcome to my hangout." Lancaster's words thundered in the dank, secret chamber that had been his home. "I'm glad to see you didn't bring more of your friends," he said, pointing to Mills lying on his back in the corner of the large room.

A dim fluorescent lantern dangling from above illuminated the detective's blood-soaked white shirt and a small pool of blood next to him.

"I hit him so hard he didn't notice when I stuck my knife in his gut," Lancaster said matter-of-factly. He paused. "And now, for my next trick."

With his right hand he yanked away a black sheet covering an object in the middle of the room.

O'Riley's heart skipped a beat. Nancy was hanging from a beam, her arms above her, feet just touching the ground. Her mouth was bound with gray duct tape, her face pale with fear and fatigue. A hand-lettered sign bearing the word EVELYN hung across her chest.

She wore a long-sleeve, blue and white gingham check shirt-waist dress, the exact dress Evelyn had worn in the 1955 picture of the couple that rested on a table in O'Riley's living room. The choker strand of pearls given to his wife on their fifth anniversary hung around Nancy's neck.

"You're sick, Lancaster," O'Riley snarled, realizing the killer had been in his house stealing cherished keepsakes from his attic. "Or is it Seabold?"

"Take your pick. I'm whoever you want. I just have a lot more fun when I'm Jimmy Seabold."

O'Riley had kept his eyes on Nancy. "Let the lady go. I'm the one you want."

"Sorry. Can't do that. You missed out when I carved up your wife the first time around. I don't want you to miss the encore. After all," he said, pulling a card from behind his back and flashing it in O'Riley's face, "she's *my* Queen of Hearts, too!"

"What's that make me, the King of Hearts? Your last victim?"

"Not so fast," chided Lancaster. "You're losing it in your old age. There are two jokers in every deck. You're the second one." He waved the joker in front of the former chief's face. "You and the artist are wild cards from my past. I'm not the *Hollywood Killer. I'm* the *King of Hearts!*" He laughed, a wildness showing in his eyes as he held the King of Hearts above his head. "You call yourselves detectives. You're just a bunch of incompetent fools. Couldn't you figure it out?" He tucked the card into O'Riley's shirt pocket.

"Your cards have run out. Is this the end of the line?"

"For you and your girlfriend. I may move on. All I need is a new deck." His eyes, the left one blue and the right one green, flicked coldly from victim to victim.

O'Riley had seen those eyes before. At Brushy Mountain Penitentiary. On Jimmy Seabold's execution night.

Lancaster eased toward Nancy. "Time for some fun," he announced, as he unbuttoned the whimpering woman's dress.

O'Riley watched helplessly, tugging in vain at the rope binding his hands.

Lancaster's right eye twitched wildly as he rubbed his fingers across Nancy's smooth cheeks. "Such a shame that I have to transform this warm, beautiful body into a cold, lifeless corpse, don't you think?"

Powerless, his face flushed with rage, his hands feverishly worked the rope, trying to emulate Houdini, as he had done so many times before.

Lancaster raised his axe into the air.

O'Riley's heart pounded as his voice rose in panic. "No!" he screamed. "*Nooooo!*"

Suddenly a form bolted from the darkness, slamming into Lancaster who dropped the axe and grabbed at Nancy to keep his balance. The old beam snapped with a crack under their weight, sending the three crashing to the floor.

Lancaster quickly recovered and lunged at Mills, knocking him side-ways. Nancy, her hands still bound, took refuge behind a large crate near O'Riley.

Lancaster brought his right fist back, hitting the detective in the face once, twice, three times. Mills retaliated with a kick to the groin, sending Lancaster backwards. The detective struggled to his feet and charged, arms swinging.

The wooden floor creaked under the shifting weight of the frenzied combatants. Mills wrapped an arm around Lancaster's neck and threw him down. Landing with a dull thump, he was momentarily dazed. Mills reached down, tightly grabbing the murderer's neck as Lancaster's hand shot up, digging into Mills' wound. Screaming, the detective fell backwards.

Spotting the axe, Lancaster grabbed for it and swung the weapon at Mills, planting it squarely in his shoulder.

Mills cried out and slumped to the floor, unconscious.

Sweat ran down the sides of O'Riley's face as he desperately tried to pull his hands free. He had never known such fear.

Then he felt a human touch behind his back. His hands slipped free and he was on his feet. The fear in his eyes vanished.

They ran at each other, meeting in the middle of the room with arms swinging savagely. A right from O'Riley met Lancaster's chin but he was no match for the killer's youth. Three quick jabs to the older man's stomach knocked the wind out of him. Reeling from the impact, his knees buckled and he dropped to the floor, gasping for air.

Lancaster picked up the axe. "Say goodnight!" he snarled.

O'Riley instinctively raised a hand, closing his eyes.

A guttural "Uuuurgh!" broke the silence in the room.

Lancaster's body tightened, his eyes locked open. He collapsed in a heap. Two four-inch nails that had been jutting from a piece of the broken beam were buried in the back of his head.

Nancy stood over him, hands trembling.

Suddenly Harris, Crosby, Norton, and Harvey burst into the room with guns drawn.

Nancy collapsed into O'Riley's arms.

"It's all right," he whispered softly. He then motioned toward Mills. "Harris. Get an ambulance. He's in pretty bad shape. Lost a lot of blood."

Harris barked into his radio. "Need an ambulance at the old Lamar theater at Lamar and Felix. Officer down."

"How'd you find us?" O'Riley asked.

"Dispatch alerted us when Mills didn't respond to the radio," Harris replied. "I was talking to Calicutt, the cop who shot Lancaster. He remembered hearing the artist say something about Lamar. This old dump came to mind. We spotted Mills' cruiser close to the theater. Pretty obvious."

The detectives tended to Mills as O'Riley comforted Nancy.

Clutching her tightly to his chest, tears glazed his eyes. He thought he had lost her forever.

"Please," she whimpered, her voice muffled in his chest, "please don't ever let me go."

"I won't," he promised, as he gently rocked her. "I'm going to hold on to you for the rest of my life."

A siren wailed in the distance.

After a few minutes, the ambulance crew was carrying Mills out on a stretcher. "O'Riley," he called out faintly, sweat beading on his chalk white face.

O'Riley and Nancy moved to his side. "I'm here, Mills."

"Did we get him?" Mills whispered, gritting his teeth in pain.

"He won't be bothering anybody ever again," replied O'Riley. "At least, not in *my* lifetime."

42

The next afternoon O'Riley and Nancy arrived at The Med in the mid-town Memphis medical center to find Chief Charlie Perry standing in the hallway down from the intensive care unit.

"How you doing, Joe?" Perry asked, eyeing the patch of gauze on O'Riley's head.

"Only took twelve stitches. What's the story on Mills?"

"The doc says he'll be all right. Has a concussion, snapped collar-bone, broken nose, and assorted bruises to go along with the axe cut to his shoulder and the stab wound in his gut. He's lucky no major organs got punctured. Three months of rehab and he'll be pushing his pencil back in Homicide."

O'Riley breathed a sigh of relief.

"How's the artist?" the chief asked.

"Just saw her. Concussion and a few bruises. Not too serious. Smells like a goddam florist shop in her room. Flowers wall to wall. It's got her so inspired she's talking about painting floral arrangements." He paused a mo-ment and then added, "When she's not painting portraits."

"How long's she in for?" Perry asked.

"Two, maybe three days. She had us promise to feed the pigeons and squirrels until she gets back." He slipped his hands into his pants pockets and yanked upward, positioning his waistband firmly on his hips.

A crew-cut figure dressed in blue scrubs suddenly appeared in the corridor. "Ever think of tightening your belt?" he yelled.

O'Riley shook his head as the medical examiner walked up. "You gettin' to work on live ones these days?"

"Nah, not my cup of tea," Davenport said. "They complain too much. Just checking on Mills. How's the head?"

O'Riley touched a forefinger to the bandage. "I'll live. Takes more than a good whack to keep me down."

Davenport turned to Nancy. "And how are you after all this?"

"Physically, I'm fine," she replied, "not mentally. Might take a while."

"I understand," Davenport responded, nodding. "Mind if I borrow this security blanket of yours for a few minutes?"

"Not if you promise to return him in the same shape you're getting him in," she said with a smile.

The two men walked down the hall out of earshot, stopping beside a rollaway bed.

"What's on your mind?" O'Riley asked.

"I just finished up the autopsy on your man."

"And?"

"Never seen one quite like it."

"You mean the nails?"

"No," Davenport replied, "not that. I see penetrating trauma a few times a week. Bullets, knives, other sharp objects. It was his brain. The tissue itself. Looked like it had been trying to regrow." He looked straight into O'Riley's eyes. "Mills told me what you thought. About Lancaster and that Seabold guy."

O'Riley whispered, "You think I'm nuts?"

A grin crossed the medical examiner's face. "I'm a big fan of Shirley MacLaine. If I can accept her reincarnation claims with a grain of salt, there's no way I'm not giving you the benefit of the doubt. Especially now." He drew in a deep breath and exhaled. "During the autopsy I expected to see cystic scar tissue. What I found was an abnormal growth of cerebral cortical tissues."

O'Riley's forehead wrinkled in confusion. "Speak English, will ya?"

"We're talking *major* scientific breakthrough here. This represents the spontaneous regeneration of central nervous system tissue. Neurogenesis. They've been trying to do this with spinal cords for years. You ever heard of the Miami Project for Paralysis?"

The former chief nodded. "Started by that Miami Dolphins player for his son?"

"Yeah, and it's the same type of research Christopher Reeve got behind. If you lose a chunk of liver, it regrows. But you lose a piece of your spinal cord or brain and that's it. Maybe until now."

"Keep going," O'Riley said.

"Given Lancaster's history, I think the surgery to remove the tumor and the experimental application of the memory drug simultaneously with high doses of radiation could have combined to produce an environment that stimulates regeneration. All around the area where the tumor had been excised were masses of regrown border cells. This memory drug might at times enhance a person's memory function by interacting somehow with the remaining cells. But, under certain circumstances, the drug could act as a cell-growth enhancer."

"Kinda like chemical fertilizer," O'Riley added.

"Precisely," replied Davenport, his eyes shining. "As much as this man was a separate individual from the original killer, his brain, his being was predominantly that of the killer. If we *are* reincarnated but only a small portion of our brain is sensitive to it *and* if that area grew to dominance somehow, in this case by regenerating, then a person might actually be influenced by his prior self or, for that matter, one of any number of prior selves."

"People are gonna think you're nuts, too."

"Wrong," Davenport fired back. "I'm keeping my mouth shut. This is somebody else's war to fight. I don't pretend to fully understand how the brain operates. I'll leave that to the experts. I can tell you what to expect

282

when the brain is damaged. I look at what passes through a brain nearly every day. But I can't read minds. Autopsies don't tell me that. I'll tell you one thing, though."

"What's that?"

"We're just scratching the surface on this one. I'm talking major federal funding. Like Nobel Prize-winning research. But, before you go opening your mouth, you might want to think about it. I'm not so sure the world's ready for this."

"What do you mean?" O'Riley responded. "Think who might be out there just walking around somewhere. Einstein. Da Vinci. Maybe Thomas Jefferson or Abraham Lincoln."

"Caligula, Attila the Hun, and Adolph Hitler," Davenport added emphatically.

O'Riley said nothing for a few moments, tugging at an earlobe. Then he stared down the hall toward Nancy. "I guess you're right," he admitted. "We better let things ride. If what you said turns out to be true, they'll figure it out soon enough." He ran his fingers through his salt and pepper hair, careful not to touch his bandage, and asked, "Where do we go from here?"

Davenport stretched his neck. "I don't know about you, but I'm heading back to the office. Got two gunshot victims from last night to autopsy. Can't keep Death waiting too long. Stay out of trouble or I might be seeing you around."

The two shook hands and soon Davenport was a tiny blue dot at the end of the long corridor.

"I got to hand it to you," Perry said as O'Riley returned. "Seems like you just about figured this case out all by yourself."

"I did have some help, you know. Mills was right in there with me. And," he said, nodding at Nancy and gently placing his hands on her shoulders, "I sure as hell wouldn't be standing here right now if it wasn't for this little lady. One thing's certain—Lancaster ain't playing with a full deck anymore."

"Can Trevor have visitors now?" Nancy asked.

"Only family," Perry replied.

"He ain't got no family," O'Riley said.

"Then I'd say you two qualify."

The couple turned to leave.

"Oh, since you're filling in for other people," Perry said, "you know we'll be one short in Homicide with Mills out of commission. I think we might be able to use you a couple of days a week. How about it?"

"Don't think so," O'Riley replied as he leaned to kiss Nancy's cheek. "My heart's just not in it."